NOWHERE PEOPLE

NOWHERE PEOPLE

Nowhere USA Book Seven

NINIE HAMMON

STERLING & STONE

Chapter One

MALACHI EDGED the door open with his backside, balancing a tray in front of him, and came into the storage-room-turned-hospital-room where Rusty lay — still, so very still. On the tray was a cup of coffee, along with packets of powdered creamer and sugar, and a plate with a pale yellow substance that could have been scrambled eggs or toe fungus, a single slice of burned toast — or maybe butter on a roof shingle — and a pink, rectangular *something*.

"What is that?"

"You're welcome. And yes, I do know how to operate a toaster. I burned it on purpose because I found the piece of bread in the back of the breadbox with something suspiciously penicillin-like growing on it. But I killed it."

"No, I mean that. The pink thingy."

"What does it look like? It's SPAM."

Sam didn't know whether to laugh or cry, and she was perilously close to doing both almost all the time now. Her look said, *you're joking.*

"Serious as a heart attack. I was afraid you'd be a

SPAM snob so I've been composing a soliloquy in its defense — Ode to a Small Ham Loaf."

She shook her head and started to speak but he held up his hand to forestall any argument. "I am here to testify that SPAM won't kill you. If it can't kill a battalion of Marines, you'll survive it." Then he shrugged his shoulders. "It was all I could find in E.J.'s cupboard — unless you count a box of stale pretzels and a jar of bean dip. Eat all the eggs you want, though, they're a renewable resource."

"If you have a chicken."

"Yeah, well, there is that." He grew serious then. "You have to eat, Sam. You can't keep going if you don't eat. And we need you." He landed a sucker punch then, and they both knew the manipulation for what it was. Gesturing with his chin at the still boy on the bed. "*He* needs you."

Malachi set the tray down on the bedside table. "So shut your mouth and eat. Okay, open your mouth and eat."

He stood over her menacingly, glowering at the pieces of fried meat. "Don't make me get ugly." He brightened. "I can get catsup, too, if that'll make it go down any smoother.

She dutifully reached out and picked up one of the pieces of SPAM with her fingers, and took a small bite.

"More."

Another bite, bigger.

"All three pieces."

"But I—"

"It's this or bean dip."

She took another bite and he sat down on the edge of Rusty's bed, careful not to disturb the boy. Malachi here, with her and Rusty. If she let herself go there …

"Did you get any sleep last night?"

She nodded. And she had. A little. Thanks to Malachi's little sojourn into the Ridge to have a talk with Roger Stovall at Stovall's Used Furniture Store. Roger was about as unpleasant a human being as Sam had ever met and somehow Malachi had talked the man into *donating* a piece of furniture to the clinic. Malachi said he would have "borrowed" one from Martha Whittiker's house, where he'd gotten Rusty's bed, but Martha didn't have one — and besides, he didn't like wandering around people's houses taking their furniture without permission. He'd tried to *buy* it, but Roger didn't want Malachi's money and plastic was no good. So Malachi'd then begun serious negotiations about *donation*.

Sam hadn't asked how he'd pulled it off. Hadn't even known he was going to talk to Roger until he came back to the Middle of Nowhere with — of all things — a *recliner* loaded up in the back of E.J.'s van. He got Pete and Charlie to help him — his almost-dislocated shoulder really needed to be in a sling, but he'd refused. The three of them then hauled the chair in through the waiting room — past the unexplained chalkboard with the picture of the autopsy of a spider, at least that's what it looked like to Sam, down the hallway and through the door of the storage room that'd been converted into a hospital room for Rusty.

Sam had been totally flabbergasted when he'd backed into the room, carting the platform end of the chair. Oh, she got it, she understood. Malachi'd gone on a chair safari to take his mind off ... *things*. The body of Rev. Duncan Norman, floating somewhere in the Rolling Fork River. And his family. His sister, shot dead. His mother ... well, just his mother. Sam suspected that doing something "good" might have been Malachi's go-to coping mechanism his whole life.

"What in the world …?"

"Charlie and I knew we'd never be able to get you to go to bed, but … if I have to, I can duct tape you to this chair. Right here beside Rusty's bed. You can lean it back, maybe doze a little."

She'd expressed her surprise and delight with grateful babble.

Malachi's only comment had been: "Roger Stovall is meaner than a serial killer with a sinus infection and a boil on his butt," and he refused to provide details about the transaction. Sam had been unprepared for the sudden tears that leapt into her eyes and flowed in rivulets down her cheeks.

Sam had believed then that the surprises of the night were over.

Not.

Half an hour after Malachi'd brought the chair, the old man had shown up. An old man nobody knew. Which, of course, was impossible.

FOOTSTEPS IN THE HALLWAY. Sam loathes that sound because it always signals a crisis.

"We got an incoming," Pete says, standing in the open doorway of Rusty's room.

"An incoming? Who …?"

"That's the thing, Sam. Nobody knows who he is."

Among the handful of people at the clinic, there wasn't anybody in the county they wouldn't recognize.

Sam casts a look at Rusty, and Pete says, "You go on now. I'll wait right here." He tried to smile but phony smiles just weren't as easy to pull off these days as they'd once been. "Got this nice recliner here. Only thing I need's a football game on television."

Sam rushes out into the parking lot to find Raylynn, Doreen Perkins — who'd come to bring her father some supper during his shift with E.J. — Charlie, Merrie and Malachi standing in a little group around a man seated on the bus stop bench.

A stranger.

"Who ...?" That's all Sam is able to say.

"You mean, you don't know him, either?" Charlie says. "I thought it was just me, being gone for so long."

"I've never met this man." Sam shoots a look at Malachi and Doreen. Both shrug and shake their heads.

"You sure he rode the Jabberwock?" Sam asks, knowing what the answer must be. If he hadn't, how had he come to be sitting in the bus shelter in the Middle of Nowhere? Except he isn't like the other "incomings."

He isn't desperately sick like Sam, Charlie, Malachi and most of the other Jabberwock riders had been. He isn't blind, like Hayley Norman, or about to choke to death like Fish. He is just ... what?

Well, the first stab at a diagnosis is easy to come by. He appears to be utterly insane.

CHARLIE AND MERRIE had been staying at Sam's house in the Ridge because it was closer to the Middle of Nowhere than going back to her mother's house at the foot of Little Bear Mountain. Oh, alright, it wasn't closer. It was farther. But the roads were better. Actually, that wasn't even true either. Charlie had taken to driving into Persimmon Ridge from the Middle of Nowhere down Danville Road to Elkhorn, then Chimney Rock Pike to Bat Cave — and that route *definitely* was neither shorter nor smoother. No, proximity didn't have anything to do with it. Charlie and

Merrie'd gone to Sam's house on Sunday night after Viola Tackett'd threatened to kill Charlie. And they'd just … stayed. Oh, it wasn't like Charlie was hiding out from Viola at Sam's. That'd be the first place the old woman would look for her. And hiding was futile, anyway. There was nowhere in Nowhere County to run from Viola Tackett.

The truth still in the husk was that Charlie flat out didn't like being alone at her mother's house anymore. Part of the reason was the omnipresence of the kiln in the backyard. She'd have hauled the thing out of there and thrown it off a cliff if she could have, had settled for having Lester Peetree remove the door. But it was there, always there, and every time she looked out into her backyard the stone building glared back at her, the gaping doorway like an open maw. An always, always reminder of the worst day of Charlie McClintock's life, the day she thought Merrie was dead, that crazy Abby Clayton had suffocated the precious little girl in that building.

Another part of the reason was the ever-spooky blackboard in her kitchen where Stuart had written "Where are you?" and the Jabberwock had told her "I want to play with you." And now the even-spookier blackboard wasn't even *there* anymore. Who had moved it to the clinic waiting room? And why? She'd been rolling that over and over in her head ever since Merrie'd shown it to her last night. Well, when she'd had time and energy to think about it. Time and energy were in extremely short supply right now in Charlie McClintock's life.

As she put away the last of a meager breakfast's dishes in Sam's cabinet, she acknowledged that the real reason she'd been staying at Sam's house was that she had bonded to Sam. They were closer now than they'd ever been as children, and they'd been inseparable then, playing with their baby dolls in the shade of the elementary school building. The relationship had been forged by the Jabber-wock nightmare, and it was tempered steel now. Charlie needed that. She suspected Sam did, too. Particularly now, with Rusty …

Rusty.

A crazy woman had shot him, *shot* the poor kid with a shotgun.

How could the world get this crazy so fast? How could …?

Of course, the answer to all questions was the same. Jabberwock. The monster held the keys to every lock. She and Sam and Malachi, E.J., Thelma Jackson … all of them together or any one of them separately had to figure out the monster or Rusty Sheridan could lie in that makeshift hospital room and die. As E.J. would die.

As they all would die.

"I've decided, Mommy," Merrie announced as she came bouncing into Sam's kitchen, where Charlie had poured herself a final cup of coffee before returning to the Middle of Nowhere. She only came home … came here, now, so Merrie could sleep in a bed, could have some semblance of normal in her life. Not that the kid cared. She was indisputably the most resilient of all of them — bubbly and cheerful in the face of horror too big for her to comprehend. She was a breath of fresh air … and a reminder of what was at stake if they didn't figure this out.

"Decided what, sweet pea?" Then she saw the outfit the little girl had selected to wear. A bright pink tee-shirt with figures of unicorns on it … over a pair of bright red plaid shorts. Charlie sighed. After all, Merrie didn't have a particularly stellar wardrobe to choose from. Just what Charlie'd snatched from the Dollar General Store and the little bit Charlie'd packed for her when they left Chicago.

Chicago.

Stuart.

Charlie wondered how long he'd stayed in Hawaii. He and "Mrs. McClintock" had been playing bump and tickle in a motel there when Charlie had called before J-Day. He was supposed to be in Portland working, had said it was a big deal. Yeah, it was a big deal, alright.

But he was here now, though. Wherever *here* was. He'd written a desperate *Where Are You* message on the blackboard — and Pete had confirmed a stick-pin message on his county map. Stuart had come looking for her and Merrie. And when that had sunk in, oozing into the pores of her being like butter into hot cornbread, she discovered she couldn't fit both images of the man in her head at the same time. There simply wasn't room, not now. Not *now*. She couldn't hold onto two different realities.

Stuart — her best friend, her husband, her lover and Merrie's father.

And Stuart lying on the beach with … somebody. Some other woman.

The two were mutually exclusive and if she tried to embrace both images at once, it would rip her apart at her core. So she locked the unthinkable in a solid stone box, set it on a mental shelf in an empty room in her mind, then walked away and left it there, slammed the door behind her. Oh, sure, the corrosive evil inside that box would eat through the stone and the metal and the door eventually. She knew that. One day, the reeking corruption would begin to eat away at the rest of her mind. She'd deal with that when the time came. If she lived that long, she'd deal with that part. Right now, the only Stuart whose existence she acknowledged was the man who had come to Kentucky looking for his wife and daughter. And found … yeah, what? What was there on the other side of the Jabberwock?

"… one that bited me *and* the one wiff white paws. Pleeeeease, Mommy."

"What? What are you talking about?"

Merrie looked at her with a strangely adult expression on her face.

"You wasn't listenin', was you Mommy. You never listen to me anymore." And she unexpectedly burst into tears.

Charlie dropped to her knees and gathered the crying child into her arms, awash in guilt and sorrow.

"I'm sorry, baby, Mommy's sorry. I never, ever intended to ignore you. I love you, precious. Please forgive Mommy. Please."

The little girl pulled back out of her embrace, tears streaming down her face and a smile on her lips.

"I lube you, too, Mommy. So, can I?"

"Can you what?"

"Can I have *both* puppies? The one that bited me *and* the one wiff socks. Pleeeease."

Charlie deftly sidestepped the question by telling the little girl she would need to see and inspect both the puppies in question before she could render a decision, then handed Merrie the bag of clean clothes she'd selected for Sam — who'd been sleeping in the clothes she was wearing — and told her to take it out to the car.

Charlie's back was turned when Merrie opened the front door and cried, "Toby! You comed to play wiff me!"

She turned around slowly and saw Sarah Throck-morton standing with Toby beside the open door or her ancient Chevrolet parked behind Charlie's mother Honda Legend in Sam's driveway.

The look on Sarah's face told Charlie something was very, very wrong.

Chapter Two

"So okay, the SPAM's good," Sam said grudgingly.

Malachi did a fist pump.

He really hadn't expected to be able to entice Sam into eating anything, but two bites of SPAM, hey, that was something. On a roll, he tried to distract her so maybe she wouldn't realize she was eating and reflex would take over.

"I've been sitting with our new friend and it's clear to me he was at least half a bubble off plumb long before he hit the Jabberwock."

The new friend was the old man who'd shown up in the bus shelter last night, clearly transported there by the Jabberwock but displaying none of the Jabberwock-ride symptoms other passengers on that train had suffered.

Well, except his brains were scrambled. And stayed scrambled. He made no sense when he talked, didn't seem to understand or responded inappropriately to what was said to him, and had a strange, creepy vacant look in his eyes.

He was a bent old man with wispy white hair, wearing a leather apron beneath a raincoat. His gnarled fingers told

Malachi he'd likely spent his life working with his hands — an assumption borne out by the business card in his wallet: "Moses Weiss, Craftsman Cobbler, shoe repairs, insoles, shoe laces."

Beneath that: "A journey of a thousand miles begins with a single step." Lao Tzu, 4th Century A.D.

And beneath that: "Every journey *seems* like a thousand miles if your feet hurt." Moses Weiss, 1945.

Malachi liked the card, would likely have liked the man in whose wallet he'd found it — along with a Tennessee driver's license identifying him as Moses Habakuk Weiss, 73 — if the man had been lucid. They'd all assumed he would "come back to himself" in a little while, like all the other Jabberwock victims. But he didn't. Three hours after they'd found him in the parking lot, Malachi had led him upstairs and put him to bed on the couch in E.J.s apartment. He'd followed along as obediently as a child.

And like a child … he had wet himself.

Yep, sure did.

As he'd cleaned the old man up, Malachi'd tried very hard to be grateful he'd done it standing in the doorway and not after Malachi had gotten him settled on the couch. He had put Mr. Weiss in a pair of E.J.'s old jeans. Clearly the dude's circuits were seriously fried.

"What is he saying?"

"Everything. Nothing. I've been listening to him ever since he woke up this morning — at five o'clock, by the way. No, not listening. Hearing. There's a difference. He just talks. Random. Babbles. Nonsense."

Malachi hadn't had a chance to tell the others about Mr. Weiss's little accident last night. He'd fed him some breakfast this morning — supplies were low and choices were limited so Malachi'd chosen a can of Campbell's chicken noodle soup. He heated it and set a bowl of it in front of the man. He didn't appear to notice. But when Malachi spooned the soup into his mouth, he chewed and swallowed. Same with a glass of water — he drank.

Malachi had taken that as a good sign and decided to take him into the bathroom and just see if he'd … He had done as instructed. But Malachi was pretty sure he wouldn't do it on his own. It felt a little like house training a puppy — Malachi would have to remember to "take him out" every couple of hours, but it sure beat cleaning up a mess.

Malachi'd brought Mr. Weiss downstairs and parked him in a chair in the waiting room. He'd been content to follow, sit where he was placed. Malachi hoped this morning's adventures in potty training had been a harbinger of better times ahead. Life was already icky enough without having to care for an incontinent stranger.

"I'm hoping that several of us — you, me, Charlie, Pete … whoever — could get together and talk to him all at the same time, try to focus him so he'll make sense. Find out how he got here."

"He couldn't possibly have been here since before J-Day … could he?"

Malachi shrugged. "I would think somebody would have noticed a dithered Away-From-Here who's not potty trained."

"Not potty trained?"

Malachi tried to blow it off. "A little accident. No biggie." He quickly deflected the conversation. "And if he wasn't trapped here like the rest of us, he's from" — Malachi made a vague gesture that indicated everything out beyond the walls of the room — "out there. So how'd he wind up with a ticket on the Jabberwock to the Middle of Nowhere?"

They'd asked all those questions last night, of course.

Had batted around one hypothesis after another until they were all exhausted. Malachi had watched Sam struggle to stay awake and focused and made an executive decision. Rest. Sleep. They'd come at it with fresh minds in the morning.

Well, it was morning. And Malachi's fresh mind was no closer to an understanding of what was going on than his tired mind had been last night.

After he'd fed Mr. Weiss his breakfast, one of the elders of Duncan Norman's church arrived. When Pete got back from delivering the news about Duncan to his family last night, he'd said that members of Norman's congregation were forming up in teams to go out with lanterns and flashlights to search for the pastor's body — on the rocks below the cliff face or in the river. Elder McEntire said they'd found nothing, so it must have washed downstream. They'd keep looking, of course, but … the Rolling Fork River wound in and out of Nower and Beaufort counties. What if the body had washed into Beaufort County … what did that mean? Would the body …? Then Malachi'd stopped himself. He just didn't have enough space in this mind to consider the ramifications of a thing like that. Right now, he had to concentrate on the living instead of the dead.

During the pause in the conversation, Malachi could hear the old man's voice from the waiting room. He was either hard of hearing — certainly a possibility — or just talked loud.

"You missed a spot shaving." A pause. "Collect payment upfront. If they don't pay — hold their wing-tips hostage until they do." Another pause. "You have shaving cream under your ear." A third pause, it had the cadence and rhythm of a conversation, like listening to someone talking on the phone where you only hear half of what's being said. "Smile once in a while, it won't break your face, and don't break your tooth on that hamburger meat. There's a ring in it."

Nonsense.

The old man's voice grew softer then, but still clear. "She's dead. My baby girl's dead."

Like Malachi's sister, Esther Ruth. Dead.

He grabbed hold of his emotions and wrenched his thought processes back away from that abyss. But not before the whole of it kicked him in the belly with a hiking boot.

Somebody had shot that poor little girl — and Essie was still a little girl — a small child in a woman's body. Everyone knew Essie would never grow up, but Malachi had never considered the possibility that she'd be robbed of the opportunity to grow older.

Who would shoot an innocent like Essie? What for?

Of course, he knew what for. Payback. Revenge. His mother had done something bad to somebody — and there were dozens, hundreds of those somebodies out there — and they'd taken out their impotent rage on poor little Essie.

Impotent rage. He knew that feeling, had felt it well up from the pit of his soul at so many things his mother had done over the years. It horrified him how easy it was to identify with the monster who'd shot Essie. Viola Tackett had earned the rage and hatred of just about everybody in Nowhere County.

But Essie hadn't. Why shoot poor simple-minded Essie?

"I'm sorry," Sam said, her husky voice quiet, and he felt the light touch of her hand on his arm. He looked into her hazel eyes, saw the faint shadow of a dimple in her right cheek. "You loved your sister a lot, didn't you?"

He discovered he couldn't speak over the lump in his throat. He merely nodded. Then he found his voice. "She was a single, pure thing. Just good … only good. When you looked into her face, you saw no guile in her. She was the only … perfect thing my mother ever did."

"She sang to her." Sam's face was swimming in the tears in his eyes. "When Essie was … when she was dying, your mother sang to her. It was some nonsense song, not even a song, really—"

"Ahhh-nah, gahma-gahma-gahma." Malachi's soft words were tear-clotted. "So-so-wissy-wheeee."

"Yes, that's it. Your mother sang that to Essie. Those were the last words she ever heard."

How was it that Sam knew just the right thing, the only thing to say that would comfort Malachi right now? Sam, whose son lay too quiet on the bed, might be dying as well. Still, she'd had the heart and compassion to reach out to Malachi.

Sam Sheridan was a remarkable woman.

Charlie suddenly appeared in the doorway of Rusty's room. Her face was pale, her eyes wide.

Merrie, who was with her, announced, "Dat old man in the waiting room …" She wrinkled up her nose. "He pooped his pants."

Goody.

"What is it?" Sam asked Charlie, reading her distress.

"I just talked to Sarah Throckmorton." She turned to Malachi. "I think your mother knows about Howie. Well, *something* about Howie. Viola showed up at Sarah's house yesterday. She and Toby hid in the woods, so Viola didn't see Toby there. But this morning, Sarah noticed Toby's baseball cap was missing. She said there was only one place it could have gone. Sarah thinks Viola took it with her when she left."

Chapter Three

WAS IT A TOMB OR A VAULT? Or perhaps an ossuary?

There were interesting distinctions, of course, Fish thought, occupying his mind with the distraction of figuring out the proper noun to use for the place he was going, so that perhaps he could manage to pull himself back at the last minute and not go there at all.

Not likely.

Still.

It was surprising to Fish how clear and sharp his mind had become after he stopped drowning his synapses in alcohol every day. Sharp was the proper word, of course. It was sharp, as in razor sharp — so sharp, getting near it was likely to result in a nasty cut.

Fish really should *not* get anywhere near his own mind, but of course, it was not a thing he could avoid.

Serrated edges, maybe, too. His thinking was so vivid, so pointed, so *clear,* that it felt like his every thought sliced into him whenever he allowed himself to think.

And since he had sobered up — last drink fifty-six hours and twenty-five minutes ago, if he were counting, of course, and he absolutely, one hundred percent *was* counting — he had not yet figured out a way to direct his outrageously clear mind away from the thoughts, images and memories he had spent more than a decade obscuring with booze.

Holmes Fischer's clear mind knew exactly what he had done. It knew how he had done it, and was likely to offer up for his viewing enjoyment images from those times just to prove that he did remember.

He crossed the street in front of the Methodist church, where he had spent the night, not sleeping but spent the night, and headed north on Main Street.

At every step, he tried to stop himself from taking the next one, but he moved recently onward, propelled by a need that was far stronger than his pitiful ability to hold it in check. The walk to the cemetery was quite a hike on foot, but it was a beautiful spring morning. Exactly the same as every other morning had been for more than two weeks now. Cloudless blue sky, warm but not hot. Just perfect. Too perfect. He couldn't be the only person in Nowhere County who was yearning now for bad weather. How about a thunderstorm? Or not even that much varia-tion — overcast would be nice. Or not even that. Just cloudy. Clouds. Okay, one cloud. One measly cloud in the sky. How he longed to see that. But the Jabberwock controlled the weather now ... and the time ... and access and egress into and out of the county. The rest of the mere mortals here had no say in the matter.

Don't do it.

He pleaded with himself, begged himself, would have gotten down on his knees in front of himself, though that was, of course, physiologically impossible, but he'd have done it if it would have dissuaded him.

Please, don't do it.

But, of course, he was going to do it. Every step he took confirmed it. All the arguing to the contrary, Fish was going to do what he shouldn't, couldn't, mustn't do. If he did. If he took even one sip …

He had not been sober in such a long time, he hadn't realized how too-clear and too-crisp reality unmuted by booze was, hadn't remembered what it was like to have ordered thoughts, purpose and direction unhindered by the obsession, the constant need to find that next drink.

The moment he had opened his eyes this morning, he knew he was lost.

He had only dozed, of course. Even though he was exhausted — must have walked … what? Ten miles, maybe fifteen — never leaving the church basement, of course. Around and around and around he had paced after his conversation with Charlie McClintock. After he had ripped the scab off his most grievous wound, after he had allowed the pus and putrefaction to flow out of it into the world, he had felt utterly empty, and strangely at peace.

For a little while.

For ten minutes after she left. And then the awful memories had raced down the field after him. He ran, as hard as he could. Not literally, but in his mind, as his body circumlocuted the basement for hour after hour. But in the end they had tackled him, brought him down, held him crushed beneath them by the sheer weight of their bulk.

And he had confronted yet again — sober this time — his encounter with the Jabberwock. The death of Jamie Forrester. And Martha Whittiker. And Dylan Shaw.

He was, after all, quite the murderer. Serial killer. Yeah, that's what Holmes Fischer was. A serial killer.

Sometime before dawn, he'd realized he couldn't do it. It was not the surrender of a wrestler, who has struggled and fought and given all his strength to the effort to defeat his opponent. It was a simple concession. An acknowledgement of the nature of the universe.

Holmes Fischer was a drunk. Right now, he was what the alcoholics called a dry drunk. A sober drunk. But he was a drunk nonetheless. He simply could not remain sober. Could not remain sober *and* remain sane, that is. He either had to blunt, obscure, blur the images that ate up his soul … or he had to kill himself.

Long before the sun rose up above the horizon somewhere out there on the flat, he came to accept that it was suicide or booze. One or the other. Those were the only choices his life afforded him.

And, of course, Holmes Fischer made the choice of a coward. Of course. Why, he would expect no less of himself. He was a sniveling weakling who caused the deaths of innocents, but who didn't have the guts, the cajones, to take his own life.

Morning light had not yet begun to filter through the trees at the top of the mountains when he set out for the Mason family crypt. Or vault. Or tomb.

One of those words.

It was one of the many places the county's token homeless person had laid his head in the past ten years, as he wandered the highways and byways of the county in a state of near falling-down inebriation all the time. And it was the only place where he'd left a stash. Not much of one. A single bottle of whiskey, but it was mostly full.

He had poured all the booze in his possession down the sink Sunday night, when he staggered back to the church basement after Viola Tackett had hanged an innocent teenager for the crime she knew Fish had committed. He had dumped it all, had gotten rid of every drop. Then he had suffered the ravages of the DTs, lived through it unassisted — which was something of a physical accomplishment, or so he had read. Unmedicated DTs killed a lot of people.

But it hadn't killed Fish. He had survived. He had slowly become again the human being he had been pre-booze. Well, a reasonable facsimile. He had lived in that reality. Had even shared the horror of that reality with Charlie McClintock. But after he did that … he found he just flat out couldn't live the rest of his life with the clarity of what he had done, like a bright light shining onto a dark stage where he writhed in its white-hot glare, naked and alone, sobriety laid his soul bare.

And he made a decision to leave sobriety behind, and crawl back into the bottle where he had lived in something like comfortable oblivion for all the years after the monster ripped off Jamie Forrester's face and sliced open Fish's chest. He hadn't just given in to a compulsion. He had made a rational decision, at least he had done that much. He had decided to live what was hopefully a blessedly short time on this earth in a drunken haze.

So he'd set out for his stash.

He had made a little "nest" in the alcove behind the stone structure that held the Mason family's … what had John called it? His jewels.

It was a mighty stone building that dominated the otherwise ordinary cemetery where the dead of Persimmon Ridge had been interred since the Nower family crossed the Cumberland Gap, whenever that was. Set off to the side in the back beneath the spreading limbs of a huge cherry tree, Jonathan Mason had built a stone structure fit for a king, into which he put the bodies of his wife and two little girls.

Rebecca Mason and her daughters, Melanie, and Marianne, had been killed in the fire that consumed their stately home on a hundred acres of prime bottom land in

Nate's Creek Hollow. John Mason had been away at the time. The best it could be determined, the fire had started in the wall next to the chimney — not an uncommon occurrence in houses with fireplaces if the chimneys were not kept scrupulously cleared of creosote.

It had turned out to be an unseasonably cold night in early September, and Rebecca had started a fire in the fireplace. John had not yet cleaned out the chimneys, the creosote buildup had caught fire, and the fire had spread through a crack in the bricks into the wall of the upstairs bedroom.

John Mason had been utterly devastated by his loss, and had built a stone edifice with a statue of the Virgin Mary on top and steps leading down into the ... crypt, tomb ... burial chamber below, where the bodies lay entombed in side-by-side chambers with names inscribed.

There was a space between the stonework in which the bodies where interred and the back wall of the burial chamber. It was warm in the winter, cool in the summer, dry all year round and one of Fish's favorite home-away-from-homes in the county.

He kept a sleeping bag there that he'd been given by Lester Peetree. The last time he had spent the night in that particular abode, he taken four bottles of wine and a bottle of whiskey down into the dark confines with him, had drunk all the wine and passed out. But the whiskey was still there, or so Fish's memory assured him, gleaning that information from fuzzy images, like out-of-focus photographs.

It was the only place he'd ever left booze — since it was safe there. Nobody ever went down there. John Mason had married again later in life and had two children, but they had grown up and moved away, and there was nobody left to mourn Rebecca and little girls.

And then Fish was there. He had been walking down the street in Persimmon Ridge and then he was crossing the cattle grate beneath the archway that said Cherry Blossom Acres into the cemetery. He had no memory of the miles in between. Perhaps his sharp mind was not as razor-edged as he'd thought.

Well, it was about to become even more blunted.

Fish crossed the cemetery to the back corner, walking in the lanes that had been laid out with stepping stones between the graves. He wouldn't walk on someone's grave.

There was no door on the stone building beneath the gigantic Mary, just stone steps leading down into the room below where the three bodies were encased in their own chambers. There were dried leaves on the stone steps and the crunching sound they made under Fish's feet had an oddly ominous sound. He had never been creeped out by the fact that he chose to make a nest and sleep in a building with three white-boned skeletons, but he felt a chill down his spine now.

The only light was what little filtered in through the doorway. In the dim interior, Fish went around to the back side of the stone structure that held the entombed caskets, knelt in the cool darkness of the alcove and felt around for

…

Yes, there it was. His eyes had not yet adjusted to the darkness, but he didn't need to see it to know that the bottle was almost full.

Letting out a sigh of relief — it might not have been there, you know! — and resignation, he sat down with his back against the wall, opened the bottle and gulped a drink, felt the fiery liquid warm him all the way down.

He hadn't even taken a second swallow when he heard the voices outside.

Chapter Four

"WHAT'S the matter with you, Neb?" Obie asked as the three brothers got out of Obie's new black pickup truck. "You's grouchy as a bobcat with a boil on its butt."

"Essie's dead," Neb cried, hadn't meant to say it like that, but he didn't seem to have no control over how he said things, not since yesterday when he had looked down at Essie lying on her back on the porch in a growing puddle of her own blood.

And he had to keep it together, had to be careful what he said, he couldn't just blurt something out and then everybody'd know.

"I know she's dead," Obie said. "It's a pure D shame for a fact, but you ain't acting sad. You acting pissed off."

"Naaa, he's actin' scared," Zach said.

Neb froze, averted his eyes so the other two couldn't see. He'd never imagined his brothers was smart enough to pick up on a thing like that, on how he was acting about Essie's death. Wasn't neither one of them the sharpest knives in the drawer and Neb was both surprised and frightened that they'd figured it out. They was just makin' conversation without even knowing they'd stumbled on the truth of it.

He *was* pissed. And he was scared, too. Way more scared than pissed.

He was pissed that it had happened at all. Like you get mad at yourself when you get caught sneaking off to smoke weed instead of tending to the garden like Mama said. You knew you hadn't ought to do a thing like that, knew Mama always caught them when they didn't get their chores done, so you's mad at yourself for not listening to yourself when you'd thought better of it and almost didn't go.

He was mad at himself like that now. Why'd he have to go practicing shooting in the front yard, for crying out loud? There Essie was, sitting on the porch, big as life, except now she wasn't alive anymore, she was dead. He shoulda stayed in the backyard to practice. But really wasn't his fault because she wasn't happy nowhere but the front porch and wouldn't come out to the back. It scared her. And he had to stay close to her — being alone scared her, too.

Still, he shoulda known better.

Of course, he couldn't rightly be blamed for what happened because how was he to know the trigger pull on that Colt .45 was so loose? Who'd a thunk a thing like that? Revolvers always had stiff triggers — unless you cocked them first — because the trigger had to do all the work of pulling the hammer back. Them kinds of guns was hard to aim right because it took so much strength just to pull the trigger you was like to yank the gun barrel off the target. How was he supposed to know this gun was different? Wasn't his fault.

That's what he was mad about — for not having the

sense not to practice in the front yard and at that trigger that pulled light when it wasn't supposed to.

But he was way, way more scared than he was mad. If Mama found out ...

He hadn't never in all his years on the earth seen anybody look like Mama looked when she told Malachi yesterday that she was gonna find out who done it and make them pay.

What would she do if she knew it was him? Would she shoot him? Might be she would. Mama always favored Essie over the boys — well, all except Malachi — took up for her against the boys. But that didn't happen very often because Essie never gave nobody no trouble, not Mama nor her brothers neither. She was like ... kinda like a puppy, wagging its tail and just being happy and not causing no trouble for anybody.

Yeah, if Mama knew, she might shoot Neb. Or ...

He couldn't even imagine or what else. But it'd be awful, that's for sure. He sure as Jackson didn't want to find out.

"Yeah, I'm mad. Course I'm mad. Ain't you mad? Somebody shot Essie, just drove by the house and bam, blew her away. Poor little Essie, wouldn't hurt a fly — don't that make you mad?"

"Sure it does," Zach said, but he didn't sound like he was mad. "Only you're acting ... I don't know. Funny, that's all. Like you's scared Mama was coming after you 'stead of whoever shot Essie."

Neb whirled on Zach.

"I ain't scared of no such thing. Don't you say a thing like that or I'll bust you in the mouth. You take it back."

Obie stepped in between them, shoving Zach one way and Neb the other.

"Knock it off. Ain't got time for fooling around. We got to fill up our tanks and go cruising."

Mama had said she wanted all three of the boys to fill up the tanks on their vehicles and drive all over the county showing folks how they had plenty of gas. Neb'd had no idea Big Ed had fixed hisself up his own private gas station, but it was just like Mama to know a thing like that and take advantage of it. Big Ed musta been out of town on J Day 'cause he wasn't home when they went out there before sunup to fill up. Mama'd let Neb take Howie Witherspoon's Dodge after all, and Howie's house was on the way to Big Ed's.

"Don't it strike you odd that Big Ed was gone but all his cars was there and his pickup, too?" Zach said.

Obie elbowed Neb in the ribs. "'Pears little brother ain't figured it out that Mama got rid of Big Ed."

"How you know that?"

"I just know Mama."

The boys had crossed the cemetery to the Mason family's tomb-thing, or whatever it was called, and Neb looked up into the stone eyes of the Virgin Mary standing guard on the top.

"I don't like this business," he said miserably.

"What — you scared of ghosts?"

"It ain't about being scared, you moron. It's about not wanting to open up a grave. You know how … gross that's gonna be?"

"Oh, no it ain't. All the gross part's over by now. Ain't gonna be nothing in these boxes 'cept bones. You got the crowbar?"

The three men went down the concrete steps into the cool interior of the vault.

"Mama said to open up the one marked Rebecca,"

Obie said. "She was a grown woman and the boxes they put them little girls in might be too small to fit Essie."

"It don't feel right," Neb said. "Throwin' out somebody's bones and putting Essie's body in their place. I don't want to get buried in a borrowed grave."

"We ain't borrowin' it, big brother," Obie said. "We *stealing* it. Mama said she was gonna get somebody to change the names, so it says Tackett instead of Mason. You best get used to it because this is where you're gonna be laid out when you die."

"The Nower House. The Mason family's grave. It don't feel right."

"Bobby Griffith's 'Vette, Earl Jackson's pickup, and now Howie Witherspoon's Dodge," Zach scoffed. "Them's *ours*. We took 'em. Things b'long to whoever can keep 'em, and they couldn't."

Neb didn't say anything else. Now he just wanted to open this grave up, get the bones out and get out of here.

Obie worked the end of the crowbar into the crack of the little doorway to the box where the bones of Rebecca Mason lay.

"How many you think it'll take?" he said as he worked.

"Take to what?"

"How many people you think Mama's gonna have to shoot before somebody comes forward and admits they killed Essie?"

Neb felt like he might throw up.

"Might take a right smart lot of them. You gonna have to threaten to shoot somebody who knows who done it — scare 'em into giving the shooter up. You might have to kill a lot of people 'fore you get the right one."

Neb suddenly turned and made for the steps, rushed up out of the tomb and upchucked his breakfast into the grass.

He leaned against the building panting, his eyes watering.

"You alright up there?" Obie called out.

"Just get the job done and don't worry about me."

He refused to go back down into the tomb, not even when they said they needed his help to pry open the final door to get to the box. He stood right where he was when they come back up the steps with the black plastic leaf bag full of bones.

"What're we gonna do with these?" Obie asked.

"Throw 'em out the car window," Zach suggested. He grinned. "See if you can hit one of them Do Not Litter signs."

The others headed back toward the truck but Neb stood where he was, leaned against the rock building. They was throwing away somebody's bones, then they was gonna bring Essie here and stick her in that box, and after that Mama was gonna start shooting people. And all of it was his fault.

"I didn't mean to," he said aloud, choking back tears. "As God is my witness, it was an accident."

He turned and started for the truck. Maybe after it was all over, he'd come here and put flowers on Essie's grave. Real regular like. Maybe every week, he'd bring her flowers.

Yeah, he'd do that.

He noticed as he walked across the graves back to the truck parked by the entrance how isolated and still the cemetery was. It'd be a great place to practice his quick draw.

～

FISH LISTENED to the Tackett boys outside the building, and to Zach and Obie when they came down the steps inside. Viola Tackett would never cease to amaze him. She was even stealing a grave for her daughter.

But the shock of that revelation was quickly eclipsed by the horror of what the men discussed next.

Fish didn't know the specifics of what was going on but it wasn't hard to figure out the gist of it. Somebody had shot Essie, drove by the house and shot her, and Viola was determined to find the shooter. She must have called a county meeting, summoned everybody from the four corners of Nowhere County to assemble them in once place so she could catch the murderer.

But how she intended to do it ... staggering.

"How many people you think Mama's gonna have to shoot before somebody comes forward and admits they killed Essie?"

"Might take a right smart lot of them. You gonna have to threaten to shoot somebody who knows the one done it — to make them give the shooter up. You might have to kill a lot of people to do that."

Could that really mean Viola Tackett intended to just ... just randomly *shoot* people, one after the other, until somebody confessed they'd done it or fingered the person who did.

Even Viola Tacket ...

No, that was not outside the realm of what that woman was capable of.

She had known Dylan Shaw didn't kill his grandmother. Fish had stood right in front of her and confessed, told her he had accidentally killed Martha Whittiker when she caught him stealing booze. Viola knew that boy was innocent. But she hanged him anyway. Killed, *murdered* an innocent teenager because ...

Yeah, why?

Fish didn't have any idea what the reason could be but he did know it was useless to try to understand the workings of a mind as depraved as hers.

Shoot one person after another.

Fish was grateful he was already sitting because he would have fallen down at that revelation if he'd been standing up.

Then they'd broken open the crypt, taken the bones and put them in a garbage bag and hauled them away, leaving Fish sitting in silence in his little nest in the darkness.

What should he do? What could he do?

Well, one thing he couldn't do … he looked at the bottle of whisky from which he had already taken a lone swallow, the bottle every fiber of his being was demanding he lift to his lips again and swallow more and more, feel the burning liquid slide down his throat and the blessed fuzziness cloud his thinking.

But he couldn't do that. He wouldn't. He rose to his feet and with trembling fingers, turned the bottle upside down and started to pour out the contents on the floor. A small amount splashed around his feet before he yanked the bottle upright again, panting.

Fine, then … he'd put the cap on and set it right back where he'd found it. Then he could come back. If he got desperate enough, he could come back.

But right now he had to focus on what to do. Warn people. Get help. *Something!*

Then he heard a voice from above. One of the Tacketts … it was Neb … was still there, had remained behind. Fish froze.

"I never meant no harm," Fish heard Neb whisper, his

voice anguished. "As God is my witness, I done it on accident."

Then he heard footsteps as Neb hurried away.

Didn't mean to. *An accident.*

The full understanding slammed down on Fish like a wrecking ball, hit him in the chest. The knowing and understanding of it almost knocked him to his knees in the little puddle of whisky by his shoe. If anybody on the planet knew how it felt to … to be responsible for the death of somebody, to kill someone by accident, it was Holmes Fischer, knew it in his guts, in his bones. In his very soul.

He heard that feeling in Neb Tackett's voice, was attuned to it, his own guilt reaching out to touch the same sensation in another.

Neb had killed someone. It'd been an accident, but he had taken a life. Fish would have bet his own life on that. And who else could it be?

Neb Tackett had killed his little sister. And now their mother was intent on killing one person after another until she found the killer. Which meant … would she really keep killing and killing and …?

In the opinion of Holmes Fischer, she absolutely would.

Fish had to find help.

The Middle of Nowhere! He had to get to there, tell Sam and Malachi and Charlie. They'd know what to do.

Chapter Five

*S*HEP. *It's time.*

Shepherd Clayton's head snapped up, but he didn't look around like he done at first, trying to see who'd called his name. He knew now it was Abby, though she didn't sound in his head no more like she done at first, when he first sat in their wrecked house off Sawmill Lane in Poorfolk Hollow, listening to the whispers. Then she'd just sounded like Abby, a voice like little bells ringing. Of course, then, she just told Shep what she thought about things, and suggested what she thought he'd ought to do about them.

Wasn't that way no more, though. The voice didn't sound like Abby at all, though it was Abby, had to be, who else could it be? And the voice didn't just say that Shep might oughta do a thing. The voice was in charge now. It had taken over Shepherd Clayton as surely as somebody shoving the driver out of his seat and driving off with the bus. Shepherd done whatever the voice said to do. Mostly, he didn't even talk no more, Shep didn't. Wasn't no need. The voice spoke out his mouth, said things as if it was Shep talking but it wasn't. He was just along for the ride.

Shep supposed he was okay with that. Wouldn't have mattered if he hadn't been. If he'd wanted it to be different he shoulda done something about it a long time ago because it was way past too late to take his body back now.

And if that was the way it had to be for him to get his Abby back, then Shep was more than alright with that, so's him and her and little Cody could be a family again. He'd find them another place to live. He'd get hisself a job to support them, or go on the gubmint dole if he had to, so's they'd have enough money to eat. That's all they needed — a place to live, food and each other. The three of them a family. Shep would give his life for that. He would kill for that.

And it appeared that was what Abby intended to do, kill them as was sticking their noses in where they didn't belong — Jolene Rutherford and them black men, Cotton Jackson and Stuart McClintock.

They was getting in the way of the Jabberwock's plans and so it was gonna take them out, using Shep and Claude to do it. But they'd already tried once and failed. Wasn't their fault that time, but Abby wanted to make sure this time the job got done. So she sent Shep and Claude out to round up reinforcements. Shep'd gone out yesterday, stopped at Hankey's Tavern off Ferguson Road just inside Beaufort County when he seen a bunch of familiar cars and trucks in the parking lot.

"Shep, are you alright?" Jasper Tucker'd asked, eyeing him suspiciously over the rim of his beer.

"Ain't nothing wrong with me. I'm fine."

"You don't seem fine. You seem ..."

"What?"

"I don't know, just not like yourself, is all. Queer-like."

Ronnie Potter'd chimed in then.

"Jasper's right. You …" He stopped, musta seen something on Shep's face that pulled him up short.

"Look, I get it. Of course I do. I lost my family, too. But … *shooting* people? Just going out and shooting people down like dogs—"

"It's a girl."

Huh?

"Yore baby. Becky Sue named her Marilee."

Ronnie looked like Shep had kicked him in the belly.

"What are you talking …?"

"Abby said. You wanted a boy and Becky Sue told you she did, too, but she really wanted a girl."

"A girl." Ronny almost choked on the word.

"*Marilee* just because Becky Sue liked that name, thought it was pretty. And *Winona* for Becky Sue's aunt Winona."

"How do you know that?" Ronny lost it then, started shouting. "How could you possibly know a thing like that? How?" He grabbed Shep's shirt at the shoulder and shook him. Then he let go, spoke soft. "If it was a girl, I's gonna suggest maybe we'd ought to name her Winnie after Becky Sue's aunt, but I hadn't never said nothing about it. How could you …? How …?"

"Abby." Shep's one-word answer.

Then Abby kept talking out Shep's mouth.

"If'n you ever want to see Becky Sue and that baby girl, you got to stop them meddlers. The Jabberwock don't like them messing in its affairs. It ain't never gonna let them people go unless we do what it says."

"And if we do?" Robbie asked. "If we … shoot them people, kill them, then—?"

"Then Becky Sue and Abby and all the others ..." Shep looked around the room at the men gathered there.

"Jethro, you want yore Trina back, do ya?"

Trina was his girlfriend. They'd been living together long's anybody could remember. The woman was ugly as a mud fence, but Jethro did love her something fierce.

Jethro didn't say nothing, appeared he couldn't. But he nodded. He set his jaw and nodded.

"Jim Bob," Shep said to the man who'd helped him run the McGintys' tractor into a creek when they were drunk teenagers. "You want to see them boys again? Want to watch Derek play baseball next summer? Jason'll be old enough for tee ball by then, won't he? Hope he ain't on the Food Town team with them ugly tee shirts Oscar Manning got 'em. The color of mashed peas. Abby said it was Oscar's girl, Chastity, picked 'em out."

Jim Bob's voice was ragged. "You telling me if I do what you say, if I go out and shoot these people I'll get my boys back? Jenny and the boys?"

"That's what I'm telling you." Shep paused, looking from one man to the next, making eye contact with each one. "And I'm also tellin' you that if you *don't* get rid of them meddlin' outsiders ..." Shep lowered his voice to a whisper for effect. No, Abby lowered his voice. "They's gone for good. You ain't never gonna see hide nor hair of any of 'em ever again."

"You done lost yore mind," Wilbur Gibson said. Then he looked around at the men who'd stopped drinking to listen to Shep when he'd come in. "Ya'll can't honestly be considerin' this." He looked at Jim Bob Claywell. "Listen to yourself, Jim Bob. *If I go out and shoot these people* ... You're a decent Christian man and" — he turned and looked at Shep — "and Shep Clayton here is crazier'n a soup sandwich."

They argued it back and forth, got loud, almost come to blows a time or two, but in the end, none of them agreed to help Shep and Claude. Some of them wanted to. Actually, most of them wanted to, but they flat out couldn't wrap their minds around what it was gonna take to get their kin back.

He didn't know what Abby was gonna do without no army to make sure they got rid of the meddlers, but apparently Abby had figured something out. Might be she'd found her own army because she told Shep later that him and Claude would have "help." Said they wouldn't be by theirselves.

It'd been pouring rain on Monday when they'd first tried to stop the meddlers. Shep figured he might have hit one or the other of them but there wasn't no way to be sure. He *was* sure, though, that he hadn't done enough damage to stop them. They was coming back — *today.* Abby said.

When it was just him and Claude shooting at them people, they'd gone up into the woods on the mountainside opposite Buzzard Knob to give them an unobstructed view of the buildings and the streets of Gideon below.

That wasn't the plan no more, though. Now they was supposed to hide up in the woods above the Gideon cemetery. Abby knew that's where them troublemakers was going and what they planned to do once they got there. But wasn't gonna work out like they had planned.

Might be some dead people in the cemetery today, but wasn't gonna be the ones them folks figured. The onliest dead bodies was gonna b'long to Stuart McClintock, Jolene Rutherford and Cotton Jackson.

~

SAM WAS HORRIFIED by the desperation she saw in Charlie's face. Even more horrified that it was mirrored in Malachi's.

"What are we going to do?" Sam launched the words out into the air of Rusty's not-hospital room and neither Charlie nor Malachi had an answer.

Charlie had said Sarah Throckmorton believed Viola knew Toby Witherspoon was staying at Sarah's house.

"Maybe she doesn't know for certain, but she sure enough suspects. Why else would she go to Sarah's house? And why take Toby's hat?"

"But how could she possibly—?"

Malachi waved off her question. "What difference does it make now? I have spent my whole life amazed by what my mother could figure out. Somehow ... some little thing ... somebody. I'd bet she doesn't know much for sure, but all she has to do is talk to Sarah ..."

There were chairs in Rusty's room, where the three of them had pulled them together yesterday to try to figure out what they would do next. Charlie sank down into one of them, struggling hard not to cry.

"She'll come after me," she said, trying to keep the tremor out of her voice. "As soon as she knows for sure ..."

"I think there's something you need to know." The words came from the doorway where Raylynn Bennett stood, looking wan and thin and ... She was calm, though. There was an eerie peace in the girl's demeanor. Sam had had neither the time nor the fortitude to question. But she did consider it now, looking at her. Raylynn Bennett had matured twenty years in the past two weeks. She might be a teenager in years, but the person standing in front of them now was a young woman who ... who has faced some profound sorrow and somehow survived it.

"Merrie's okay, she's not—"

"She's fine. She put half the litter of puppies together in a kennel with half the litter of kittens, and she's lying there while they crawl all over her."

Charlie gave the scraps of a smile to that description.

"I'll get right back to her, but I think you need to know that Viola Tackett has called a county meeting for today. She put the word out on the phone tree yesterday afternoon and I just heard about it. Margaret Atwood told her neighbor Agnes Wheatley, who told her cousin, Gladys Copley, and her best friend is my Aunt Effie. She just called me."

That's what Zach had been doing yesterday. Sam had seen Viola talking intently to her son right after she brought his dying sister into the clinic. Then Zach had gone down the hallway … and obviously into E.J.'s office to use the phone.

"A meeting …" Charlie's eyes were wide.

The last time Viola Tackett had called county residents together, she had murdered Liam Montgomery.

"What did she say it was for?" Malachi asked.

"She *said* it was so she could give everybody gasoline."

"What?" That made no sense.

"I didn't think it made sense, either," Raylynn said. "But that's what she's telling people. She said she has an 'inexhaustible' supply of gasoline, that she wasn't going to 'be selfish' with it, that she intended to give it away free because everybody needs it."

Malachi coughed in derision. "Riiiiight. Like Mama ever did anything even remotely altruistic in her whole life."

"Surely, nobody is falling for that line," Charlie said.

"Oh, people are suspicious. Still … Margaret Atwood said that Viola was putting it out there that the only thing people had to do to get the gas was to show up at noon today and put their names on a list."

"Then *that's* the point. The gasoline is a carrot to lure everybody to her meeting."

"So she can … what? What does she want everybody in town for?"

Suddenly, Malachi looked pale.

"Essie," he said. Sam felt the bottom fall out of her stomach. "She is trying to find out who shot Essie."

"So she gets everybody together … then what?" Sam asked.

"All the suspects … but how does she find out who did it?" Charlie wondered aloud.

Nobody answered.

"She must know something about Essie's shooting that she's not telling," Malachi said. "Neb must have seen more than she said he did. She's planning to use whatever that is to flush out the killer." Malachi paused for a beat. "People are going to get hurt. The frame of mind Mama's in …" Malachi stood and Sam knew he intended to go into the Ridge and … and deal with his mother.

"I need to get back to E.J.," Raylynn said. "But …" She looked uncomfortable.

"What?" Charlie asked.

"The old man in the waiting room … I think he may have … he smells bad."

Malachi rolled his eyes. "I washed the pants he had on. I hope they're dry." He started for the door. "I'll clean him up before—"

"Wait!" Sam cried. She could hear the desperation in the word but there was nothing she could do about it. He and Charlie turned to her.

"I know you're worried about what your mother might do," Sam said, "but right now … what are *we* supposed to do? Where do *we* go from here? It's one thing after another and we never have a chance to …" She shot a look at Rusty, lying so still on the bed. "We have to figure this out! Us, the three of us. It's here because of *us*. It's our fault. We have to … *do* something."

She hadn't meant for her voice to break, but she was too tired, too scared to keep her emotions in check. All the air seemed to drain out of Malachi.

"Okay, you're right. We need to … talk. Let me deal with …" He didn't finish, just gestured with his chin toward the waiting room. "Then … I think we have to find out how he showed up here. That matters. If Moses Weiss came from … out there —"

"But we've tried to talk to him," Sam said.

"He doesn't make any sense," Charlie said.

"We have to keep trying, keep at it. He's all we've got. Maybe the three of us *together* can make some sense out of his ramblings."

Twenty minutes and a clean pair of pants later, the three of them sat in a semi-circle around the dithered old man babbling nonsense to himself in the waiting room. Sam left Rusty with Pete, who had shown up this morning with his own mystery.

"My map's gone," he'd said. "Left here last night and went home and it wasn't on the wall no more. Somebody come in and took it".

One more *impossible*. Like the blackboard. Who … why? None of it made any more sense than the words coming out the mouth of the old man sitting there in damp pants that still smelled vaguely of urine.

"So sorry, just so, such a shame. Winona, did you say? Pretty name, Winona. Baby girls are carried high, and boys low. We didn't have children, should have. Flossie left after that first year, except she didn't go anywhere."

"Flossie? Who's Flossie?" Sam asked, but the man paid no more attention to the question than he had to the dozens of previous questions.

"A ring frozen in hamburger meat, can you beat that?"

"Who's Flossie?" Charlie countered. "Is she your wife?"

"Flossie bossy." He looked horrified. "I never said that, never did. Didn't think it either. Wouldn't have. Never."

"So Flossie was bossy?"

"She never breathed. Little Marilee never drew breath. Just a cold lump in Becky Sue's belly."

Becky Sue.

"Becky Sue *Potter?*" Sam asked. Charlie's brow furrowed trying to place the name. "She's pregnant, due any day. We thought she was in labor the day E.J. got bit by Judd's dog. She lives with Ronnie's mother and sister in that little red brick house on Elkhorn Road just off—"

"The one that had the walking bridge?" Charlie asked.

Sam nodded.

"It's old now," Charlie said. "That house ... I passed it this morning on my way here. A couple of days ago, it was fine. But this morning ..."

"That means ... they're all dead there. So this guy couldn't have had a recent conversation with Becky Sue—"

"Unless he talked to her after she died."

"How do you know Becky Sue Potter?" Malachi asked the old man. He didn't answer, but he did keep talking.

"Gone, all gone. Dead and cold. Selma and Amelia, too. Gone. Cotton said the Potters would be kind, he promised."

"Cotton *Jackson?*" The three exchanged a startled look. "You know Thelma's husband?"

"Jolene shouldn't have come with us, though."

"Pete's daughter's name is Jolene, isn't it?" Sam said. "I haven't seen her in years."

"Oh, no, not with that gunshot wound. Jolene should have stayed in bed."

"Are you talking about Jolene *Rutherford?*" Charlie asked. "Jolene Rutherford *got shot?*"

"Stuart said it was nothing, but I could see — the look on Jolene's face — it *hurt.*"

Charlie had frozen as solid as a block of ice at the mention of the name.

"Stuart …" Charlie gasped out the question, "*McClintock?*"

"Big football player like that, of course it wouldn't hurt him, but poor little Jolene …"

Sam's mind was racing, staggering and stumbling, trying to put it all together. Jolene *Rutherford.* Pete's daughter. Pete … who had communicated with *Stuart McClintock* using stickpins on his map on Monday. The map Pete said this morning was missing. Were Stuart and Jolene *with* Cotton Jackson? On the outside, the three of them together there? Talking to Becky Sue Potter … a *dead* Becky Sue Potter with a dead baby?

"Jolene should have stayed in bed like the old lady Cotton talked to in that nursing home."

Cotton's wife, Thelma, had told them she'd talked to the Witch of Gideon's daughter *in a nursing home.*

"Cotton *Jackson,* Jolene *Rutherford* and Stuart *McClintock?*" Malachi demanded. "Is that who you're talking about?"

Moses Weiss nodded his head but it might not have been a response to Malachi's question.

"They're going to face down the monster. Main Street in Gideon. High Noon."

"What monster?" Malachi asked.

This time the old man answered. Maybe. Or maybe the word just happened to be the next one lined up by his randomly firing synapses.

"Jabberwock."

Then a look of such utter terror stamped itself on the old man's face that it knocked the breath out of the other three. His eyes moved like a frightened rabbit's, seeing something their eyes could not.

"No, please, no, don't take me!" He shook his head frantically. "Forget it all. Never happened. *Please.*"

Then he screamed. Shrieked. Wailed.

The sound was as fierce and abrupt as a single bleat of a police siren and then was instantly cut off. His mouth kept working, though, screaming silently. And he wet himself.

Chapter Six

CHARLIE WENT next door to the ravaged Dollar General Store, dug around in the piles of discarded merchandise, and came back with a box of adult diapers. Malachi looked profoundly grateful. He got the old man into one, covered it with a borrowed pair of E.J.'s sweatpants, and parked Moses in the waiting room, babbling nonsense.

Now, she sat with Malachi, Sam and Pete in Rusty's not-hospital room, trying to process, make some sense of it all.

"You're saying my Jolene was … *shot*," Pete asked. He had been thunderstruck when they told him what the dithered old man had said, and that they believed Pete's daughter was with Cotton Jackson and Stuart — *Stuart!* — outside, and that they were doing there the same things the four of them were doing in Rusty's room. Trying to figure it out, trying to *do something about it.*

"That's what the old guy said," Malachi said. "But it wasn't a bad wound. He said she shouldn't have gone with them to see Becky Sue Potter, should have stayed behind.

44

But she didn't so she was obviously not hurt that bad, even if it did hurt."

"Jolene, here." Pete was having trouble fitting it into his head. "Shot? Who shot her … and why?" They all shrugged.

"We just got random information, whatever the old guy babbled," Malachi said.

"She came *here*. Why would …?"

"For the same reason Stuart came," Charlie said. "And Cotton Jackson. They're looking for us, trying to find us. I'd be willing to bet what they found in the whole county was what that little girl Lily Topple found when she went back into Gideon after she ran away from home. Everybody gone. Every house empty."

"And she said it," Sam said, excited to fit a little piece into the puzzle. "She said there was nothing left in the houses *except what was on the walls*. That would make sense, then, wouldn't it. Pete's map. Your mother's blackboard. They'd still be over there on that side … the outside."

"Following that train of thought — both of those things got moved last night. The map and the blackboard," Malachi said. "You don't suppose …

He let it dangle and Sam finished his sentence.

"Maybe *they* moved them. Jolene and Stuart and Cotton. Maybe they took down the blackboard and the map and moved them."

"What for?" Pete said.

That question hung out there unanswered.

"And where'd they put my map? Why didn't they bring it here? And, why'd they bring the blackboard *here*? What for?"

Nobody had an answer for those questions either and the conversation faltered, then Malachi let out a long breath.

"Okay, let's regroup. What do we know now that we didn't know before?" He held up one finger. "There are people out there searching for us, trying to … do something about the Jabberwock just like we are." He held up a second finger. "And we know they're going to Gideon today, *at noon today,* to … confront it somehow. To challenge it."

"And your point?" Charlie asked.

"I think we have to be there when they do."

That was a conversation stopper.

"We've danced around and around this. We know—"

"*Believe*—" Charlie countered.

"*Know* that the Jabberwock has come … out of hiding, out of hibernation, out of—"

"Like a cicada?" Pete put in, but Malachi didn't pause to respond.

"It's here because the three of us are here." Malachi was adamant. "And we know what Abby said, that it won't leave until it gets what it wants."

"And what it wants is …?" Pete asked.

"To play with us — me, Charlie and Sam."

"*Play with you?*" Pete was incredulous. "What does *that*—?"

Malachi was on a roll and didn't pause. "It captured the whole county just so it could capture the three of us."

Pete shook his head and stood. "The three of you got a whole lot more of this figured out than I have. How about I go look in on E.J. and Merrie — I ain't got nothing more to say that'll help."

As he walked out, Charlie put into words the "fly in the buttermilk" she'd found in Malachi's reasoning.

"I've been thinking about this ever since we decided we were the cause of the whole thing … so why now?"

"Because we're all here for the first time since graduation night," Sam said.

"No, we're not."

"Yes, we—"

"We were here for years, all three of us. We grew up here. Sam and I played baby dolls in the shade of the elementary school. You were a football hero, got cheered all the way down the field. If it wanted us, the three of us, why didn't it take us when we were little kids? We were all here together for years after that first-grade field trip."

"Until you left for college," Sam said.

"The morning after we graduated," Charlie said. And when she spoke again, she gave voice to the memories as they surfaced in her mind. Old, stored-away memories she had to blow the dust off before she could think them. But as soon as she did, they were crystal clear in her mind. "After the night of graduation … *when we went to Fearsome Hollow together.*"

Malachi looked confused.

"Went to Fearsome Hollow? You and me and Sam?"

Sam looked … what? Charlie couldn't read the look. Horrified? Yeah, but scared, too. Not the reaction Charlie would have expected.

"You're saying the three of us …?" Malachi began.

"Just like when we were first-graders, it was *your idea,*" Charlie said. "Don't you remember? You dared Sam and me to go with you to Gideon."

"Seriously?" Malachi's brow was furrowed with concentration.

"We went to Fearsome Hollow on graduation night … and got drunk," Charlie said. "And the next morning — nursing the worst hangover of my life — I left for college and the three of us were never together in Nowhere County at the same time again—"

"Until J-Day," Malachi said. "The Witch of Gideon said when we were first-graders that we shouldn't have come ... 'making it want,' remember?"

Charlie did. "We were playing in the woods, laughing, happy little first-graders."

"Making it want," Sam said, and her voice sounded haunted.

"Making it want ... to play with us?" Charlie asked. "To be like us? What?"

"It wanted what we had," Malachi said. "What we *were*. Carefree children."

"But it didn't take those children until *after*—" Charlie began.

"Yeah, why did it wait? There had to be something else. Something more than making it want when we were children."

"Graduation night." Charlie was thinking out loud. "We must have ... what? We made it 'want' on graduation night, too? Made it want more than we did that day on the field trip?"

"I have a vague, vague memory of maybe being there," Malachi said. "Maybe. I must have been smashed out of my gourd. Didn't learn to drink like a man until the Marines. You're sure we went there?"

"I'm sure," Charlie said. "I even remember going ... Sam's car, she drove and we sang along with the radio. Don't you remember?"

Malachi shook his head.

"There's just the ghost of ... We were in a car. I sat in the back seat. You were in front. I ..." He paused, frustrated. "After that? I don't remember ... what did we do?"

Charlie concentrated, willing her mind to retrieve the foggy images.

"There was a full moon."

"And a porch ..." Malachi was trying just as hard. "Didn't we ... were we sitting on a porch?"

Charlie shook her head in frustration. "I don't *know*! I don't remember."

No one spoke. Then Sam dropped words into the silence.

"I do." Her voice was as pleasantly husky as it always was, but now it was ... *hollow*, so full of unspent emotion that the words sounded like each one of them weighed a ton.

Holmes Fischer had walked to the cemetery from Persimmon Ridge and it had taken him ... how long? He had no idea. But he hadn't been in any hurry then, had just ambled along on his way to alcoholic oblivion. A bit like a pirate walking the plank ... he hadn't been in any hurry to get to the end of it.

Now, he had to get help fast! Walking all the way back to town would take too long. He had to find a phone. Looking around him, up and down the road leading to the cemetery, he couldn't see a single house anywhere.

Then what ...?

He had no choice and started walking. Urgency turned the walk into a run, or the best a man in Fish's physical condition could approximate a run. He didn't make it half a mile before he was gasping for breath, his head swimming, fearful he was about to vomit.

He had nothing in his stomach to throw up, only the single gulp of whiskey that ... he had left the bottle in the crypt. He actually had to catch himself, will his legs to continue walking forward when every muscle in his body was crying out that he go back.

Go back and get the bottle. No, don't get it. Go back and settle in with the bottle. Sit there in the cool dark as he had intended to do, and drink the bottle. Drink every drop. Allow the booze to transport him to that fuzzy not-reality of inebriation. That was about as far as he had been able to sink into drunkenness in the past few years with his cells so saturated with booze. But it was enough, blunted reality. It kept the memories at bay, allowed him to lie to himself successfully, tell himself that all was right with the world, that Holmes Fischer was a decent human being after all, who had chosen homelessness as a way of life and was grateful he had made a success of it.

He had hoped, *prayed* this morning, that the lack of all alcohol for four days had reset his internal drunk-meter. That when he did feel the hot liquid course through his veins, he would be able to push the needle farther than warm fuzzy. That he would achieve true drunkenness. True mindless inebriation. He'd gone out to the crypt this morning intending on banishing all reality, wiping his mind clean with the pure fire of bourbon whiskey.

Now he was running the other direction from that. Actually *running*. Alright, hobbling.

Then his feet got tangled up and he tripped. The momentum of his hobbling run carried him forward and he hit the pavement hard and rolled sideways into the ditch beside the road. His head connected with something solid and the world went blessedly dark.

Chapter Seven

Sam Sheridan remembered graduation night, all right. It was a night that changed everything about the whole rest of her life.

Sam tries to keep her eyes on the road, watch where she's going. But that's not easy given what else is going on in the car. All the windows are open, so the roar of the wind thrums inside the car, making pressure in Sam's ears. But it's a hot night and her car has no air-conditioning and besides, Malachi and Charlie definitely need the fresh air.

Above the roar of the wind is the sound of the radio, blasting full tilt, as loud as it will go. Charlie and Malachi are singing along, one country song after another. Charlie has a good voice, a little off key, tends toward sharp. Malachi's is a deep, clear baritone, but when they try to harmonize, then they're both off key and they can hear it, so they burst out laughing.

Suddenly, the crisp, clear sound of a piano fills the car, single notes in a haunting melody.

Charlie squeals in delight. "I loooove that song!"

"Lady." Kenny Rogers croons the lone word. Poignant. Wistful.

"Oh, turn it up, turn it up," Charlie cries. She's in the front seat beside Sam and she fumbles with the dials and knobs, trying to make the sound louder.

"It's up as high as it will go," Sam tells her, yelling so she can be heard.

But Charlie keeps begging Sam to turn up the volume anyway, either doesn't hear, doesn't understand or doesn't believe Sam. In Charlie's current state of inebriation, any of the three is possible.

"I'm your knight in shining armor and I love you," Kenny sings, and Charlie wails an inarticulate sound of pure extasy. "You have made me what I am ..."

"And I am yo- o-ours," Malachi joins in from the back seat, warbling the "yours" convincingly. He doesn't sound like Kenny Rogers, but it's a nice sound.

Charlie and Malachi sing along with the next few lines. Sam joins in the chorus. "And ohhhhhh, we belong together. Won't you believe in my song?"

Together they all three sing the ending. "You're my ..." and wail/groan the final word "lady."

Charlie falls back on the seat and literally kicks her feet in the floorboard in delight.

"That is the best song ever written!" she cries. Turning to the back seat. "Don't you think so, Malachi? The beeeest song e-var!" Sam can see him in the rearview mirror. He takes a long pull on the whiskey bottle he's holding, wipes his mouth with the back of his hand, and bleats a slurred "E-var!" in response before handing the bottle to Charlie, who dribbles a little of the amber liquid down her chin when she turns it up to her mouth.

It's possible the two of them will both pass out before they ever even get to Fearsome Hollow. Which might not be the bad news, though Sam isn't sure what she will do with them if they do. Just like she isn't sure how she came to be here in the first place, driving through the hot summer night toward Gideon, hauling her two soon-to-be-passed-out friends to the ghost town.

No, not friends.

Well, okay, friends, but the three of them have definitely scaled the societal barricades of standard high school striation of humanity to be here with each other tonight. Sam is a jock, loves sports, eats, sleeps and breathes basketball. Charlie is … Charlie. Beautiful. Aloof. Unattainable. And Malachi …

Malachi is the heartthrob quarterback every girl in the stands drools over.

Sam has been in love with him for years.

No, no … not "in love." Not that. A crush. She's just had a crush on him, that's all, as has every other female human being in a five-county area. And she had been brought into his orbit, and Charlie's, their senior year in Mr. Fischer's English class, where the three of them became Tolkien groupies, fascinated, addicted to, enamored of, confounded by, and obsessed with The Lord of the Rings. *Sam could not figure out why it was just the three of them, why every other senior, every other reader with opposable thumbs, hadn't fallen under the trilogy's spell.*

Jimbo'd had no idea what she saw in the books.

Her boyfriend's face flashes in front of her eyes — hair the color of sand on a beach, brown eyes, thick eyebrows, a pleasant face, not "handsome," but definitely good-looking. A really good guy. But no, Jimbo Mattingly is not her boyfriend. Not anymore. They had broken up three weeks before graduation and this time Sam is determined the split is going to last. As soon as school is out, Jimbo will go off to summer school at the University of Kentucky in Lexington and the distance will make the break easier. He'll accept that it's over. And in truth, it has been over for … she can't remember a time when she'd done anything more than coast along with Jimbo. And after … her face … she'd clung to him out of something like desperation — which was not fair to him.

She instinctively glances in the rearview mirror. Not much of her face is visible, but she can see enough, and she experiences anew the wave of self-loathing, the revulsion she feels every time she sees the gross acne spread across her skin. It had come out of nowhere last summer and overnight she felt like a leper, wanted to crawl into a hole and pull the dirt in after her.

She gets it, can quote the "causes and treatment options for adolescent acne" like a catechism. She knows it won't be permanent. "This too shall pass." But knowing it will eventually go away and living in the daily misery of sudden, acute ugliness are two entirely different things. Her self-esteem had taken a nose dive the day she saw the first bump, the first ugly, gross, yellow, pus-filled pimple, and she would not feel human again until it was gone, all gone.

Ugly was such an … ugly word. But it is the word that came to mind whenever Sam thought of herself. She had been pretty. Might even have teetered on the brink of beautiful. But now …

She shudders as Charlie takes up the chant and Malachi chimes in:

"Look out, world! You best run. We're the class of '81! Whoot, whoot, whoo-hoo!"

She shouts and hoots along with them. Malachi takes the tassel and chain with the gold letters "1981" off his cap and tosses it into the front seat, trying to hook it around the rearview mirror post where Sam and Charlie have hung theirs. He misses and intones from the back seat his imitation of Mr. Locklear's voice, calling out the names of the graduates so they can file across the stage, shake his hand and receive their diplomas from the stack of faux-leather binders on the table beside him.

"Ryan, Charlene Reneé … Sheridan, Martha Ann … Tackett, Abraham Malachi."

"Idiot," Charlie says and giggles. "Doesn't even know the alphabet." She and Malachi burst into a roar of laughter.

That's how the three of them had come to be here, driving through the dark toward a ghost town high up in Fearsome Hollow. Their diplomas had gotten mixed up. Sam had gone home right after the ceremony, didn't want to run into Jimbo in the crowd of celebrating seniors, grateful he'd been lined up two rows ahead —

Mattingly, *between* **L***arson and* **N***obles. When she finally opened up the faux leather folder and read the words "Tackett, Abraham Malachi" in scrolled letters on the diploma inside, she got in the car and went back to the high school, hoping to swap his diploma for hers before Malachi took hers home, all the way out to the other side of Killarney.*

She didn't actually expect to find Malachi at the school. The students had scattered like roaches on the kitchen floor as soon as the ceremony was over — all of them intent on celebrations that would spawn a county full of hungover teenagers in the morning. She only hoped he'd left his car in the parking lot — as a lot of the kids had, piling in together to go off partying. Maybe he'd left her diploma on the front seat; it was worth a shot, or at least she could put his there if his car was in the lot.

What she had found in the parking lot was not just Malachi's car, but Malachi himself. With Charlie Ryan. They were already well on their way to drunk when she pulled into the parking space next to them.

Seems Malachi hadn't gotten Sam's diploma, he'd gotten Charlie's, had caught her in the parking lot to make the exchange, where Charlie discovered, to her dismay, that she couldn't give him his diploma because she didn't have it. She had Sam's.

And then, well …

Malachi's football buddies had left for a party at some cabin out in the woods somewhere and he was supposed to meet them there. Charlie was to bring the booze to the gathering of her friends, showed the whiskey to Malachi and the two of them had decided to sample Charlie's wares before she left. One thing led to another and …

Somehow the straightening out of diplomas had devolved. Malachi had held one up and pretended to read from it … the speech Bilbo had given at his birthday gathering in the first book of Lord of the Rings.

Then they'd all taken a turn at quoting scenes from the trilogy.

Charlie had bemoaned the lack of adventure in their lives.

Malachi had said he would love to fight a battle with a Balrog like Gandalf.

Sam had said he could have her spot fighting Shelob any day.

Malachi'd said he bet there were even worse creatures than giant spiders lurking in the nooks and crannies of Nowhere County, did a spooky bwa-ha-ha-ha Boris Karloff laugh. And somehow that had led to Malachi daring Charlie and Sam to go with him to the creepiest of Nowhere County's crannies — the ghost town of Gideon, where the three of them would draw their swords and challenge whatever monstrosity happened to stroll by. Or something like that.

The raspy voice of Lionel Richie fills Sam's car.

"My Love ... there's only you in my life. The only thing that's right."

Charlie starts squealing again, telling Sam to "turn it up, turn it up — I love that song."

Sam pretends to turn the dial to keep Charlie from messing with it and accidentally changing the station.

The three of them sing along with "Endless Love" and by the time the song is over, Sam is pulling into the ghost town, her headlights illuminating the empty buildings and the huge tree in the center of town. She stops by the tree, and Charlie scrambles out of the front seat, almost falls to the ground and walks unsteadily to the nearest building where she sits/falls down on the porch steps.

Sam kills the lights and gets out of the car to join Charlie and now Malachi, also seated on the steps. She has always wondered how it is that this town, these houses, have remained so long, have not collapsed into piles of kindling long ago, as has been the fate of just about every other coal camp in the mountains. But Gideon ... it's like the town is somehow preserved ...

There's a full moon, the eerie light casting long, dark shadows down from the tree and between the buildings on the street.

"Look out world, you best run ..." Charlie begins and Malachi joins in, reaching into a sack and withdrawing a full whiskey bottle, mumbling "last one" as he opens it and offers a drink to Charlie.

Sam looks around. Their voices echo off the buildings and ring out in the cooling night air.

"Have a drink, Sam," Malachi says, takes her hand and pulls her down to sit beside him. "The chauffeur's off duty. You don't have to be the designated driver anymore."

He garbles the word "designated," but smiles at her with such a winning smile that she takes the bottle from him. She turns it up and takes a long swallow, almost choking. The liquid burns all the way down.

Chapter Eight

MALACHI LISTENED in fascination as Sam told him and Charlie what she remembered about the night the three of them graduated from high school. She'd been the only sober one, so she remembered it all.

As she spoke, vague images formed in his mind. Charlie instantly recalled that they had met in the high school parking lot to swap diplomas after the high school principal had given them the wrong ones. Malachi could fish a foggy image of that out of his mind, too. He recalled calling out to Charlie as she stood behind her car, the lid of the trunk up. And the rest of the memory took shape.

"WE HAVE A PROBLEM," he says, walking up to her, holding a diploma in one hand and his wadded-up black robe in the other.

"How so?"

"I got yours." He extends the diploma toward her. "Old man Locklear couldn't find his big toe with a tracking dog and a searchlight.

"Then I must have gotten …"

Leaving the trunk lid open, she steps around to the driver's side of the car, opens the door and reaches inside, where she had dropped her diploma on the front seat.

Malachi follows. "You don't want to spend the rest of your life with a diploma on your wall that says Abraham Malachi Tackett. But be grateful for small favors; if it'd been my brother's, you'd have had Nebuchadnezzar Ezekiel Tackett, which would have taken two, maybe three lines."

Neb hadn't graduated, of course. Hadn't made it out of eighth grade, even. And in those eight years of school, he had never even learned to spell the first name their mother had hung around his neck like an albatross.

Charlie opens the diploma in her hand and giggles.

"What's so funny?"

"Well, actually, I wouldn't have had to live with Malachi Tackett immortalized on my wall." She straightens up out of the car and holds the folder out to him. He opens it and reads, "Martha Ann Sheridan."

"What the …?"

Then Charlie laughs out loud. "You got mine. I got Sam's. Which means …"

"Sam got mine." He joins her in laughter.

"Guess I need to go track Sam down."

"Before you go, why don't you have one for the road."

She goes back around to the trunk of her car, opens a grocery sack and extracts from it a full bottle of Jim Beam. She cracks it open and holds it out.

"Don't have a glass or ice or a mixer, but …"

Malachi lifts the bottle.

"I take my bourbon neat." He turns it up and drinks.

• • •

"I was soooo trying to impress you," he said to Charlie. "All macho. Oh, I don't need a glass or ice. I drink from a bottle all the time. Which was a total crock. Oh, I drank — beer, strictly beer. That whiskey was a new thing. Probably why I got so smashed."

"It wasn't like I was an accomplished drinker myself," Charlie said. "That's why I'd been given the job of bringing the booze. Kim and Liza thought I could be trusted not to sample it before I got there."

"A tactical error on their part."

More silence. Both he and Charlie looked back to Sam.

"Then what happened?" Charlie asked.

Sam who looked … what? Awful. The dark circles under her eyes seemed to have deepened just since they'd begun the conversation. Maybe because there was color in her face now. She'd been pale, but now there was color. Her cheeks had flushed.

She took a deep, almost shuddering breath and seemed to grab hold of herself. Her back straightened and she looked from one to the other. The haunted look in her eyes broke Malachi's heart.

"What happened was … we sat together on the porch steps of the house closest to the Carthage Oak, passing the bottle around from one to the other. It got very quiet. Still. I … wasn't a drinker. Like, not *ever.* The basketball coach would have tossed me off the team if … so drinking whiskey straight from the bottle …"

"… must have knocked you on your keister quick," Charlie said.

"It did. But later, not until after …" She took a breath. "Before I … lost it, I remember it was too quiet. There'd been crickets when we first got there. And the usual night sounds. Tree frogs, an occasional hoot owl. Like that. But the longer we were there, the quieter it got. I can see now

… maybe I could even tell then, but wouldn't admit it, but the quiet wasn't natural quiet."

Sam looked away from them, focused on a spot high on the wall above Rusty's bed.

"I think … I think the mist came, too. But not then. Not until … later."

She stopped again, then turned slowly back to look at Malachi.

"You don't remember what happened? Really don't remember a thing? Think about it?"

Her gaze was penetrating and he called up the haze of memories back into the front of his mind. Examined the blurred images. The night flying by outside the windows of a car, where the wind roared and music blared.

He tried to pull up later images. He could see the Carthage Oak. Charlie sat on one side of him, Sam on the other. They were on a porch.

Blurred images. Movement. He's walking … staggering away from the tree. His arm is around somebody, who's holding him up. Sam.

He's singing.

Then … nothing.

"I can't remember anything after … you and I walked away. To the car, maybe? Do you remember? What happened after that?"

She takes one breath. Two. Looks directly into his eyes.

"Charlie passed out on the porch. You and I went back to the car. We got in the back seat. And …"

Then she just looked at him, couldn't seem to say anything else.

The images slowly washed back into his mind, like a wave moving up the shore and then retreating, leaving a delicate lace of foam on the sand.

• • •

HER HAIR IS SO SOFT. She leans against him, puts her head on his shoulder and her hair … it's so silky. He runs his fingers through it. Smells it, like fruit. She lifts her head and looks at him, her eyes bright. He leans in and kisses her.

THE SHOCK OF RECOGNITION, of sudden understanding must have shown on his face because Sam looked like he'd slapped her. She recoiled physically, made a kind of sound, strangled, like a sob, then dropped her chin and her hair fell around her face, hiding it. But he could hear her crying.

"Oh, Sam …" It was all he could say. He shot a glance at Charlie and her face registered some combination of understanding, horror, recognition and sympathy. He saw her reach out toward Sam, then stop and withdraw her hand.

Malachi knew Sam was *mortified* to call up a memory like that out of the depths of the past — in front of other people. But he had no idea what to say, how to put out the red glow of humiliation from her cheeks.

"Sam … I never. I didn't know. I … I'm so sorry."

She sniffed loudly, shook her head and looked up. Her fiery-red cheeks were wet.

"Nothing to be sorry about. Consenting adults and all that. We were both eighteen." He watched her force herself to go on. "Besides … you can't be sorry, because I'm not. I will never be sorry about that night. If it hadn't happened …" Her voice trailed off.

He followed her gaze to the boy, lying too still on the bed.

And the whole bottom fell out of Malachi Tackett's world.

~

Stuart McClintock pulled his rented Lexus to a stop in front of a building in the Middle of Nowhere with a sign declaring Healthy Pets Animal Clinic and Hospital. He and Jolene Rutherford had been here yesterday, had put up the blackboard from Charlie's mother's kitchen on the wall in the waiting room.

He turned off the motor but made no effort to get out.

"You don't want to see, do you?" Jolene asked.

He said nothing.

"Want me to go look and come out and tell you?"

Letting out a breath, Stuart shook his head.

"I'll wait in the car," Cotton Jackson said from the back seat.

Stuart and Jolene got out and went into the building. They had had a hard time getting the blackboard off the wall in Charlie's mother's kitchen the day before — only because Stuart had been determined not to mess up the paint. The blackboard was affixed with screws, the kind that fastened into expandable wing nuts inside the open space behind the drywall. If he just pulled one out, it'd leave a big hole in the wall.

They'd been careful, left nothing but an empty space behind when they finally had the blackboard down. Clearly, it'd been there a long time. The paint was darker in the spot where it had hung. Sunlight over the years had faded the paint in the rest of the room.

Then they decided what to write on it. Stuart did the actual writing, so Charlie would recognize his handwriting. He wanted her to *know he was here!* Being careful not to smear the words Charlie had obviously left on the black-board on purpose, Stuart wrote the message in as small a script as possible, but even so, there wasn't enough space to say all he wanted to say to Charlie. Of course, there wouldn't have been enough space to do that on a blackboard the size of a football field.

They hadn't bothered to affix the blackboard to the wall in the waiting room of the veterinary clinic, just balanced it on the backs of a row of chairs and leaned it back against the wall. And it was still there, right where they'd left it. But the words he had written on it were gone. In their place was not a response to the message. It was … a child's drawing.

Merrie!

Stuart sucked in an involuntary gasp of air. She'd drawn it. He was positive, absolutely certain it was his little girl's artwork. A strange shape that might have been … maybe a tree and limbs. Or an octopus on the ocean floor. Whatever it was had a fat center and appendages extending out from it in all directions.

A flower maybe.

He couldn't see it very well because his eyes had suddenly filled with tears. He walked slowly across the room and put out his hand, touched the chalk on the surface of the blackboard.

Merrie had drawn this picture.

Which meant … what?

The only thing it could have meant was that the people on the other side couldn't see the message he'd left there, the one he had so carefully crafted, using small letters so they could say as much as possible.

Careful not to erase the message about bird seed, he'd put down who they are, that they were looking, that it appeared everybody and everything in the whole county had just vanished. He'd explained that the Jabberwock wiped out memories so people who left didn't remember what they saw here. And about the suddenly-old houses.

All of that had been erased.

"Don't guess there's any sense in going into the Ridge to see if there's a stickpin message on the map." His voice was thick.

They had come here first. It was on the way from Cotton's house to Fearsome Hollow and Persimmon Ridge was the opposite direction. They'd decided if they found a message here, they would go there to see what message might have been left on the map.

"Guess not," Jolene said.

Stuart grew still, closed his eyes. Merrie had been here. Right here in this room. Not long ago. She had drawn that picture on the blackboard. He was sure of it. And so he stood trying to … sense her. Feel her essence, some part of her essential being that still lingered in the air.

Like her spirit.

Yeah, maybe that.

"We need to go," Jolene said softly, and when he opened his eyes, he saw sympathy in hers.

"Right, wouldn't want to be late to the party where we're going to be torn apart or get our heads shot off."

But Stuart didn't turn to go. Couldn't. He reached out his hand to the child's drawing on the blackboard, touched the chalk and pulled his hand away, rubbing the chalk between his fingers. Then he picked up the eraser off the chalkboard shelf and used it to clean off a spot right in the middle of Merrie's flower. He picked up the chalk and wrote in clear, block letters on the bare spot.

Daddy loves, you, pumpkin.

He stepped back, eyed his work and then turned for the door, walked out, got into the car and started down County

Road 278 East toward Fearsome Hollow. The locals called it Lexington Road.

Looking at his watch, he thought about what Jolene had said yesterday.

A showdown on Main Street. High noon.

Chapter Nine

Charlie didn't mean to blurt it out like that, but surprise had exploded the word out of her throat.

She shot a look at Malachi and back to Sam.

Sam couldn't possibly mean …

"But I thought Jimbo—"

Charlie hadn't meant to blurt that out either. Would have done anything to grab the words back.

She reached out, touched Sam's knee.

"Uh … would you wait here while I go get a crowbar to pry my foot out of my mouth?"

Sam looked at her kindly. Malachi looked … like he had swallowed a live hand grenade and it had just detonated in his belly.

"Everybody thought so. So I just let them. Jimbo was … he'd already been killed before I found out I was pregnant. And his mother … I think it might have been … a *comfort* to her before she died."

Jimbo's mother had had cancer, if Charlie remembered right. Didn't live until Christmas and she was the only family Jimbo had.

Sam took a breath and looked at Malachi.

"I'm sorry. I certainly never intended for you to find out … this way. Not *now*."

Malachi was staring at Rusty, his eyes unreadable.

"You need to know, it's not like I'm not sure. Like *maybe* Jimbo was …" She couldn't seem to get it all out in one piece. "Jimbo couldn't have been Rusty's father because Jimbo and I never …"

She let the words dangle out there in the air, and Charlie ached for her. What a horrible way to have to reveal your most private secrets.

"We didn't … I *couldn't* because I didn't love him. I wanted to love him. I tried to. I was *supposed to*, for crying out loud — we went together for three years. But it just wasn't there. Everybody assumed he and I would get married and settle down and have babies, so let it be written, so let it be done, but I didn't want that. Not with Jimbo. And Jimbo was pressuring me to sleep with him, so we kept breaking up. Then he would come back and apologize and I'd …"

Malachi's eyes snapped to Sam and Charlie realized what he'd just put together in his head.

"That night … graduation. You and I … it was … your *first* …"

Sam actually managed the scraps of a smile.

"How about we save that conversation for some other time," she said and coughed. Then the moment of levity passed as quickly as it had come and the haunted look returned to her eyes. "There's more we need to talk about."

"Sam, I'm sorry, I …"

"Let me finish because this is the important part." She

looked at Charlie and included her in what she said next. "The mist came. It was there. I saw it, outside the windows of the car while we ... And I heard the whispers — *them* — like that day in the woods."

"The Jabberwock," Charlie gasped. Sam nodded.

She reached up and wiped her face, her jaw set, clearly would have given all she owned not to be here saying this. But she soldiered through.

"And ever since J-Day ... no, not then, but after Charlie showed us those pictures and we remembered when we were first-graders, I've been thinking about it. About what the witch said."

She took another breath.

"When we were kids, the witch said we should not have come, 'making it want.' Want to play with us, to be like us ... to *be* us. Carefree children."

She drew another shaky breath.

"That's what we made the Jabberwock want when we were seven years old." She stopped again. "And the night of graduation, I think we made it want ... *more*. Different. It wanted what Malachi and I had. It wanted the touching and the comfort and the affection. The *humanity*."

"Fish said it, that the Jabberwock was *plural*. Not an it. A *them*. More than one. Each individual. Like people. Maybe used to *be* people but isn't anymore. And when Malachi and I ... it wanted *that* — that most intimately human of all experiences."

"But then we were gone," Charlie said. "I left the next morning and for the next dozen years it ... what?"

"Waited," Malachi whispered.

"And then we came back here, the three of us ... the carefree children," Charlie said. "And ... the rest. It wants—"

"What we have. What we *are*. And it won't leave, it will never let go until we give it what it wants."

The room was silent then. Malachi's breathing was rapid. Charlie knew his thoughts must be spinning around in pirouettes, ballerinas on a stage. His emotions showed on his face, a thundering waterfall of feelings that was probably making so much noise, thundering and vibrating, that he couldn't shut any of it out.

"We have to go there, don't we," Charlie heard herself say, and recognized it for the truth when she heard it. Her voice was shaky, but clear. "It's the only thing we can do. We have to go there … and *play with it*."

"That's what it wants," Sam said.

"If we don't give it what it wants," Charlie said, "it'll stay here taking one person after another until … it will absorb us all."

"Today," Malachi said.

"At noon." Again Charlie heard herself speak and recognized the truth. "High noon. While the others outside …" Her voice broke. "While Stuart and the others are there, we have to be there, too. All of us together, fighting together at the same time." Charlie looked at her watch. "High noon … we better get after it."

Malachi got to his feet, crossed the space between him and Sam in two steps, then stood beside her. He put his hand on her shoulder.

"Sam, I—"

"Don't." The word was a whisper on a breath and Malachi withdrew his hand. But he stood there beside her, looking down at her.

Then he raised his eyes to the boy on the bed. Sam couldn't see his face, but Charlie could. The mix of feelings that washed over it was the most amazing display of unreserved, transparent emotion she'd ever seen.

How did you do that, discover over the course of a half hour, that you have a son? A son who might … die.

Malachi had obviously had the same thought.

"We have to do this"— his voice was ragged — *"now."*

Then he turned and walked to the door, turned back and waited for Sam and Charlie.

"Give me a minute," Sam said. "With Rusty."

And then it landed on Charlie's chest, too, the force of an avalanche falling down on top of her.

Merrie.

She and Sam and Malachi were about to walk into the mouth of a roaring lion. Charlie had seen the claw marks on Fish's chest. She had listened to his horror description of the monsters that had rushed at him from the trees. The teeth and claws. That's what the three of them were going out to face. With no weapons, no plan. No do-overs. No backstop.

They all could … die.

RAYLYNN LOOKED AT E.J.'s sleeping face. Watched his chest move up and down. He looked bad, so haggard, worn out and in pain. The growth of beard on his cheeks was beginning to form a solid surface. He hadn't shaved in almost a week and when the beard grew all the way in, it would be mostly gray.

Except it wouldn't grow in.

She reached into her pocket and withdrew the full bottle of oxycontin. Today was the day, for a lot of reasons. Mostly because it was time, she knew it and so did E.J., but also because Sam would definitely miss pills out of her bottle today. The only way Raylynn could get the number of pills she needed was to take almost every remaining pill.

When she went to the bottle to get E.J.'s every-four-hours dose, Sam would notice.

Today.

"I'm not asleep," E.J. said.

She could tell by the tension in his voice he was in pain. It wouldn't be long now.

"I was having the most terrible dream. I dreamed …" He looked at her, and some recognition came into his face then. "It wasn't a dream, was it? You did tell me that your father …"

She put out her finger and touched his lips.

"Doesn't matter now. Nothing matters now." She held up the full bottle. "I've got enough. We can … we can go today."

"No." His voice had a firmness she hadn't heard in a long time. "No, not *we*, Raylynn. I'm not taking those pills unless you swear to me an oath that you won't take the ones you saved for yourself."

"We've been over this. It's all right, everything's all right."

And on so many levels, it was all *right*. Raylynn had made her peace with a lot of things. Something in her had shifted. Perhaps it was giving up any image of a future. Perhaps it was embracing not just the concept of her own mortality but the reality of it. Not just the idea that yes, she would die someday, but the reality that the someday was today. That life on this planet for Raylynn Bennet was about to be over.

That was fine with her. As long as she could stay with E.J., she didn't care if where they were going was … the other side. She would die with him because she wanted to be with him, and because she could not, would not countenance an existence without him.

"Raylynn, listen to me." There was strength in his

words, so much that it was a little like ... when she was a little girl, her mother would make cookies and just the smell of them from the kitchen would make Raylynn's mouth water. The vestige of power in E.J.'s words had the aroma of the old E.J., the strong man she had fallen so totally in love with. Just a whiff, but it made her mouth water for the real thing. That's how it would be ... on the other side.

The strength in his hand when he clasped her arm was surprising.

"You don't get it and you have to. You have to understand. I don't want to die of rabies, but I will do exactly that ... or of whatever the infection is that's eating up my leg. I'll die of whatever cause is out there to bite me and take my life. I will NOT take a handful of pills and exit this world *with you*. I won't let your kill yourself with me."

"But ..."

He was so strong, so adamant and determined.

"I'm sorry. I am so, so sorry I asked you to help me. It was a weak, cowardly thing to do and I apologize. I never should have dragged you into my exit fantasy. Because that's what it was, all it was. Just a fantasy. I wanted to go to sleep and never wake up. But that's not ... I inserted a quarter and did *not* get the song I wanted. But I have to sing along with the one that's playing."

"No, E.J., you can't ... you'll ..."

"Get rabies. *Die of rabies* — that's an unimaginably horrible thought." His grip on her arm actually grew stronger.

"But you're a beautiful young woman with—"

"Don't you dare say 'with your whole life ahead of you.' People always say that. What life? What about the Jabberwock? And ... my father?"

"Well ..." Something like a grin tried and almost

succeeded in capturing his face. "I never promised you a rose garden."

"What?"

"Never mind. Just … don't make me into the hero who marched bravely into the jaws of a horrible death. Not! I'm so scared I almost wet myself when I think about it."

"But you don't *have* to—"

"Yeah, I do. We both do. Can't just pop a pill — plop-plop, fizz-fizz, oh what a relief it is."

She didn't know what that meant and apparently her lack of comprehension showed, because this time the grin made it all the way across his face.

Then the strength drained out of him, and she realized he had summoned his last reserves to say to her what he'd said. He let go of her arm, could no longer grip it, and collapsed back on the bed into the pain-riddled body he'd managed to escape for a couple of minutes.

"Raylynn." The voice came from the doorway and she turned to see Charlie McClintock standing there. Like maybe she had been standing there for a while. Maybe she had seen.

"I have to talk to you. It's very important."

Chapter Ten

THERE WAS A LARGE, rectangular room that ran along the back wall of the clinic where wire kennels had been set up to keep E.J.'s recovering patients, the "hospital" part of the Healthy Pets Veterinary Clinic and Hospital. It was where Merrie's private menagerie was housed. A couple of litters of puppies, and one of kittens that had grown so fast in the past two weeks, they no longer had to be fed from the little bottle Raylynn had rigged up to give them nourishment after E.J. had had to put their mother to sleep.

Charlie stood in the doorway of the room, soaking up the sound of her little girl's laughter. Merrie had the most glorious laugh. Maybe because her name was Merrie. It was all warmth and rounded tones, a tinkling sound that was a little like wind chimes and a little like what Charlie imagined must be the sound of bells in monasteries high up in the Himalayan mountains.

The little girl was inside the biggest of the kennels, rolling around on the floor with a litter of more than half a dozen puppies. Just lying there as the puppies crawled all over her, laughing at the feel of them.

She was babbling something that might have been real words if Charlie'd concentrated to make sense out of it. But they were just sounds to her now, seasoned with words, "… tickles me … widdle claws are sharp … Tinkerbell … tongue so pink … whee …"

It didn't matter what she was saying because she was only talking to the puppies and her intent and meaning was clear by the tone of her voice and the love in every word.

Charlie sucked in a little gasp to keep from sobbing, stepped back so Merrie wouldn't look up and see her standing there. If she did, she would leap to her feet, casting puppies every which way, and race to Charlie, begging please-oh-please-oh-please, can I have three puppies? Pleeeeease.

It had started out with one, of course. Can I have a puppy, please, Mommy? Not a surprising request. But then, Merrie hadn't been able to decide between her two favorite ones. This morning, she had announced that she wanted *three* of them because the puppies from the other litter had finally opened their eyes and one of them had blue eyes. It *did!* Charlie couldn't see the color, but she was sure Merrie could.

Charlie had come here to … say goodbye to the little girl. To lie to her, tell her Mommy was going somewhere with "Aunt Sam" and "Uncle Malachi." Not far. Wouldn't be gone long at all.

The truth was she might never come back. Probably wouldn't. But she could let none of that reality show on her face. It would frighten the little girl and Charlie couldn't stand the thought of little Merrie being afraid. She'd have to keep it light, just go in and pop a kiss on the child's little nose and …

No.

No, no, no! Charlie couldn't do it. Couldn't leave her. Could *not*. She had already almost lost her, had come so close that the frayed ends of her nerves sometimes felt the pain and terror of it when she wasn't even remembering what had happened. Sitting beside the kiln as the sun began to light the black sky. Singing to the little girl she thought was dead inside.

Hush little baby don't you cry. Mama's gonna sing you a lullaby.

Charlie'd broken off all her fingernails, didn't even realize it until hours later. Every one of the acrylic nails she had paid more than the gross national product of some Third World countries for — they were lying in pieces in the grass beside the kiln. Some of them were stuck in the almost imperceptible crack where the door fit into the jamb of the box. Charlie'd broken them off clawing at it. She supposed that was what she'd done. She didn't remember. Much of that time was blessedly a total blur.

She didn't even have to remember now, to feel the agony of being bereft.

She could *not* leave Merrie here and go off to … Absolutely, one hundred percent could *not*. She could not walk out the door, get in the car with Sam and Malachi and drive into such harrowing danger that there was almost no chance she'd survive. An image of Fish's chest, the thick bands of scar tissue crisscrossing it, like he'd been savaged by a grizzly bear.

She loved that precious child far too much to leave her!

And the power of that love was the only force in the universe strong enough to make her go.

For Merrie to survive, they had to beat the Jabberwock. The three of them, the Breakfast Club, had to walk innocently into its lair and … play kiddie games with it.

"Mommie!" Merrie had spotted her through the tangle of animals crawling on her and got to her feet. She flung open the kennel door, then realized she'd have to chase all the puppies down and catch them — she'd already had to do that once before — if she didn't fasten the door shut behind her.

Charlie knelt on one knee and as quickly as Merrie's little fingers could flip the catch, she turned and raced into Charlie's arms.

"Three of dem. All three. Pleeeeease, Mommy."

Charlie was afraid if she opened her mouth, if she tried to speak, she would burst into tears and be unable to stop sobbing. So she just smiled a tremulous smile and nodded.

Merrie was thunderstruck.

"Yes? You mean … I can have dim?"

Charlie nodded again.

"All three?"

"Sure, the more the merrier," Charlie was finally able to say, then grabbed the little girl in a hug that was so tight Merrie struggled to be free.

"How come?" she asked, pulling out of her mother's arms so she could look at her face. "How come now I can have dem, but not when I asked this morning?"

"Because I love you more now than I did this morning." She realized she probably shouldn't have put it that way. "And I will love you more this afternoon than I do now. I love you to the moon and back."

Merrie studied her face.

"What's wrong, Mommy?"

Charlie had to get away. This was taking too long.

"Nothing's wrong, pumpkin." That's what Stuart called her. She stammered, struggled for something, anything to say.

"What are you going to name your three new puppies?"

"Oh, all da puppies already gots names. Santa Claus has da biggest claws, the one wiff a black spot on his head is the one that bitted me, his name's Poopy. The solid black one wiff white paws is Twinkle Sparkle."

She flung herself back into Charlies arms and squeezed her neck so tight Charlie could barely breathe.

"Thank you, Mommy. I love you. Can I take den home to Aunt Sam's tonight? Can day sleep wiff me?"

"I'll let you know when I get back."

"Where you goin?"

Charlie heard apprehension in the voice.

"I'll be back before you even know I've been gone."

It took every speck of strength Charlie had to pull the rest of the way out of Merrie's embrace and stand up.

"Take care of Santa Claus and Poopy and well, whatever the third one is."

She leaned over and planted the peck of a kiss on Merrie's nose.

"I love you. I'll see you in a little while."

She turned around, holding her breath, because if she'd breathed she would burst out sobbing. She heard Merrie squealing behind her.

"Poopy, Santa Claus, Twinkle Sparkle — Mommy said I could take you home wiff me and you'll be *my* doggies." She heard the little girl open the latch of the kennel, then fasten it back when she closed the door behind her.

"I love you Mommy!" Merrie called after her, but Charlie didn't dare turn to reply.

Charlie went to E.J.'s room. Raylynn was there and E.J. was speaking earnestly to her. Charlie paused at the door, didn't want to interrupt that moment.

"… fizz-fizz, oh, what a relief it is," E.J. said and then collapsed back onto the bed, panting from pain.

"Raylynn, I have to talk to you," Charlie said. "It's very important."

Raylynn started to get up but E.J.'s weak voice came from the bed, "I thought we already settled this part. The we're-going-to-hide-all-the-bad-stuff-from-E.J. part."

Charlie nodded, spilled the whole story in a few short sentences, blurted out what she and the others were about to do.

"I need you to take care of Merrie," she told Raylynn.

"Oh, no problem, she's playing with the puppies right now—"

"I don't mean just for the next little while, or the rest of the day."

Raylynn backed up from what she was driving at.

"If I don't come back then … we lost. Our side … the Jabberwock took us. If that happens …"

She couldn't catch her breath, staring into the girl's horrified eyes. "If that happens, you and everybody else … I'm just asking you to please, please take care of her."

Her voice broke then, and she let the tears flow. "Hold her tight and don't let her be afraid. Tell her to close her eyes and it'll be over soon … and she and I will be together again."

Chapter Eleven

SAM WAS ON HER KNEES. She didn't remember how she'd gotten there, must simply have slid out of the chair beside Rusty's bed. She was holding his limp hand, had her forehead pressed against it as she prayed.

Sam had never been what she'd have described as a "religious" person. In truth, those kinds of people, the sanctimonious ones who were far more interested in your behavior than the nature of your heart, were the reason she hadn't gone to church for years. Oh, she was a Christian, understood Christianity well enough to grasp that Jesus himself didn't like sanctimonious people either.

As soon as Rusty was old enough for it to matter, she had choked back her dislike of religiosity and took the boy to church every Sunday.

She had always prayed, but never saw it as an activity separate from the rest of her life. Like, now I'll go to the grocery store, now I'll do the laundry, now I'll pray. It was a part of all the activities, a part of who she was, as essential and elemental as breathing. She talked to God in her head almost constantly, and out loud when she drove along the mountain roads on her way from one patient who lived so far out in the boondocks, the sun only shone there once a week, to another patient who lived equally far out in the sticks on the other side of the county.

That was one of the many reasons Sam loved her job. The enforced solitude of traveling from one patient to another, the beauty all around her on the hillsides, the creeks and the wildflowers. She'd listen to the radio — country music. Or to her Walkman, on which she'd loaded classical music. Or she'd pray out loud, talking to the God of the universe as casually as she had spoken to her own father, who had adored her in the same unconditional way she knew God loved her.

And loved Rusty.

She had prayed for God to spare the boy almost non-stop since she had knelt by his side on the asphalt in front of the clinic, and saw how terribly the boy had been hurt. He had been shot. *Shot.* She always yanked her mind away from the knowing of that, the reality of it, or she would be filled with such rage she … But when she veered away from that thought, she was always served up the image of the blood dripping out of his ear.

At the end of the day, *that* was the injury that mattered.

He could have brain damage.

Abby Clayton had had a stroke after she rode the Jabberwock a second time. The stroke had sent her off into a madness that almost cost Merrie and Malachi their lives.

Clearly, Rusty had suffered a traumatic brain injury of some sort. You could call it a stroke or a brain bleed or … didn't matter the label. Rusty needed a neurologist — now. He needed …

What he couldn't get as long as the Jabberwock imprisoned the county.

So now Sam knelt beside his bed, not just begging God to heal him, as she had begged with every inhalation and exhalation of breath for the past … how long? A lifetime. Now, she begged God to protect him and to protect her and the Breakfast Club. To protect them and intervene on their behalf.

She begged God to help them … kill the monster and release its prisoners — to release Rusty. She begged God to spare her son and all the other children of God in the county that the Jabberwock was systematically murdering.

"Please …" The word escaped in a strangled whisper. "Help us. Show us how to … just help. Help us and heal my son."

Our son.

Malachi's son.

There was no room anywhere inside Sam right now to process the enormity of the events of the past hour. The revelation. She'd told Malachi he was Rusty's father. Finally, *told him.* And what that might mean …

Didn't matter beans right now. The only thing that mattered was that Rusty open his eyes, that he get well. And she didn't believe he had a chance at that unless she and the others could defeat the monster.

Pete'd said he'd "see to the boy if …" He hadn't needed to say "if you don't come back." And if that if happened, everybody in the county would die.

So she prayed for all that. No words needed. She heard herself make some kind of sound that was like a moan, a pain so deep and profound it could not be expressed. And that was her prayer.

"Sam."

Malachi's voice. He hadn't come into the room, just called her name from the door.

"We need to go now."

She lifted her chin and gently kissed the little boy's hand she clutched so tightly in her own. Then she got to her feet. A little kiss, light, on his forehead. Twelve-year-old boys did *not* need their mothers fawning all over them. Rusty would have called that just-shoot-me embarrassing.

She turned then, didn't dare linger looking at him or she would not have been able to leave. Malachi reached out his hand to her. She crossed the room and took it, walked out and didn't look back.

VIOLA'D CLEANED Essie up best as she could last night, but there was still an odor. Dead bodies stank, wasn't no way around that and all the scrubbing with good-smelling soap wouldn't erase that. They needed to get Essie in the ground soon. Well, not in the ground, in her rightful burial place.

The boys had got the spot all cleaned out for her in the Mason family crypt early this morning. Of course, Viola'd have the name changed. Wouldn't say Mason no more on the outside. It would say Tackett. And she'd add more caskets, have places prepared there for her and all her kin, their final resting place—

But might be there'd be no time for them to be laid out together. Might be they would be took by the Jabberwock before—

No! That wasn't gonna be the way of it. She'd thought it all through, figured it all out — them houses that had aged, they'd been the houses of people who wasn't as strong as Viola Tackett. Grace Tibbits ... Abner Riley ... the Tungates ... they was weak. They was *prey,* but Viola Tackett and her clan was *predators.* The Jabberwock would recognize that, being a predator its own self. It'd respect her and hers. To her way of thinking, the Jabberwock was just culling the herd of weaklings, stragglers. Wasn't nothing to be gained by pondering who it would take and who it would leave. There'd still be plenty of people around to do for Viola Tackett. That was all that mattered.

Now wasn't the time to think on all that. Right now, she had to stay focused, had to do the next thing. That's how you got by in this life, you just done the next thing and her next thing was finding out who had shot down her baby girl. And punishing them. She hadn't decided yet how she's gonna kill whoever it was had done it. It'd be a slow death, though, not no bullet in the head. The how of it would depend on who it was. Figuring the best way to kill a person, the most awfullest way, kinda depended on who the person was.

Viola wished it was as easy to keep somebody alive as it was to kill them. She'd been thinking about that as she lay awake in the dark last night, Essie's body just beginning to smell bad in the next room. All night long, she'd seen a single image in her head. A little boy's face. Rusty Sheridan. No, rightful, that boy was Rusty *Tackett*. He was Malachi's git, plain to see, was amazing she hadn't never seen it before but that was a thing you didn't notice unless things was just right. The boy lying there with his eyes closed like he was, looking just like Malachi'd looked as a twelve-year-old asleep.

Rusty Sheridan wasn't asleep, though. He was unconscious. And might be that boy wouldn't never wake up.

The pain that thought shot through her heart surprised her. And she took it out and examined it.

What if he didn't wake up? What if he died?

Well … if he did, he did. Wasn't nothing Viola Tackett could do about it one way or another. So she had best just concern herself with what she could do if he *did* wake up.

When he did wake up. What was Viola Tackett gonna do about the fact that the young man with not-red hair — whose mama had raised him well — was Viola Tackett's seed?

Viola wasn't quite sure about that, about exactly what she'd do. She only knew one thing for certain. That boy belonged to Viola Tackett. He had her lineage. Was as fine a boy as his father'd been. But his father had gone down his own path and wasn't no way Viola was gonna let a thing like that happen a second time. Rusty … Tackett would become everything his father shoulda been but wasn't. Viola wouldn't allow that boy to grow up wild and disrespectful as his father'd done. She'd been too easy on Malachi, had been so taken by what a fine boy he'd been that she hadn't been tough enough on him. Hadn't made him toe the line, so he'd grow up obedient like his brothers done. She wouldn't make that mistake with Rusty. No sir, she would see to it that boy was disciplined right and …

Sam.

What about Sam?

Shoot, Viola'd just about forgot about Sam. She was his mother, after all, and it wasn't likely Sam Sheridan would take it well that Viola Tackett intended to take over the raising of her son.

Well, it'd be a shame, but it was clear Viola would just have to put Sam Sheridan down. She would hate to do a thing like that, she surely would, but wasn't nothing in the world going to stand between Viola Tackett and her heir. And Sam would interfere — wouldn't be able to help herself.

Viola would have to get rid of Sam. The sooner the better, too, since the boy needed to find out who he was, what his rightful place was in the world, who was his kin and how he was supposed to behave toward them as was his family now.

In fact, might be the best plan to take the bull by the horns and do the deed soon as she could. Yeah, she would have to wait until the boy woke up, but he would wake up soon. The more Viola thought about it the more certain she was of that. The boy would wake up and soon's he did, Viola would take over the raising of him.

It made sense, would likely be best all around if she put Sam down 'fore the boy woke up, do it the same time she did that Charlie woman, the mother of the little half-breed kid, the butt-in-sky woman who'd dared to cross Viola Tackett in front of people. She should have killed the woman right then and there, would have, too, if it hadn't been for Malachi.

Malachi. Ah, yes. Malachi. The best of her git. What a fine man he had grown up to be. What a pure D shame it was going to be when she had to put him out of the family. Oh, she couldn't kill him. Not her boy, not Malachi. But it was clear he had defied her. He'd done something to Howie Witherspoon after she had expressly forbidden it. She didn't know what or when or where. She would find out, of course, soon's she had time. She would find out the whole tale, starting with Sarah Throckmorton and the snot-nosed kid of Howie's, Toby. She'd get the truth out of them, and then do what she had to do.

She'd kill Charlie and Sam at the same time. Just made sense to do it that way. The little half-breed girl, too. She'd get his brothers to keep Malachi out of the way, probably have to rope and hogtie him to get him to behave while she done the business she had to do. With the women out of the way, she'd spell out the lay of the land for Malachi. He'd had his chance to join up with her and live a life of absolute power in his own little kingdom. He'd give that up and wasn't no second chances at a thing like that. She'd tell him he was out. Period. He could go do whatever it suited him to do but she didn't want to have nothing more to do with him.

And if he ever crossed her again … well … she sighed at the thought, she'd just have to put him down, too.

Chapter Twelve

THE OLD MAN sat quietly where Malachi had parked him in the waiting room. He was now wearing an adult diaper, so maybe they'd be spared yet another pair of wet pants.

Of course, it might be that none of the three of them would come back alive from Fearsome Hollow, in which case Moses Weiss's soiled diaper would become somebody else's problem besides Malachi's.

Malachi.

She'd told him.

The staggering enormity of that left her too breathless to think.

Malachi *knew he was Rusty's father.* How many times had she conjured up images of what it would be like when he did. Because she knew she'd have to tell him someday. He had a right to know. And so did Rusty. But it just never seemed to be the right time.

Malachi had come home on leave occasionally when he was in the military. Sam would catch sight of him on the street or in a store. Once, she literally bumped into him coming out of the bank in Carlisle. She'd dropped her bank papers and purse in stunned surprise and he'd thought he'd knocked them out of her hands. He got down on his knees in front of her, scrambling to pick up all the papers, apologizing profusely. She had been so tongue-tied, she couldn't manage anything more articulate than an inane, "Oh, hi, Malachi. How've you been?"

And one after the other, time ticked away the years.

When she'd heard he'd been injured, had left the military for good and had returned to Fearsome Hollow, she knew she had to do it soon. She couldn't let him drift back out of the county and maybe not return again for five years. No, it had to be now. But then … she'd seen him crouching in the bus shelter in the Middle of Nowhere, fighting a battle with enemies that didn't exist. And after that, there'd been no …

Malachi knew.

Waves of emotion flowed over her at the mere word. He *knew!*

Now, she'd *have to* tell Rusty and she didn't know how the boy would …

She couldn't tell Rusty, might never be able to tell her son who his father was. All that — *everything* — was riding on what happened in Fearsome Hollow today.

She suddenly turned to Charlie.

"It's just like you wrote. The three intrepid friends — the Alphabet Gang — going off together to slay a dragon."

Then she saw it and stopped in her tracks. They were crossing the waiting room to the front door of the clinic when Sam's eye fell on the blackboard that had "magically" appeared, moved from the kitchen in Charlie's mother's house at the foot of Little Bear Mountain to the lobby of the vet clinic in the Middle of Nowhere.

Only they'd decided maybe it wasn't by magic. Perhaps

the people who were looking for them — Pete's daughter Jolene, Thelma Jackson's husband, Cotton and Charlie's husband Stuart — had brought it here, for what purpose they didn't know.

Charlie must have seen it then, too, because she gasped and a little cry escaped her throat.

"What …?" Malachi began, then followed the looks of the two women to the blackboard.

There was a bare spot in the center of the flower Merrie had drawn on the chalkboard. The image had been erased there and in that spot somebody had written the words, "Daddy loves you, pumpkin."

"Stuart," Charlie cried and ran to the words, putting out a trembling hand.

But how … when?

"It wasn't there before, earlier this morning," Charlie said, awed, her fingers almost caressing the chalk on the blackboard. "When I came in this morning, it was just the flower."

Then she looked from one to the other. "It's Stuart's handwriting and he wrote it *this morning*."

She looked around, as if she half-expected to see the man standing in the shadows of the room.

"He was *here* this morning."

"If he was, if he could write on the board, why—?" Malachi began.

"He was here. He saw the picture and knew Merrie drew it."

"But if he could … if *they* could write on the black-board and we could see it, why didn't they …?"

Malachi's voice trailed off. He might have figured it out, too, but it was Sam who tacked words on the reality.

"Maybe he did. They did. Maybe there was something written on the blackboard and—"

Charlie finished the sentence in awed understanding. "But Merrie erased what they wrote. She found the blackboard and erased it — my mother's 'buy bird seed' and *whatever else* was on it. So she'd have room to draw a picture 'big as the sky.'"

"That'd make sense," Sam said. "They put the blackboard here to communicate with us, but whatever they wrote, we never saw. Merrie erased it."

"They were here *this morning*. And Mr. Weiss said they were going …"

They all paused to look at the man seated in the lobby, staring mindlessly out in front of him. He had stopped babbling. Sometimes he'd say a sentence or two. Single words. Mostly he just sat and stared. Sam had the awful sense that if she could look inside his mind, what she would see there was a burned-out crater. A hole. The lifeless expanse of scorched earth left behind when they dropped the atomic bomb on Hiroshima. The man's mind was gone, had been fried away. By the Jabberwock.

"They must have stopped by here on their way to Fearsome Hollow. They're going to 'face down the monster on Main Street in Gideon' today. High noon."

Stuart McClintock, Cotton Jackson and Jolene Rutherford were walking into the jaws of the Jabberwock, the monster the three of them were about to confront at the same time. Sam shivered.

Then a different emotion surged up in Sam's chest. An emotion that felt empowering instead of debilitating. Sam felt anger. Rage.

How dare this monster wreak havoc on the lives of thousands of people. Imprisoning them, killing them, *adsorbing* them, making them crazy. How dare—?

She realized her hands had balled into fists at her sides, the way they had done when she'd spotted Claire McFarland advancing on them with a shotgun. The shotgun she had used to shoot Rusty.

All the insanity — all the deaths. It was the Jabberwock's fault, all of it.

The Jabberwock had to be stopped.

It had to end. Here, today.

She would reach out and rip the face off the monster, so she could get Rusty and E.J. the medical care they needed. *She would kill it with her bare hands* if she had to.

Or it would kill her.

~

FISH DID WHAT FISH DO. He swam. No, floated. Up, up, up like a bubble to the surface.

He opened his eyes. Sunlight speared into them and he squeezed them shut. He knew the drill, of course. Knew when you'd passed out drunk, the return to reality always involved squinting eyes and—

His eyes popped open and he gasped. No, he hadn't passed out, he'd … what? Tripped, fallen. He'd been running, trying to find help.

Viola Tackett! *She was going to kill people.*

He knew better than to leap up, so he rose carefully, weathered the dizziness and looked around. Persimmon Ridge was … that way. He took out running again.

Fish had been running/hobbling/stumbling down the road for long enough to work up a full body sweat when he heard the sound of an approaching car. He turned so rapidly the motion knocked him off balance and he almost fell in the middle of the road. Which, as it turned out, was a good thing because Orville Chandler had to stop or run over him. He blared his horn, rolled down his window and yelled at Fish.

"Get out of the road, you old fool, 'fore you get yourself run over."

Fish had the presence of mind to remain standing in front of Orville's car so he couldn't drive away.

"Please, help, you have to—"

"I don't have to do jack squat. All's I have to do is get into town and get signed up on that list of Viola's Tackett's."

"List?"

"Oh, come on, get out of the way."

"What list?"

"Gus Hinkle called last night. He heard from Buster Willard who heard from Sam Hunt that Viola's gonna be handing out gasoline, but you got to sign up."

"Gasoline?"

"Yeah, gas. She's gonna be giving it out free—"

That's how she was going to gather up all the suspects in the murder of her daughter.

"Orville, listen to me, that's *not* why Viola Tackett wants everybody to—"

"She tell you something different, did she?"

"No, but—"

"Didn't think so. Just get out of my way, you old drunk, or I swear I'll run you down where you stand."

Would Orville really run over him?

Fish was about to find out. He stood frozen for only a moment, then he collapsed into the asphalt, suspected he looked like the scarecrow on *The Wizard of Oz* dropping boneless into the cornfield dirt.

"What the—?"

Orville hammered his horn. Hammered it again, held it for a long blast.

Then Fish heard him open his door, cursing and sputtering, "Worthless drunk … oughta mash you like roadkill …"

Fish was not a big man, and the years of all unbridled alcoholism had ravaged his body, leaving him *literally* scarecrow thin, and pitifully weak.

But desperation fueled him that day, and when Orville Chandler leaned down to grab his foot, preparing to drag his limp body out of the road, Fish kicked out with the force of a mule. He caught Orville smack in the middle of the family jewels and then it was Orville who was splayed out in the middle of the road. Fish leapt to his feet, ran to the door Orville had left open and jumped behind the wheel. Orville had dropped to his knees and then rolled over onto his side, clutching his gonads, too shocked and in too much pain to speak. But as Fish put the car in reverse and pulled back from his body, Orville began to yell.

"You drunken …" followed by expletives as profane and colorful as any Fish had ever heard.

The words faded into the distance behind Fish as he drove away from Orville's body, away from the cemetery in the direction of the Middle of Nowhere.

He literally slid to a stop in the parking lot of the veterinary clinic, likely looked like a slalom skier at the bottom of a hill. If there'd been snow, he'd have plowed a wave of it up onto the clinic steps.

Leaping out of the car, he almost fell. He was weak, nothing to eat, and the adrenaline that had fueled his car theft was leaving him. Only a little farther, he told himself, ping-ponging off the roof post, and then the door jamb as he staggered into the waiting room.

Nobody was seated at the reception desk. The room's only occupant was an old man he didn't recognize, so he ran through the doorway into the hallway of the clinic. Nobody was there, either so he just yelled out.

"Hey, *somebody*. Charlie, Sam, Malachi. Somebody ..." Then the last of his energy reserves gave out and he drooped to his knees.

"Help. Somebody, help."

Raylynn Bennett appeared at a doorway about halfway down the hall.

"Where's Charlie?" Fish cried. "Sam or Malachi ... where?"

"They're not here. You just missed them. They went to Fearsome Hollow to—"

"Not here?" Fish couldn't process that. "When will they be back?"

Raylynn shook her head slowly, a frightened little girl.

"I don't know ... they might not—"

"Might be they ain't coming back." Pete Rutherford had appeared in a doorway farther down the hallway. His already gruff voice had a ragged edge.

Fish stared at him in disbelief.

"But ... but I have to talk ..." He looked beseechingly into Pete's eyes. "You don't understand. They have to stop her."

"Stop who?"

"Viola Tackett. She's ... she's going to shoot people."

"What people?"

"Anybody. Everybody. And she won't stop until ..." His voice failed and he drew a shuddering breath. "She won't stop. Not ever. Not until they're all dead."

Chapter Thirteen

Judd Perkins' phone rang as he was closing his back door behind him and he almost didn't bother to go back inside to answer it. But it might be Doreen, something with the girls. He'd finally convinced her to move back into the house with him, so he could look after them. She was packing them up today and they'd be here when he got back tonight from his turn sitting up with E.J.

E.J. was going to die. Judd wasn't no doctor, but you didn't have to have no medical degree to see that the man was failing. He wouldn't likely live long enough to get rabies, which was not a bad thing. Not a bad thing at all. Oh, it wasn't that Judd had given up hope that they'd get out of this thing, that somebody'd ... well, do something and the Jabberwock would vanish quick as it'd come and they'd get E.J. to a doctor in time. He still hoped ...

No, he didn't. He wouldn't let anybody — Doreen or the girls or E.J., anybody — know that, of course, know he didn't believe no more. Shoot, he wouldn't even let himself know it most of the time. But in his heart of hearts a coldness had settled in. Partly fear, maybe mostly fear. But resignation, too. Like he'd felt when he finally accepted that Mildred's cancer wasn't going to get no better, that she wasn't going to get well and grow all her hair back and fix him eggs and pancakes for breakfast and train Buster to answer commands in German.

When he'd understood the reality of that, had shifted that gear, his whole world perspective had changed. The hole in his belly where hope had been was so huge at first he was afraid his whole self would fall into it and disappear. But his focus had been sharper, too. Like tunnel vision, seeing something through binoculars. Every second, every breath his precious Mildred took was significant after that. He took note of every one. Paused on every one, appreciated and was grateful for the breath and didn't demand anything beyond that. In that instant, he was merely grateful for that frozen moment of time, didn't spoil it by pining away for what he didn't have.

He had felt that shift in himself again in the past couple of days. Ever since E.J. had given his life to save Michelle and Julie Ann, Judd'd watched E.J. slip away and hope slipped away with him. Now, when Judd was honest with himself, which he wouldn't allow himself to be very often, he acknowledged that every breath of every person in the county — his daughter and precious granddaughters — everybody, was to be treasured and appreciated. They wouldn't last.

Soon's he got home tonight, he was gonna set both them girls in his lap and tell them funny stories like Mildred used to do when they was little. He'd tell tales about Buster, too. He hadn't mentioned the dog's name to the girls since ... Judd had dug a deep hole near the back fence and buried what was left of the poor thing soon's he got home from taking E.J. to Sam. But tonight, he was gonna talk about Buster. Wasn't the dog's fault what'd happened. It was Judd's for not getting him vaccinated. All the dog had ever done was be a good, loyal friend and Judd wasn't going to dishonor his memory by acting like he hadn't never existed. He was going to hug the little girls close, smell the fruity clean smell of their freshly washed hair, and glory in every breath they took.

He didn't know what form their end would take, but he would be there with his family to love and protect them until that final breath. He hoped they'd be 'lowed to take that one together.

Stepping back into the house, Judd went to the phone on the kitchen wall and lifted the receiver.

"'Lo."

"Pete Rutherford, here. We got ourselves a problem." Judd coulda said, "Tell me something I don't already know," but the tone of Pete's voice silenced him. "Need you to get your rifle and lots of ammunition. Meet me and Lester at the hardware store."

Then Pete told him why.

$\sim$

"IT SEEMS to me that once in your life before you die you ought to see a country where they don't talk in English and don't even want to."

Lester Peetree smiled as the words formed in his head. *Our Town.* Mr. Fischer had let Lester's son, William Lester Peetree, Jr. — just Willie — read the part of the narrator of the play when the boy was in high school — because Lester had begged Fish to. He'd thought the experience of reading it aloud would paint the words on his son's soul the way his own reading of it, alone in his bedroom, squinting at the words on the library book page, had done for him. He'd been wrong. Willie hadn't cared a fig about *Our Town,* had been bored by the experience of reading it aloud in front of a bunch of disinterested, pimple-faced teenagers in Holmes Fischer's English class. Even though the play had completely changed his father's whole life.

Okay, maybe not changed it, but certainly informed it. That play, superimposed on all the years since he'd read it, had been the lens through which Lester Peetree had viewed the world. He sometimes thought that just about all the wisdom there was in all the world was contained within that single Pulitzer Prize-winning drama.

Well, except the part about going to a country where they didn't speak English. He'd done that. He had for a fact, and he had returned to testify, if anybody'd asked and nobody ever did, that it was way, way better to stay home, right where you was at, live life there and die there and never know what kind of incredible evil dwelled out there in the world beyond.

Lester would say that today with as much conviction as he'd said it when he got home from Vietnam, spent miserable months enduring flashbacks of little kids with their clothes on fire, or dead bodies swollen and bloated and stinking — cows, pigs, people. Or the unrecognizable corpses of dead friends. Or a leg. Just a leg. Ripped off at the thigh, naked — no uniform pants, no socks or boots. Lester had been ridiculously troubled by that at the time, thought about it for months. George Phillips. Lester had seen him just moments before the world erupted into tiny points of brilliant light and the man's body had been completely blown apart by a mortar shell, pieces flung into the faces of his friends. So … where were George's pants? How could a mortar shell blow your boots and socks off? How could that be?

Lester would have said then that the most profound evil in the world could be defined with one little word, three simple letters. W. A. R. War was all evil. Every second, every breath, every eye blink, nothing but evil.

But war wasn't all the evil there was. He had learned that, too, over the years. Certainly had had his nose rubbed in that reality since J-Day when an impossibility had changed reality and everybody in the county's understanding of it. The thing, the Jabberwock, the monster that was systematically — what was it Charlie McClintock called it? *Absorbing* — everybody within the county's borders was evil, too.

It wasn't all the evil, though. Human hearts ... evil resided in human hearts, blackened and shriveled them.

You couldn't let that evil win. Not in war. Not in everyday life. You stood up to it or you couldn't lay claim to any good in your own soul.

Lester Peetree hadn't fired his rifle in more than thirty years. To this day, didn't know why he'd said yes when his sergeant offered to let him keep the weapon. He'd put the gun and his uniform away, along with the box of medals he had resolutely refused to allow anybody to see. Not even his wife. Willie had found them when he was ten years old and hauled them out, asked what they were. Lester'd sent the boy to his room, wouldn't let him come down even for supper because he'd disobeyed Lester's ironclad rule that nobody ... nobody *ever* went into that storage room in the back corner of the hardware store. After that, Lester kept it secure with a padlock as big as his fist.

Lester stood in the storage room now, lifting the rifle out of the scabbard and hating how natural it felt to hold the thing again. He slicked his hand over his bald head — shaved because bald was more attractive, or so Ramona had said, than the ever-expanding patch of bare skin that had attacked him before he even turned forty.

He glanced at his watch. He was supposed to meet Pete

Rutherford in the store at 11:30. Pete had said he'd be bringing along Judd Perkins. Judd was maybe ten years older, hadn't served in Vietnam. But he was the acknowledged "best shot" in the county, as evidenced by all the game he'd felled — some from six, seven hundred yards — with one shot over the years and all the blue ribbons he'd won in the shooting contests at the county fair. Lester never entered those contests, so nobody ever knew he could likely out-shoot Judd Perkins seven ways to Sunday. Nobody ever would know, because Lester had put his rifle away when he got back home and never fired it again. Oh, he kept the rifle immaculate and in perfect working order, maintained like it was brand new. Every gun owner owed that kind of respect to his weapon. Just left it locked up was all. Same as everybody else in the county, he had other weapons he used for hunting, and sold all manner of them in the store — or had until somebody broke into it a week ago and stole every bit of inventory.

They hadn't stolen this rifle because didn't nobody but Ramona know it even existed — well, Willie'd seen it that one time when he was a kid. It was locked away where nobody would ever steal it, where nobody would ever even fire it again — or so Lester had assumed when he put the gun out of sight, out of mind, in that storage room all those years ago.

It was a Ruger 10/22 automatic with a suppressor. A sniper rifle.

Lester Peetree had been a sniper. Served at a base in Da Nang in what the military called "Arizona Territory."

He never thought about it, had learned how not to think about it, but as he held the weapon now in his hands he considered the number again. Seventy-one. Lester Peetree had seventy-one confirmed kills from a two-year tour in Vietnam. There'd been more than that. Lots more.

Those were just the ones that'd been "confirmed" by observers. Lester Peetree had killed way more than seventy-one Cong. Not as many as the Marine, Chuck Mawhinney, though, who had once landed sixteen head-shots in thirty seconds in pitch black darkness. Mawhinney had 103 confirmed and 216 probable kills in just sixteen months in country.

Lester'd never talked to the man — though he served in the Arizona Territory same as Lester — but he bet the Marine felt the same way Lester did about it. Lester's job was to wipe evil off the face of the earth. Pure and simple. The Cong had been verifiably evil, demonstrably so. They were the enemy, of course, but they were way more than that. They were soul-less monsters who strapped bombs to little kids, burned old people alive and roasted rats on a stick in the flames. They stalked the jungles, killing whole villages full of innocent people, shooting them one after another, looking for a single American sympathizer.

That's what Pete Rutherford said Viola Tackett intended to do right here in Nowhere County.

"She's just gonna pick people at random and shoot 'em, one after another until she finds out who killed her daughter. Fish said he thinks it was her own boy, Neb, done it. Accidental. But you ain't never gonna convince Viola Tackett of that."

Lester had been at the county meeting where Liam'd got shot, believed it was Viola done it, though he had been where he couldn't see so he didn't know for sure. He *did* know she'd hanged that teenage boy, Martha Whittiker's grandson ... Dylan something. Just hanged him. It had fallen to Lester to take charge of the morgue in the base-ment of Bascum's so he seen it all, up close and personal, had been the one took the rope off the boy's neck where it had dug in so deep it would have bled, except there was no heart to pump blood by then.

Wasn't a doubt in Lester's mind that Viola Tackett was evil, same's the Cong. He was certain she would make good on her threat. Only thing standing between her and a mass murder was him, Pete and Judd Perkins. That woman didn't have no conscience, no soul. Wasn't no way to stop her but to put her down. Either him, Pete or Judd Perkins was gonna have to do just that.

Chapter Fourteen

THE BOYS HAD GOT BACK from they errands and most everything had gone according to Viola's plan.

She'd sent Zach in his fancy Vette to Pine Bluff Hollow, around Hollow Tree Ridge down to Poorfolk Hollow. She'd sent Obie to Nate's Creek Hollow, through Killarney to Turkey Neck Hollow and back through Harrow Woods.

She didn't have nobody to send to Soloman Hollow, Little McGuire Hollow and down Lexington Road to Route 19 and Frogtown, but Zach got done quick so she sent him there. Didn't send nobody to Fearsome Hollow cause didn't hardly anybody live there.

The boys honked they horns and called folks out of they houses to see their full tanks of gasoline, and handed out five-gallon cans to them as didn't have enough gas to get to town for the meeting.

Neb was driving Howie Witherspoon's pokey old Dodge and he had stayed close, starting in Bugtussle Hollow, around Bishop Mountain to Freeman Hollow, then through Wiley to Chicory Hollow.

Something was wrong with Neb. Viola didn't know

what it was, but something had got his goat. Must be the awful of finding his sister like that, shot and dying on the porch. Well, whoever'd done that grievous deed was gonna be held to account for it this day, and the group of men gathered before her on the too-tall grass in the front yard of the *Tackett House* was gonna help her administer justice.

She looked out over the group of lowlifes and sighed. Ever one of them was dumber than the next.

Merl Pickett had a dent in the middle of his forehead — you could see it — where his daddy'd throwed him out of the car while it was still moving. His brother said it was 'cause he'd farted in the car, but Viola wondered sometimes if he'd just made that part up. Merl wasn't as stupid as he looked, though, with that dent and that one black eyebrow stretching across both eyes. He might have been the smartest of the lot, but that wasn't saying much.

Hoyt Wilmer had a wad of snuff under his front lip big as a golf ball. He spit juice out onto the ground when he talked, about every fourth word, and it'd dribbled down the front of his red-and-black checked shirt.

Bolyard and Delbert Scully was brothers, or so they thought, and so did they daddy. Viola didn't. She was sure Bolyard was not Angus Scully's seed, that his Mamie had gone out and found her somebody else to rut around with because that boy absolutely did *not* fit in that family.

Viola knew about such things. But Malachi looked a whole lot more like his half-brothers than Bolyard Scully looked like his. Bolyard's brothers was all red-headed and freckle-faced, had blue eyes so pale it was creepy to look at them. Bolyard was dark, brown hair and muddy brown eyes. He looked like a Mexican and maybe he was. They was illegals worked on the horse farms up around Lexington and maybe Mamie had spread her legs for one of them.

They was others, Clarence Thacker, Buster Willard, Jethro Bodean and the Monroe brothers, Bubba and Felix, whose matching beards put Viola in mind of the Smith Brothers on a box of cough drops. Fifteen, maybe sixteen or seventeen altogether. She didn't count noses and Bufford Pettigrew and Hulan Gibson was still getting out of they truck. She didn't need half this many! Coulda done it with her boys and three or four more. But she'd throwed out a net and these here was what she'd caught and a show of force this big would be intimidating — wouldn't nobody go up against this many guns.

All them men standing in her front yard was in her debt in some way, and she'd called in every single chip she had, and she had a lifetime's worth. Wasn't nothing she'd ever done mattered to her as much as finding out this day who had shot poor Essie down like a dog, and she intended to administer righteous wrath upon that person. When she had the time, she was gonna question Neb more about what'd happened, but he didn't want to talk about it much. She hadn't never seen him so upset over a thing and it made her proud he'd thought so much of Essie — though he sure hadn't never showed it when she was alive. Didn't none of them pay her no mind except Malachi. She had been able to pry out of Neb that he'd heard hollering and carrying on from the car that roared down the street, like maybe they was a bunch of people in it and maybe they'd been drinking. Bunch of drinking buddies, out tearing up stuff, might even be they didn't mean no harm, though didn't matter a fig whether they did or no, they'd caused harm and they was gonna pay dearly for it.

Viola's plan had been the first thing she'd thought of, but the more she organized what was gonna go down, the more sure she was that the plan was solid. Might take a few shootings to get there, but soon's she aimed her gun at one of them dudes as was in the car, or one of their kin they'd bragged to about it, the person with the gun to his temple would sing like a canary. She was gonna kill them all, soon's she found out who they was. Ever man jack as was in that car was gonna die this day. She wasn't gonna tell them that in the beginning, of course. But the triggerman, she had special plans for him.

All she needed was time to execute her way to the information she needed, and these boys was gonna join with her and her boys to make it all happen.

Merl Pickett owed her because she hadn't ratted him out to the feds that time the DEA found dope on the back of his farm that bordered on hers. She'd told the law she'd seen Bert and Billy Ray Cummings going down the road toward the back of the farm, hadn't never seen Merl anywhere near it, though.

Bert and Billy Ray was already in federal prison serving mandatory twenty-year sentences for their part in the Cornbread Mafia from Marion County. They'd got sent off right before the feds busted that field so's it was easy to lay blame on them. They denied it, of course, but didn't nobody b'lieve 'em.

Hoyt Wilmer owed her money. A considerable sum if she'd been a bank and added in interest and late fees and the like. He'd bought dope off her to sell and his man run off with the profits. Or so Hoyt said. She'd been meaning to send Obie and Zach around to his house to do some persuading to call in the debt. But that was before the Jabberwock had handed Viola Tackett her own private kingdom on a silver platter.

"I ain't asking for yore help," she told the men standing there, armed with rifles ... well, Bufford Pettigrew had a shotgun ..., "I ain't *asking* for nothing. You owe me and this makes us square. We clear on that?"

"Neb said you was gonna shoot people," Hoyt said and spit out a wad of juice on the grass.

"You got a problem with that?"

"Depends on who the people is."

"The people is gonna be whoever I decide it is, and if you ain't in, leave now and take the worthless brother of yours along with you. And you best get ten thousand dollars quick, and it ain't easy to scrape together that kind of cash, given the way the world is now, so you best have some kinda plan. I will be calling on you and you will have my money ready for me, or ..." She didn't finish, of course. She didn't have to.

"I didn't say I wasn't in, just wanted to know, that's all."

"You ain't gonna have to shoot nobody, if that's what you're asking. Well, 'less somebody tries something you ain't. You just got to stand there. I'll do the shooting."

She hadn't told them exactly what her plan was, just that she was looking for the drive-by shooters of her girl, and she needed them for "crowd control."

"So we good?" she asked Hoyt, who nodded, and then she directed the question out to the others. They nodded, too. "All's you got to do is keep folks in line, don't let nobody try nothing. Me'n the boys will take care of the rest of it."

She looked at her watch. The fireworks was s'posed to start at noon.

High noon.

IMAGES PLAYED across the screen of Pete Rutherford's mind that he hadn't seen in years. Hadn't allowed himself to see. When he had come home from the South Pacific in 1945, he had done his dead level best to leave behind all that he had seen in the preceding four years. He had actually thought that. As he stepped down off the gangplank of the troopship onto the dock, he had actually made a kind of mental symbolic gesture. He paused for a beat, imagined himself taking off his backpack and leaving it on the dock before he stepped off it onto shore.

All the blood.

Guadalcanal.

The Philippines.

The Solomons.

His best friend from boot camp had died in the battle for Midway Island when a sniper put a bullet right in the center of his forehead.

He had gotten his own first wound on Tarawa, not one severe enough to get him sent home, just went to an army hospital then back to the front.

While he was gone, three of his buddies had been killed.

He had tried very hard to leave the war behind him, as soldiers before him had done and others after him would do. He had tried. But the images had assaulted him, in nightmares in the dark and hallucinations during the day for years.

But he silenced them eventually. Put it behind him.

Pete had been so sympathetic when he'd seen Malachi Tackett crouched in the bus shelter on J-Day because he'd been overwhelmed by a profound been-there, done-that feeling.

He'd never thought he would take up arms against another human being ever again, yet here he stood with his M1 rifle, waiting for Lester to come out of the storage room in the back of his store.

He would be lining up a human being in his sights today, would likely be taking a life. Maybe more than one.

But it was either that or let Viola Tackett murder people and he was flat out done with that.

The other images that filled his mind when he shoved images of battle away were those of his daughter. His little girl. He used to call her Tater Head.

Jolene. She was here. Well, here … wherever *here* was. She had come home, looking for him.

He was staggered by that revelation, surprised by the depth of the feelings he had capped off and sealed after she left home.

He had genuinely believed he would never see her again. After his cancer diagnosis, he had briefly considered getting in touch with her, trying to make amends. Briefly. He hadn't contacted her, though, because he knew a lost cause when he seen one. He had lost his daughter, had so alienated her by how he had responded to finding out she was a … a what? A ghost hunter, apparently.

He made a humph sound in his throat. As if he gave a Fig Newton about a thing like that now. The cancer, and then the Jabberwock, had burned the scales off Pete Rutherford's eyes as nothing else could have done. He'd realized then he didn't care what his daughter did for a living. He had just been a cantankerous old man bent on having his own way, offended that his offspring had chosen to live life on her own terms. Just who did he think he was, getting to decide for another person what was good and right for them? And when he got sick, he thought about trying to tell her that, but he'd pushed her away and now he was just gonna have to live with the consequences of his bullheadedness.

But Jolene had come home! Had come looking for him. If the crazy old man who kept peeing in his pants in the waiting room of the clinic was to be trusted, she and Stuart

McClintock and Cotton Jackson were trying to find the people who'd vanished.

Well, if he and Lester and Judd didn't do something, there'd be a whole lot fewer people to find.

Lester stepped out the door that led to his storage room carrying a Ruger 10/22, so shined up it looked brand new. A sniper rifle. A fine weapon.

"You know, I ain't fired this thing in a couple of decades," Lester said.

"It'll come back to you." Their eyes met and acknowledged that it was so.

"You got this all figured out, have you?" Lester asked.

"Pretty much."

Funny how the military was.

Pete hadn't never had conversation one with Lester Peetree about Vietnam. But it didn't take half a minute before the both of them was on the same page. They were soldiers, after all. They had civilians to protect. It was that simple.

The bell on the front door of the hardware store jangled and the stout form of Judd Perkins walked through it. He was carrying a rifle, but Judd Perkins wasn't no soldier.

Chapter Fifteen

Viola went back into the house while the men she'd called on got in their vehicles and cleared out of her driveway. She stood for a time looking at the body of her daughter, laid out there on the couch in the living room, wrapped up in the quilt off Obie's bed and that lacy white bedspread that looked kinda like a wedding dress.

Yeah, she was definitely starting to smell bad. They needed to get her into that crypt soon's they could, but Viola was determined to do it in the right order. She would not lay her baby girl to rest until she found out who'd killed her. Until she had made that person pay for the horrible deed. Pay with pain ten times greater than poor little Essie'd felt when the lowlife shot her.

She turned and crossed the living room. She had left her pistol in a fancy box she'd found on a table beside the front door, made outta all kinda wood she hadn't never seen the like of. She thought the gun looked right fine in there.

Zach was waiting for her in his snazzy car. He liked playing the role of chauffeur. Mostly, he just liked driving that thing, anywhere and everywhere. He'd drive it from the front door down the driveway to the street to pick up the mail out of the box if she'd let him. He'd just got back from Frogtown. Him and Obie didn't have no trouble, but Neb had run into some meanness when he pulled up at the Coltrain place in Chicory Hollow. They come out with guns, didn't 'xactly threaten him but come as close as you could get 'thout rubbing elbows. They didn't trust Viola and let Neb know they would *not* be coming to her county meeting, thank you very much, to collect gasoline they knew for a pure D fact would *not* be free like she said.

Might be the truth was that them or one of their kin had driven down Main Street yesterday and shot poor Essie where she sat on the porch, and they didn't want to face Viola and that was the real reason they wouldn't come to town. But Viola didn't think so. They was lots of people had it in for Viola Tackett, had their noses out of joint at her for one thing or another she done to them through the years. But the Coltrains didn't have no bone to pick with her, least none she could think of. They was just ornery people was all. Wasn't no reason for them to have come roaring down the street with guns blazing, intent on causing harm to Viola and her kin.

Besides, the family didn't have nothing but that big old Chevy Malibu held together with duct tape and Bondo. That car didn't have no muffler and you coulda heard them coming a mile out. She'd asked and Neb'd said he didn't see nor hear nothing he recognized. Nothing at all. So unless they borrowed somebody else's wheels, it couldn't have been the Coltrains.

She'd sent Merl Pickett and the Scullys on ahead to get in position, all casual-like. She crossed the yard to where Zach was parked, revving his engine, and kicked something in the tall grass that *still* hadn't got mowed yet. She glanced down at it. Something made outta leather with what looked like catsup smeared on it. Then she noticed that Obie was standing beside the door of his truck, arguing with Neb.

"You boys come on now," she called out.

"Neb won't come," Obie said. "Said he was staying here." She stopped, changed direction and walked up to where her oldest son stood beside the open door of Obie's stolen black pickup truck. In truth, the boy didn't look good. White as a sheet. No, actually his face looked kinda green. Like maybe he was gonna upchuck and lose his breakfast.

"S'matter with you, boy?" she demanded, and he looked at her with such hound dog eyes she wanted to look away.

"Nuthin'. I just don't feel good's all. I'm sick."

He did look sick, actually hadn't looked right since she found him staggering under the weight of his fat sister, carrying her body to the truck in back to get her help. Was actin' peculiar, too. Middle of the night last night she seen him out in the front yard with a flashlight, just wandering around, said he couldn't sleep. She made him come back in the house and go to bed. Might be he was sick then, too. But sick or well, he was coming with her.

"I don't care if you's knocking on the Pearly Gates with a jackhammer. Get in that truck, you're coming with me."

He didn't argue, just drooped his head all mournful-like and went around to the passenger side of Obie's stolen pickup truck.

If his stomach was bothering him, he was likely to puke for sure at the scene she was imagining taking place on the street in front of the school. They was gonna be lots of blood, she was sure of it. Screaming and carrying on and the like. It wasn't a place for somebody whose stomach wasn't too settled to begin with. She come within an inch of telling Neb to stay home, but her thoughts got hung on the nail in her head that had been derailing every train of thought she'd put together since yesterday afternoon, when she sat at her kitchen table staring at a photograph that coulda been Rusty Sheridan … well, 'cept for the black hair.

Ever time she thought about it, the strangest stew of emotions took over. She couldn't wait until that boy come around, because she was almost sure he had pale blue eyes like his daddy. And she sure did want to see that for a fact.

She let that go, however, and concentrated on the job she had before her. She needed to get her girl in the ground and the murderer suitably punished before she had any space in her head for more. But soon's she did, soon's she had all her ducks beak to tail feathers, well … she'd go get her rightful heir. She'd settle up with his mama — people was gonna pitch a fit but wasn't nothing for it but to do what she had to do. And more importantly with that McCormick woman. She'd get rid of them all, fix everything that wasn't right in her whole life in one grand sweep.

Then she'd sit back in the lap of luxury in the Tackett House and enjoy raising her grandson to be a good, obedient boy like his father never had been.

"BEST GET this outta the way first thing," Pete Rutherford said. "Me and Lester's soldiers. We seen … we been in battle. We've taken a human life. This ain't no deer or elk you gonna be shooting, Judd. You take up arms with us today, and you gonna have to kill people. Likely more than one. Straight up — can you do it?"

The man didn't mince words.

Six months ago, a month ago … shoot, even a week ago, Judd Perkins woulda balked at a question like that. Could he kill a man? Put the crosshairs of his sight on another human being and pull the trigger?

He'd thought about it all the way into town, trying to get his arms around the enormity of what he was preparing to do. He'd backed up from it at first, had been so shocked by what Pete told him, he'd stammered agreement without even considering the ramifications. Judd was on the phone tree and Daniel Hunt had called late yesterday evening and said Judd had ought to go into town at noon today because Viola Tackett was signing people up for free gasoline. Him and Dan had talked about that — Viola Tackett giving out something free … *riiiiight.* They was some kinda catch to it, they always was with a woman vicious as she was. But even with whatever the catch was, it was still gasoline. And the tank on Judd's truck was darn near empty. He'd gone down the road to Bobby Ray Blaylock's place, who hadn't been home since the week before Memorial Day. Wherever it was Bobby Ray'd gone, he'd drove his only car to get there, but he had a tractor in the barn, and Judd'd been able to siphon out enough gasoline from it to fill two five-gallon cans. Judd was burning through that fast, though, going back and forth into the Middle of Nowhere helping to sit with E.J. When it run out, then what? Dan was in the same shape as Judd. Everybody was. So him and Dan'd finally figured that it didn't really matter what the real deal was, what kind of bait-and-switch Viola was gonna pull on 'em once she got everybody together. Whatever the price was, they'd all have to suck it up and pay. It was either that or walk.

But then Pete'd told him gasoline didn't have nothing to do with why Viola was gathering up folks in town. Judd had asked Pete to repeat himself when he heard the real reason Viola'd called the meeting, made sure he heard Pete right. Wasn't no mistaking his words the second time around, though — Viola Tackett intended to start shooting people, random people, one after the other until she found out who'd killed her daughter. The words had knocked the wind out of Judd and he'd agreed to come help just as a kinda knee-jerk reaction. Of course, he'd help stop a thing like that from happening. Anybody would.

But saying you's willing to stand up and do what was right and the actual act of standing up and doing it was two different things altogether. That's what had hit home with him when he was opening up the box of shells after he'd got his rifle down off his gun rack.

Pete'd said he'd need extra ammunition, that Judd'd probably oughta pack a full box of shells, maybe two because there was no telling how many … *people* he might have to shoot. That had brought him up short. He'd froze then, felt a queasy feeling in his belly, then slowly, kinda in a fog, he'd poured the shells out of the box into his hand.

He had a vest that he wore when he went hunting. It had padding on the right shoulder for recoil, rifle and handgun magazine pockets, shotgun shell holders — even had a handgun holster. It was hanging on a hook beside the gun rack. Judd stood there looking at it.

A hunting vest.

Then he turned away. Wasn't gonna put on no hunting vest like he was just going out into the woods to bag a deer so he could fill the freezer with venison steaks for Doreen and the girls. He wasn't going *hunting*.

He'd emptied the shells into his hand then and filled up the pockets of his overalls, went out to his truck and headed into the Ridge with his thoughts skidding around in his mind like he was trying to drive 'em on black ice.

Could he really shoot somebody? *Kill* somebody? Did Judd Perkins have the courage to do a thing like that? Then he'd thought about E.J., coming up with a plan to save the lives of Judd's precious granddaughters — a plan that meant E.J. was going to get ripped apart by a rabid dog.

Wanna know what courage was? *That* was courage. Judd'd never seen anything like it. E.J. Stephenson was the bravest man Judd Perkins had ever met. Judd had wondered at the time how he could ever repay E.J. for what he had done. Well, maybe this was how.

Maybe this was the big, awful, scary thing the good Lord had given Judd Perkins to do. Pete hadn't said so — because he didn't have to say it — but Viola and her boys wasn't just gonna sit there like ducks in a pond and let him blow them away. When him and whoever else Pete'd gathered up started shooting at the Tacketts, the Tacketts was gonna shoot back.

Judd Perkins hadn't never been shot at in his life. He could get killed here today. But if he didn't man up and do the hard thing, a whole lot of other innocent people was gonna die. *Could* he shoot somebody, *kill* somebody?

Judd squared his big shoulders and looked Pete Rutherford dead in the eye.

"Yeah, I can do it, kill somebody if it comes to that." His voice was strong and firm. "I wouldn't a' come if I wasn't sure you could count on me. I won't let you down."

Chapter Sixteen

SKEETER BURKETT WAS the one spotted the map on the wall. He'd shown up early at the West Liberty Middle School auditorium for the meeting his neighbor had called him about last night. But he hadn't come early because he was so anxious to get his hands on Viola Tackett's free gasoline. He didn't put much stock in that offer, hadn't never in his life seen Viola Tackett give away something she could make a buck selling. He was sure she planned to get everybody gathered up with her offer of free gasoline, and then tell them, oh by the way, it wasn't exactly *free*. They was gonna have to pay for it in some way — she'd give out gasoline in exchange for food or moonshine or weed or ammunition. Something. Wasn't in the nature of Viola Tackett to walk away from a transaction with her pockets empty.

Skeeter'd come early because he was curious, wanted to see what the old girl was up to this time. And because he didn't have nothing better to do. Didn't have nothing to do at all, if the truth be known, and it didn't take much to catch the interest of a man who'd opened up his eyes this morning and seen the whole of a day stretch out there in front of him, hours stacked up one on the other, and not a single task he had to do to fill them up with.

He coulda gone fishing, but that didn't appeal to him no more after he found the dead body of that preacher's girl in the river. Might not never go fishing again. Guess you could say Skeeter was just coasting, like a jon boat when you kill the engine with the bow pointed at the shore and it just glides across the glassy water without making a sound. That was Skeeter … guiding across the final days of his life all smooth, not making a sound.

He'd parked his truck out back in the parking lot and come in the back door so he was facing the back wall of the auditorium soon's he walked out that little door beside the stage. And on that back wall was … a wonder. The closer he got to it, the more of a wonder it appeared to him to be.

It was a map of Nowhere County. A huge map of Nowhere County, bigger'n any map he'd ever seen, as a matter of fact. It was drawn on canvas, like artists used to paint paintings, musta been at least ten feet across and maybe eight feet tall.

Every step he took toward it revealed greater detail, until he was just standing in front of the thing, looking up, wondering who in the world could possibly have drawn something like this.

"You make that thing, Skeeter?" said a voice behind him. It was Bud Crockett, who lived out on Blandford Lane in Little McGuire Hollow. Him and Skeeter had been on a bowling team so many years ago he couldn't have put a year to it if you'd held a gun to his head. Long time, though.

"No, I didn't make this," Skeeter said. "Obviously, you didn't neither. Who did?"

Bud had come to stand next to Skeeter, staring up at the map.

"You got me, but whoever it was done it musta spent months—"

"Months?"

"Okay, years putting it together. Look at that little print. Why, this map's got every little creek—"

"Lookit that," said a woman's voice, and Skeeter cringed. It was Wilma Thacker and she had a voice like a rooster. "You draw that, Skeeter? That's amazing."

"Folks keep trying to give me credit for it, I'm gonna start taking it," he said. "But it weren't me. I was just lookin'—"

"That there's Burnt Stump Road," said a laughing man behind the three of them and they turned to see Burt Donaldson from Poorfolk. He had come in with Clyde Biggerstaff, Jeb Pruitt and Milt Watson from Killarney. "I ain't never seen a map had Burnt Stump Road on it. I didn't know anybody knew it was there 'cept me and my daddy."

"Why shore, I know where Burnt Stump Road is." Jeb walked to the map and had to stand on tiptoe to reach the spot on it he was pointing to. "Right there. That's where I killed my first buck."

"We had a deer stand not half a mile from there on …" His eye traced along the map and the smile on his face grew bigger. "Look a'here. Now, who knew Little Bit Rock was right there in the creek. Used to fish there when I was a kid."

A crowd had gathered around the map, growing bigger and bigger and folks crowded around the outside edges, trying to get a look at the wonder of detail that had been set down.

It was like somebody'd took the time and trouble to

mark out the stones that lead across the creeks of their whole lives.

Skeeter found himself shoved a bit to the side, as others crowded around, pointing to one thing and another.

"Used to go parking there with Sue Ellen when we was …"

"That's where that black bear come out of the woods, right there by …"

"Me and Buddy Doverspike was looking for ginseng in the woods there, come upon a hornet's nest and …"

The conversation that hummed around him had a pleasant sound. Like an old sewing machine, purring along, making stitches, sewing one piece of cloth to another. He noticed stickpins on the map, groups of them — several crowded together in the same places. Couldn't figure why that was because the stickpins wasn't holding up nothing.

"Who done this?" Jimmy Dan Thacker called out. "How'd he know …? Look a'here."

He pointed to a spot on the map marked in clear block letters: "Blarnaby Stone."

"How in the world …?" Jimmy Dan was clearly flummoxed and Skeeter knew why. He'd heard about the Blarnaby Stone, but probably weren't two dozen other people in the county knew it was there.

Skeeter's daddy'd took him out to see it when he was knee high to a grasshopper, the big green rock sticking out of the ground, right at the top of Hollow Tree Ridge, like it was a chocolate chip some giant had stuck in a big cookie. The thing was bigger than a farm truck and almost round as a marble, least the part of it that was sticking out of the ground was. Of course, it was 'cause it was green that made it something worth trekking all the way up the steep ridge to see. Appeared to be something growing on it, not moss, lichen of some sort. He'd seen the green stuff growing in other places in the woods, but didn't know why — and neither did his daddy — it had growed solid all over this one rock and nothing else nearby. His daddy'd said his own daddy'd showed it to him, said it was the Blarnaby Stone, which was like some rock that was supposed to be sticking out of the ground somewhere in Ireland.

"Who drew this map?" somebody pushing through the crowd asked, but didn't nobody standing there know. They was all looking at the places they'd seen all their lives, special things like the Blarnaby Stone, or not so special, just that spot where somebody used to go fishing, fell in and danged near drowned in three feet of water. But special places to the folks looking at 'em — because just like the Blarnaby Stone, them places was *their* places, b'longed to them and their families. Never occurred to Skeeter Burkett they was so many of such places in Nowhere County.

PETE RUTHERFORD HAD GIVE it as much consideration as he'd had time to do, but in truth it wasn't a particularly quarrelsome logistical problem.

"Lester, you chime in as you see fit, make sure I didn't miss nothing." Lester nodded. For a fleeting moment Pete flashed back to his days in the army, with his platoon, about to go into enemy fire for the first time. He'd gone boots-down on Guadalcanal with the original squad of soldiers he'd gone through boot camp with. He knew them all and boot camp had a way of bonding men together like wasn't nothing else in the world could do. Ralph Bartley, the Kansas farm boy with the most pathetic set of buck teeth Pete'd ever seen. Got tagged Bucky the first day, of course, and that boy could shoot — whew, doggies could he shoot! Enrique Martinez from El Paso — they called him Poncho — had confided in the other men that he wasn't really a citizen, his parents had sneaked with him across the border when he was three years old. Pete didn't know how he'd managed to get through the military's paperwork, but he'd done it, was proud he could serve with his *fellow Americans.* There was Bonzai — the Californian who did everything full out — Hoosier from Oklahoma and the Jewish guy called The Nose from Massachusetts. The other soldiers took turns standing in the shade of The Nose on hot days. Pete knew without a doubt they would have his back as he would have theirs.

The two men who stood with him in Lester's Hardware Store were good men. Pete'd known them all his life, a lot longer than he'd known his army buddies. But he didn't know them the way you knew your fellow soldiers. When the guano connected with the air conditioning, would they ...?

Well, he supposed he was about to find out.

"Way I see it, Viola's gonna herd everybody together in front of the school." West Liberty Middle School sat in the middle of the block directly across from the courthouse. The school mirrored the architecture of the courthouse with wide steps and tall white columns and big oversized double doors, inlaid on both sides by leaded glass windows.

"I don't got no idea how many boys she's gonna have along for this rodeo. Her own boys, that's three, but I figure she's called in reinforcements for a thing like this. So she could have a dozen, maybe more, maybe less. We ain't gonna know the strength of the enemy until we see for ourselves."

"You're thinking up on the top of buildings on both sides of the courthouse," Lester said, and Pete nodded.

"The crowd'll be hemmed in front and back by the buildings, but she'll have guns on both sides to keep them from scattering up and down the street. Judd will get up on the roof of the drug store, I'll take the beauty parlor." Willingham's Drug Store was still open for business, as was the Hair Affair Beauty Parlor and Nail Salon. But there was a sad row of four closed businesses — two on either side of the courthouse — between them. "Judd can take down the men on the north side of the crowd. I'll take the south."

"You got it figured how we gonna cut down on civilian casualties?"

"That's gonna be Fish's job."

Lester raised an eyebrow at the mention of Fish, but Judd never twitched, just stood there, stoic. It was clear Judd had set his mind to doing as he was told, *exactly* as he was told, and he didn't presume to have any opinion on things one way or the other.

Pete hadn't really intended to involve Fish. But the former English teacher had definitely demonstrated initiative — stole a car, for crying out loud — to get help. As far as Pete could tell, Fish was cold sober, and Pete hadn't had time to recruit anybody else.

"Fish's gonna be in the crowd. They're gonna be boxed in by the buildings and the only place to run is north and south down the street. Can't have that. Soon's the shooting starts, Fish is gonna herd people *forward* — up *toward* the school — and then turn 'em right, down the sidewalk toward the bank, around the fountain and out the back."

Pete had told Fish he had to keep the crowd together. If they just scattered, bolted in every direction, they'd overrun Viola's gunmen on the sides, get in his and Judd's line of fire. The only opening off Main Street lay through the big courtyard next to the bank building where a spray of water once spouted out a mermaid's mouth, though water had long ago been cut off to the empty building and vandals had stolen the statue's head. On the back side, the bank's courtyard opened through an ornate archway into the parking lot behind the building.

He looked at Judd when he spoke again. "But this here ain't gonna be all neat and tidy." He thought 'bout telling Judd what his sergeant had told him all those years ago — "No plan survives after the first shot's fired." Instead, he said, "Folks is gonna panic. I hope Fish can get most of them out, but they ain't all gonna listen to him. Maybe none of them will. No telling what they'll do, where they'll run. That's why I didn't try to round up an army of hotshots and line the rooftops with them. It's just you and me and Lester because we *got* to hit what we aim at … and *nothing else*."

Judd nodded and Pete turned back to Lester.

"I'm thinking a sniper-initiated ambush."

That meant the ambush would begin after the first shot from the sniper. "Best spot for you'd be on the roof of the post office, don't you think?" The post office was a block south, on the same side of the street as Judd and Pete's positions. "There's air conditioning units on the top there you can hunker down behind. I know 'em well, probably cleaned a hundred birds' nests out of the things. There's an unobstructed line of sight to the front of the school."

He and Judd would not have to search for cover to conceal their presence. All the buildings on both sides of the street had facades that rose up at least three feet above the roof line, each unique. Several buildings had built up higher facades — ten or fifteen feet tall, all ornate and fancy-like, which presented an uneven, jagged roofline to Main Street. Pete had always thought it'd look better if they was uniform, all the same height and shape, but hadn't nobody asked his opinion on the subject. He'd selected the drug store and hair salon buildings that had facades perfect to his purpose, designed with the missing-teeth look of castle turrets, where you could hide from sight behind a yard-wide "tooth" and stick your rifle barrel out through the slot between them to fire.

The suppressor on Lester's Ruger 10/22 would make it silent, just a little coughing sound you couldn't hear six feet away. When a weapon was fired, there was two things made the gunshot sound. One was the explosion of the gun powder in the barrel and that's what the suppressor would silence. The second was the sound of the bullet breaking the sound barrier, the familiar "crack" sound. A .308 with a suppressor was still so loud it'd make your ears ring because the bullet it fired was going something like 2,600 feet per second — and the crack would give away the direction the bullet was coming from. But Lester's Ruger fired a bullet much smaller and slower. No sound. Of course, that required an even greater accuracy than a larger gun. A sniper had to land a good, solid center shot, headshot or middle of the chest or back — otherwise the shot would only wound, not kill.

"Soon's Viola starts talking, everybody'll be looking at her," he told Judd. "That's your signal to line up your shot."

He looked from Judd to Lester. "Simple plan. Lester takes the first shot." He looked at Lester and said just one word. "Viola." Lester nodded. "Won't nobody see nothing nor hear nothing, she'll just drop." He looked at Judd.

"We got to give them a chance to surrender. I'll holler for them to drop their guns — and when they don't, and they *won't* — that's our cue to open fire. Have a man in your sights so you can get at least one maybe two in the first couple of seconds while everybody's still surprised.

Judd would be firing a Browning A-bolt .270 hunting rifle with a Diamondback HP 3-12x42 scope. Pete's was an M1 carbine. Both of those weapons would blow a hole in a man big enough to stick your fist into. As opposed to Lester's sneak attack, Pete and Judd would be loud — that was part of the plan, too. The men below could tell where their bullets were coming from, and they'd turn and fire back, *shoot at the men on the rooftops* while Fish led the crowd to safety.

Both men nodded. Pete went over it one more time anyway. "Lester opens fire, takes out his target. We pick off the men guarding the right and left flanks. Fish directs the crowd forward, then right to the bank and out the back."

The men nodded again.

Pete looked at his watch. They had plenty of time to get into position before noon. He looked at Lester, then Judd, didn't say nothing stupid like good luck. Just held their gaze for a moment, didn't mess up the communication with words. The men turned without speaking then and went out the back door of the hardware store.

Chapter Seventeen

JUDD HAD MORE trouble than he'd thought he'd have climbing up the rusty, rickety old ladder on the back side of the drug store. Wasn't an easy thing to do cradling a rifle, and his knees cracked so loud it sounded like rifle shots when he bent to a crouch at the top of the ladder to duckwalk across the roof to the facade wall in front. He glanced to the right and could see Pete making his way up a ladder two roofs away. The Hair Affair building, where he was positioned, didn't have a ladder on the outside anymore, so Pete had to climb up onto the roof of the insurance agency next door and step across. The State Farm Insurance building had a tall facade so he merely bent at the waist all the way to the front of the roof, hidden behind the tall facade, before he had to hunker down and cross onto the hair salon roof.

Judd glanced to the left at the Post Office a block away with its flat roof adorned with air-conditioning units in the center, but saw nothing, didn't know if Lester was in place yet or not, suspected if he was, he was hidden so well Judd wouldn't spot him.

Judd couldn't be seen from Main Street standing at the top of the ladder on the back side of the roof, but from there to the facade, he'd be visible unless he crouched, even had to crawl the last few feet to remain hidden from view. The stone facade reminded Judd of a picket fence, 'cept the pickets wasn't pointed, and he slowly peeked out the space between them. He had a clear view of the crowd gathering in the street below, and the school's broad steps and tall white columns. He could only see about two thirds of the crowd because the rest was too close to his side of the street. He checked his weapon, then leaned back against the facade wall, panting. Not from exertion. From fear. His hands were slick with sweat and he dried first one palm and then the other on his pants.

He went over the plan for the umpteen bazillionth time in his head. As soon as Viola started talking, he was to swing around, put the barrel of the rifle through the slot on the facade and sight in on a target. Only about six inches of the barrel would be visible from below, and Pete was banking on the fact that the crowd would be facing the other way, everybody's attention would be focused on Viola, not looking over their shoulders at the roofline behind them. But whoever stood up on the school porch with Viola was facing the drug store and hair salon buildings. If they looked close, they'd see. Nothing to be done about that, though. It was what it was.

As soon as Lester shot Viola, Pete would yell for them to surrender and if they didn't ... *when* they didn't, he and Pete would open fire.

Judd found he suddenly needed to go to the bathroom. Fine time to notice a thing like that! He wondered what soldiers in battle did ... how did they ...? He let it go, might ask Pete or Lester about it when this was all over. Assuming all three of them were still alive by then.

The point of using his Browning and Pete's M1 was because they both sounded like cannons. Pete wanted the sound to distract Viola's troops from guarding the crowd, wanted them occupied with … *returning fire.*

Judd hadn't never in his life experienced the particular tingle at the base of his spine occasioned by the realization that any second now, somebody was going to start shooting at him.

Viola and her sons done like she done the night of the last public meeting, where she'd got rid of the deputy sheriff. She come into West Liberty Middle School through a door on the north side that opened into a space beside the building you couldn't see from the street. Everybody else was parked in front and was milling around in the crowd that was already pretty good-sized and the party wasn't scheduled to start until noon. When it did, her plan was to get to the point quick. Zach and the Monroe brothers, Bubba and Felix, Clarence Thacker, Hoyt Wilmer, Jethro Bodean and another couple of fellas would be in the street on the north side of the crowd, making sure didn't nobody "wander off." Obie, the Scully brothers, Bufford Pettigrew, Hulan Gibson, Merl Pickett and some others would be on the south side, doing the same thing there. She'd keep Neb with her.

She didn't even make no effort to hide her gun when she come walking in through the little door beside the stage in the auditorium. It was a Smith & Wesson Model 66 .357 magnum with a six-inch barrel. A revolver with six chambers. It was a heavy weapon, not the kind of pistol most females woulda chose, but she was a strong woman and she liked the heft of it.

Soon's they walked into the room, she spotted the crowd of people standing in front of something on the back wall. When Viola got close, she could see it was a giant map of Nowhere County.

Where in tarnation did a thing like that come from?

She shoved her way through the babbling crowd until she was standing right in front of it, and she was as floored as everybody else seemed to be at the detail shown. She seen Scott's Ridge, the bat caves in Bugtussel Hollow and the spot where there usta be a bridge on old Rabbit Run Road. But there was also a mark that showed that little spring uphill from her house that didn't even have no name. It only come out in the springtime, dried up in the summer and run again soon's the weather got damp in the fall. She didn't think there was a soul in the world had ever seen that thing whose last name wasn't Tackett. Obviously, everybody else standing around was as taken with the map as she was, babbling about this little detail and that, commenting how they hadn't realized how many unique things they was in the county until they seen all of them together like that, drawn out on the map.

"Who done this and what's it doing here?" she asked nobody in particular. Somebody said they'd heard somebody else say they thought the person drew it was Pete Rutherford, which would make sense, she supposed, him being a mailman all them years, he'd know what was located where. But to be able to remember it all, all them little things … that was *something*.

But Viola Tackett hadn't come to town today to admire a map of Nowhere County. She had other business, and she called out to them as was gathered around the map to go on outside to the street so she could talk to everybody proper. Most did, but a handful hung out at the map, and other folks was coming in the front door to see it when she walked out on the porch. She'd get Neb to gather up all the stragglers soon as she got the meeting going.

Squinting up into the almost noonday sun, Viola stood on the high porch in front of the leaded glass window beside the school door — both the left and the right double doors had been propped open. She looked out over the people who'd gathered there in the middle of the street. Hard to know how many folks was there. They was packed tight and more was coming up and filling in all the time. She'd had Zach make it plain on the phone tree message that "every adult" who showed up would have their name put on the list, so if they was a big family living up in a hollow, they'd best bring all the aunts, uncles and brothers, so everybody would get a share.

She looked at her watch. She still had a couple of minutes and she planned to start right on time. High noon.

Little kids was running around, chasing each other and making a racket. Her first feeling of annoyance — she never liked to be around little kids — was replaced with gratitude. Good thing to have some kids. Put a gun to one of them's head, they parents would fall all over themselves to save their skins, plead with they neighbors and the like.

The midday sun hung right dead overhead. Wasn't hot, though, course not. Hadn't been hot since J-Day. Not a cloud in the sky, neither. They was folks complaining about how good the weather was, how unnatural good and uniform it was, but she wasn't one of them as didn't like it. It'd be fine with her if every day from now on was just as clear and comfortably warm as this one. She put her hand over her eyes to shade them, surveying the crowd and—

Something glinted and caught her eye. There was something shiny on the roof of Willingham's Drug Store on the other side of the street about half a block down from the school.

Then it was gone. She kept looking. It blinked again and was gone. Sunlight was reflecting off something shiny. The sparkle made her uneasy in the way other things in her life had done, and though she didn't understand it, she never questioned the feeling.

She called Obie to her side and spoke in his ear without gesturing.

"Climb up on the roof of the drug store and see what's up there that's sparkling."

Chapter Eighteen

If Cotton hadn't known there was a cemetery here, Stuart would have driven right past it. Piloting his rented red Lexus around one hairpin turn and then another, he was concentrated on the road and unprepared when Cotton told him to pull over.

"Where?"

"There." Cotton indicated the ghost of a trail leaving the highway on the left side and winding back into the trees. As Stuart began to slow down, Cotton pointed down the highway ahead of them. "Around that next turn is Gideon. The first house probably isn't half a mile from here." Stuart pulled off onto the almost-not-there trail and ventured slowly along its rocky surface and Cotton gestured at the steep hillside snuggled up to it on the right side. "The town's just on the other side of that hill."

The Gideon cemetery boasted no sign or any landmark to mark its presence. It was an overgrown area about half the size of a football field between two steep inclines, next to a meadow carpeted in colorful wildflowers that had butterflies flitting around from one blossom to the next.

Stuart felt anew the sensation he'd felt when he'd first driven the winding mountain roads — the vistas, drop-offs and lush green mountains were breathtaking, but more subtle beauty like this meadow seemed to be around every corner, too. In the Detroit neighborhood where Stuart had grown up, the only bright colors were provided by graffiti, gang logos and "colorful obscenities" painted on the gray tenement buildings.

One glance at the other two and he knew he was the only one who had noticed it. When Stuart killed the engine and got out, he could actually hear what he thought might be a hive of bees somewhere. There were a couple of tree stumps in the meadow, almost covered by the flowers and grass — maybe there were bees in one of them.

"This is it, huh," Jolene said. She was seated in the back seat and didn't get out.

Cotton told Stuart, "There are little cemeteries like this all over the mountains, a few graves here, a few there. Families and neighbors take care of them."

Obviously, nobody'd been caring for this one. Stuart looked uneasily up into the surrounding woods and Cotton caught the look.

"The phrase you're searching for is *sitting ducks*," Cotton said, then he said something else, softly. "Some ducks have teeth."

That couldn't be right. Stuart's mind was so numb from exhaustion, Cotton could as easily have said "some trucks have wreaths," or "some pucks have grief" and it would have made as much sense. Stuart was too tired to ask, just looked up into the thick brush and the deep shadows of the huge trees. If you knew what you were doing, you could be hidden in plain sight right there in front of him and the city boy wouldn't spot you.

Stuart could pick out occasional grave markers where

vegetation hadn't completely taken over. Closer inspection yielded some semblance of order, what might once have been neat rows of markers under the extending arms of a huge sycamore tree near the south edge of the meadow.

Stepping to the nearest marker that lay on its side in the undergrowth, he pulled it free from the grass and entangling vines and dusted off the front side of the stone. Or maybe it was the back side. There was no way to tell because any words inscribed there had worn off long before Stuart was born.

"Lily Topple kept up the cemetery as best she could," Cotton said. "Probably some of her kin was buried here. Rose did the same after her. But these people died more than a hundred years ago, and when all the residents of Gideon vanished overnight, that left nobody to see to the graves."

Stepping to another stone lying in the undergrowth, Stuart freed it and tried to make out the words inscribed on it. All he could see for sure was the date "June" — either the birth or death month. But the year and everything else had worn away. Another toppled stone bore the family name McTavish, or McIntosh, so there must have been some Scots sprinkled among the Irish miners in the coal camp.

Cotton indicated a bare space between the headstones that might once have been a walkway or path. "How about we dig here?" Cotton almost grinned. "The royal *We*, meaning *You*, of course."

They had made something of a plan last night. Jolene and Cotton would drop Stuart at the cemetery on their way to Gideon. He would dig a grave and set up the "marker" while Cotton and Jolene went into town to retrieve the bones — if, indeed, the bones were still where Lily Topple had put them a hundred years ago.

Stuart went back to the car, hit the button on the key fob and the trunk unlocked. He lifted the lid and found the tools Cotton had purchased yesterday at Home Depot in Carlisle, picks and shovels, a flashlight and three sets of work gloves. And the wooden grave marker.

They'd made the marker last night. It had taken longer to decide what words to inscribe on it than it had to construct the small cross. Cotton had purchased wide black Magic Markers. Jolene had the clearest handwriting. Unlike the square, all-caps Stuart or Cotton would have printed, hers was fluid cursive that looked almost like calligraphy.

Truth was, they knew almost nothing about the bones that had been in the burial cave the miners had accidentally cut into. Since the mining company supervisor had assumed they had been Quakers — Christians — Stuart and Cotton had constructed a cross. But even that was just a guess. So they'd written on the marker as little as possible.

Jolene penned the words "Carthage, Kentucky, 1795" in large letters on the top. Beneath that, she wrote: "May these children of God rest here in eternal peace."

Stuart glanced again at the surrounding woods.

"If they're up there, you won't see them," Cotton said.

"Figured that."

The two men stood, looking at each other for a beat, then Cotton put his hand on Stuart's shoulder.

Neither spoke. Stuart knew his voice would be thick with emotion if he did, but Cotton merely nodded then, turned and went back to the car. He got in on the driver's side, adjusted the seat forward — he didn't have Stuart's long legs, then turned the car around and headed back down the not-quite-a-trail toward the road. Jolene looked at Stuart through the backseat window, the expression on her face unreadable. He was glad she didn't wave.

As soon as the sound of the car engine died away, Stuart became aware of the sounds of the woods. Birds calling out to each other, a dozen different varieties. A raucous cry came from the bushes, courtesy of a what sounded like huge cicadas — which Stuart understood only came out every seven years. Or fourteen. Or maybe it was twenty-one — at some regular interval, anyway. Clearly, with the ruckus they put up, this was their year to shine.

He put on the work gloves, lifted the pick high above his head and hammered it with a crunching thud into the earth at his feet. The contact was jarring, but gratefully the ground wasn't hard and the point sunk deep into the earth. Even in soft ground, digging a grave big enough to hold two duffle bags full of bones would take a while.

Concentrating on expending all his strength with every blow, he hacked at the dirt, keeping his mind fixed on landing every stroke in the same spot as the one before, driving the point of the pick as deep as he could. He refused to look up at the woods all around him.

If they're up there, you won't see them.

Chapter Nineteen

CHARLIE'D VOLUNTEERED to drive the three of them from the Middle of Nowhere to Fearsome Hollow, to Gideon *where the wild things are.*

Sam insisted Malachi ride in front because his long legs would be jammed up in the backseat, but in truth Sam's six-foot frame didn't fold up very well in Charlie's mother's 1991 Honda Legend, either.

Charlie's mind flashed briefly to the Chrysler Cirrus she'd rented at the airport in Lexington, wondering idly what had happened to it. What had happened to all the vehicles that just vanished when they hit the county line.

"You can put that stuff in the back," she instructed Malachi when he opened the car door and saw resting on the seat the envelop of information Thelma Jackson had brought to show them two days ago. "I intended to go through it, see if maybe there was something, but I just never ..."

Malachi picked up the envelope and sat down. As she pulled out of the parking space, he opened it and idly fingered through the contents. Copies of birth and death certificates, of "chits" for merchandise sold at the store in Boonesborough before the Revolutionary War, family tree charts, the list of names from the Bible Thelma found in Shakertown, copies of ledger entries, letters like the one where someone had set down the memories of the trapper Jeb Pollock, who went looking for a crying child in the woods and found "a beastie twenty feet tall, teeth sharp as knives," or Aloushous Hardy, the minister who claimed the devil "his own self came to carry me away to hell. Its teeth were daggers and its eyes were full of lost souls."

When she turned on Pebble Bottom Road and headed toward Byrne Lane and Zebulon Pike, she glanced at Malachi's face and realized he wasn't really looking at any of the pages on his lap.

His mind was somewhere else entirely. She couldn't fit it into her head what it must be like to find out you have a son … and, oh, by the way, the boy might die before you ever have a chance to have a conversation with him.

Sam sat silent in the back seat. Charlie didn't speak either. All of them were as imprisoned by their own thoughts as the county was by the sinister mirage on the county line.

Merrie.

Stuart!

Stuart had been here. No, was *still* here, at least in some "here" that approximated Nowhere County somewhere in the universe. He'd come looking for her. And she would bask in the warmth of that, not let the cold of other realities chill her. If she ever saw him again … *when* she saw him again, there would be time and space for all the rest of it. Not now. Right now, Charlie concentrated on the truth as she knew it to be. Sometime this morning, Stuart had written a message to Merrie on the chalkboard in the waiting room of the clinic. He was *here right now*, searching for her.

And if Moses Weiss was to be believed, he would be in Fearsome Hollow today, too. High noon. Fighting the Jabberwock to free his wife and little girl.

She tried to allow that reality, like the heat from a single red coal in a fireplace, to warm her and keep at bay the terror. And the agony of leaving Merrie.

She suddenly realized there were tears running down her cheeks. She reached up and wiped them away. Malachi hadn't noticed. His head was bent to the papers in his lap but there was a thousand-yard stare in his eyes. It didn't surprise her that when she glanced in the rearview mirror, she saw that Sam's cheeks were wet, too. When she rounded the final curve into Fearsome Hollow, she looked fearfully up into the trees. The last time she had been here, when she and Malachi had come with the Tungate brothers to look for Abner, she'd spotted puffs of white, like mini clouds, clustered in the trees on the mountainsides around them.

Now the Tungates were as "gone" as Abner, as gone as an uncounted number of other Nowhere People.

The bright blue sky shone above the mountaintops. There was no mist clinging to the trees today. It was here, though, somewhere. Waiting for them.

Pulling to a stop on the right side of the huge Carthage Oak, she killed the engine and the three of them sat still and silent.

Then Malachi opened his door, and they all wordlessly got out of the car and stood together in front of the tree, in the shade of its massive canopy of leaves. On the other side was a huge hole that'd been filled by rocks, but on the front side the tree's gnarled roots spread out into the street.

They looked around them at the empty buildings that

should have collapsed half a century ago but hadn't. It was quiet. Preternaturally quiet. No birds sang in the trees, no cicadas buzzed in the bushes. It was utterly still.

She found herself instinctively moving closer to the others. Malachi had taken Sam's arm, stood beside her, his head on a swivel, looking all around them. But there was nothing to see.

Or hear. Except there was.

She could hear the *silence*. It wasn't hollow-sounding, empty — the quiet of one of the gigantic cathedrals in Europe, where the walls and ceiling contained the quiet and the silence echoed in the hollow void, big and vacant.

This silence didn't feel empty. It was full, swollen silence. Silence stretched so tight over sound that it was bulging out on all the sides, about to explode.

The bulging silence … if you put your ear up to it, you could hear the sounds on the other side. Voices. Whispering. The whispers were as dry and fragile and brittle as chaff blowing across a threshing room floor. As sand blowing across ancient stone.

Whispers. And … crying.

Sam put her hands over her ears and the three exchanged terrified looks. They hadn't been here even a minute, and already …

"We're here," Malachi called out, looking around. "We came. To *play* with you."

"Kiddie games," Sam called, her husky voice an octave deeper than usual. Charlie could hear the tremor in it. "What games do you want to play — hide and seek?"

As soon as the words left her mouth, there was a sound like static — the one they'd heard inside the Jabberwock. And there were sparks in the air, a shower of sparks like from a welding torch. Sam's whole body was suddenly outlined in the glittering light, Fourth of July sparklers, and her face instantly went blank, expressionless. Except for her eyes. Her eyes were seeing "something" and clearly it wasn't a reality Charlie could see.

"Sam …?" Charlie said.

Sam stood rigid for a moment, her eyes moving frantically, and then she clamped both hands over her mouth and cried out through them in a terror-filled voice. "Indians! The Indians are coming."

Cotton Jackson pulled Stuart's rented Lexus up on the left side, as close as he could get to the behemoth trunk of the massive Carthage Oak in Gideon. The gnarled old tree stretched up more than a hundred feet into the sky, with a circumference Cotton would guess was at least twenty feet. When they had last come to Fearsome Hollow, they'd been in Jolene's van and she'd backed up next to the tree, *facing the street* … and a good thing, too, because Cotton had been driving when they left. He'd been so frantic to get away from the storm, the shadows, the shrieking *and the gunfire* that he'd have plowed smack into anything in his path.

This time he parked so it'd be easy to load up the trunk of the Lexus. If they found anything to load, that is.

Jolene got out of the car and came to stand beside him, looking up at the mammoth tree. She'd refused to wear the sling he'd made for her, just got him to put on a tight bandage, pointing out "I might need this arm."

She might indeed.

Going around to the car trunk, he retrieved from it the second of the two picks he'd purchased at Home Depot, along with the tire iron and accompanying mallet. He rejoined Jolene, who had gone around to the back side of the tree and was now on her knees in front of the sealed opening of the huge hole, the hole Rose Topple had told him was so large children had once played inside it. The bottom of the opening was a couple of feet off the ground, where roots the size of fire hoses snaked out away from the trunk. The top of the opening was about five feet from the bottom, stretching out in an oval maybe ten feet wide. You could easily have fit a chest freezer through that opening. Depending on the depth of the hole, the contents of two duffle bags of bones certainly wouldn't fill it.

If the bones were still where the Jabberwock had instructed Lily Topple to put them a century ago.

The little girl had jammed the opening full of creek rocks after she placed the bones inside, filled it completely, top to bottom. Cotton had always assumed — as he was sure everyone else did — that the entire hole was full of rocks, that they'd been used to seal the hole for some purpose related to the health of the tree. He didn't lay claim to vast knowledge about trees, but his neighbor'd had a big tree with a hole in it and an arborist had instructed him to fill the hole — to keep critters from burrowing farther into the tree, causing more damage. Not with concrete, though. Once it set up, it wouldn't "give" as the tree moved in growth. The recommended fill was spray insulation foam. But most people just filled holes in their trees, if they filled them at all, with rocks.

Cotton was sure nobody'd ever given any thought to what had been jammed into the hole in the big tree in a ghost town. If you dug back through property tax records, he would bet the land all around Gideon, and the buildings, still belonged to the Monroe Addington Coal Company. And the struggling coal company had had bigger fish to fry in the past century than curiosity about rocks in a tree.

Cotton put on the pair of gloves he'd purchased, and

handed another pair to Jolene. As she put them on, Cotton looked around, straining to see … what?

"You feel it, too, huh?" Jolene said. His eyes snapped back to her. She reached up and felt her short-cropped brown hair. "Is my hair …?" It was standing out in a halo around her head.

"When I was in grade school a little boy rubbed a balloon back and forth on the top of my head, but the static electricity wasn't this strong."

If it was, indeed, something as benign as static electricity.

Cotton had felt it the instant he stepped out of the car. A kind of tingling, buzzing sensation, but he had been studiously ignoring it, hoping he was imagining it.

"Do you hear …?" Jolene started. "I don't know what it is, but it sounds like——"

"Static," he finished for her.

"Yeah, like when you can't find a station — what's *that*?"

"What?"

"That … I don't know what——"

She pointed to something like a spark in the air on the other side of the tree. One spark, then another. Then the air in front of the tree was filled with sparks, like somebody was welding a piece of metal there. Showers of sparks rained down out of … nothing at all.

"The static's not just … static," she said. "There are voices——"

"Whispers."

"Can you hear what they're saying?"

He shook his head and they both looked around fearfully. Waited.

Nothing else happened. Oh, maybe the static got a little louder, the showering sparks thicker, but no other weird phenomena showed itself. And in the world in which Cotton Jackson now lived, only "mild" impossibility was a win.

"We need to get busy." He bent and jabbed the pointed end of the pick between two of the big rocks and began to try to pry them apart. Jolene helped out with the tire iron. It took considerable muscle to pry the rock free from the space it had occupied for a century undisturbed, and Cotton was beginning to think it would take days to finally dig them all out. But the first one was the hardest, jammed in tight by the pressure of the others around it. Once it was free, the other rocks were easier.

He pried out rock after rock, and Jolene piled them up in a stack. He lost track of time, just jammed the pick between rocks, wiggled and pried them loose, used the crowbar, then back to the pick, pulled small rocks free, then bigger ones …

Suddenly, he pulled a rock free and there was no other rock behind it. Just … black emptiness.

"Guess this means the entire hole isn't filled with rocks." He felt his arms pebble with gooseflesh.

He kept digging and prying while Jolene went back to the car trunk and got the flashlight. He tossed a big rock aside and leaned back on his haunches. Jolene handed him the flashlight wordlessly. He flipped the switch and he and Jolene leaned forward together to peer through the opening — into a darkness illuminated for the first time in more than a century.

Sweeping the beam back and forth, he saw nothing but the back side of the hole in the tree, nothing—

There! Bones. A pile of bones. A big pile of bones.

Jolene managed not to cry out but her hand went to her mouth.

The two sat still, breathless, then Cotton put the flashlight on the ground and went back to work.

His attention and focus narrowed to widening the hole, concentrating on the next rock, and the next, handing them out to Jolene and digging out the next one. And the next. He no longer needed the pick to pry them apart, could wiggle each free with his bare hands. He hadn't removed all the rocks, but had opened up a large hole in the stone wall of them, when he had to stand. His knees were killing him, and they protested with loud pops and snaps when he extended them.

Jolene remained on her knees.

"Hand me a sack," she said. "We don't have to move all these rocks. This hole's big enough for me to crawl through. Just hold the flashlight."

The wall of rocks was several feet thick. But beyond them was, indeed, a chamber. A burial chamber, full of bones.

"Are you sure you want to … to crawl in there?"

"I'm sure I absolutely, one hundred percent do *not* want to crawl in there. But it'll be quicker that way." She looked at the cascading sparks in front of the tree and he followed her gaze. The waterfall of sparks was huge now. "I think we are in a hurry. A really big hurry."

Chapter Twenty

SAM BLINKED. Gideon and the tree, Malachi, Charlie and the car … everything vanished. No, just blinked out for a moment with a sparkling light so bright it blinded her, before an entirely different reality blinked back on. It was a little like changing the channel on the television. She had been expecting any second that the Jabberwock with claws and razor teeth would appear and rip the three of them to pieces, had been so afraid, *terrified!*

Not anymore. She wasn't frightened now, she was angry. She was sitting on a rock, could feel the cold on her butt, and she was looking out on a sunshiny day *through somebody else's eyes.*

IT'S NOT FAIR.

Grace Biddle sits with her back to the other children and she's glad they can't see her face because she is crying and she doesn't want to give Hope the satisfaction of seeing her cry.

Mrs. Campbell told her she had to sit by herself until she was willing to apologize to her sister for taking her doll away. Well, that's going to be a long time because Grace isn't sorry. How can she be sorry for taking the doll away when it was her turn? Hope had the doll all morning and it was Grace's turn and when she said she wanted it, Hope started to cry.

Hope always cries.

Six years old and she still tunes up every time something doesn't go her way.

Maybe Grace should do that. She's always been the strong one of the twins, the one who knew what the two of them ought to do, who planned. Hope acts like a baby. Hope doesn't want to get mud on her skirt. Hope wants to go in the house at night as soon as it gets dark because she's scared. Pooo!

Mostly, Hope is terrified of Indians. She and Hope had both sneaked out of the house into the shadows beyond the big campfire the elders built that night and listened to the travelers from Boonesborough talking about how the raiding party of Cherokee Indians had attacked their settlement. Whooping and hollering, tried to kill everybody there. The men fought back, shot two of the Indians and all the others ran off.

After that, Hope was afraid of her own shadow. They sleep together on the corn husk mattress and after Hope heard about the Indian attack she cuddled right up next to Grace in the bed every night. It's too hot for cuddling, but Hope is so scared all the time that she has to be right up next to Grace or she can't go to sleep.

Grace hears laughter and turns to see Lydia Mullins splash water on Ruth Ann Whitt. Lydia is watching her eight-month-old brother, who's sitting in about an inch of water, clapping his hands and giggling at the girls playing.

Most of the girls are here at the creek helping their mothers do the washing. Most of the boys are out playing hide and seek. They don't have to work nearly as hard as the girls. But now that the wash is done, the women are sitting on the rocks talking before they haul their baskets back home.

Grace wishes she had a baby brother to look after. She asked Ma *for one and Ma gave Pa a look and smiled but she didn't say yes or no. Hope even chimed in, pleading with their parents for a baby.*

And then they'd told the girls to pray about it, to ask God for a baby brother and after that, whenever they got down on their knees beside the bed at night, they begged God for a baby brother but God hadn't given them one.

Ma'd said she didn't want two of them this time, so alike she'd had to tie a red ribbon on Hope's toe when she was a baby so she could tell them apart. Just one baby, she'd said, so the girls would have to share him.

Grace doesn't like that part because Hope is so selfish she probably won't even give Grace a turn holding the baby. Just like she wouldn't let Grace have the doll. Sarah and Priscilla's father had carved dolls out of wood, was going to make each of the little girls her own doll. That was before he cut his hand. Now he was in bed with a fever and the bandage on his hand smelled bad, and Ma said it would be a long time before he'd be able to carve again. Hope had gotten her doll but Grace hadn't. So Ma had said they had to share the one doll Hope got but Hope wouldn't. She kept it all the time and cried when Grace wanted to play with it. Grace asked nice this morning, but Hope said no, so Grace had taken the doll away — it was her turn — and Hope had started crying. David and Silas's mother had been standing there, holding their little sister, Leah. Mrs. Campbell listened to Hope and took Hope's word for what had happened — and had made Grace go off by herself to "pray for God to forgive her sin and soften her heart."

But she isn't praying. She's too mad to talk to God, who will be mad at her because she is mad at Hope. If Hope would just—

"Grace, are you ready to tell your sister you're sorry and ask for her forgive—"

Mrs. Campbell's words are cut off by the sound of shouting. Men's voices.

The women drop their baskets. Some of them scream. At first, Grace doesn't know what's going on, why everybody is so upset and then Hope drops the doll on the rocks and leaps to her feet, her eyes huge. Grace knows then. She covers her mouth, utters a bleat of wordless horror and cries out through her fingers, "The Indians are coming."

~

MALACHI HAD no idea what to do, no idea how to call Sam back from whatever reality had prompted her to cover her mouth in shocked terror and cry out that "the Indians are coming."

He exchanged a look with Charlie, then he called Sam's name firmly, with authority. "Sam!"

She ignored them both, continued to stare out at something in front of her they couldn't see, her red hair fairly glowing in the sparkling light.

Malachi had never felt so helpless and vulnerable, certainly not when he was a soldier. As Charlie drove along the winding mountain roads on their way to Fearsome Hollow, he had been unable to do as he had done the dozens of other times when he had willingly walked into harm's way, knowing he could be dead in seconds.

As a Marine, he'd learned to blank out everything but the immediate, didn't allow his mind to venture out there beyond right here, right now. The rifle in his hand. His buddies beside him. The enemy beyond.

But he couldn't do it now, had somehow lost control. His emotions were as tangled up as Christmas lights, twisted and tied into knots by one staggering revelation after another.

His mother intended to *kill* Charlie.

His sister was dead.

Rusty ... was *his son.*

That was the hardest. The one that totally knocked the

wind out of him. The blow that sent him to his knees.

Rusty Sheridan was *Malachi's son!*

How had he not … why couldn't he see … why didn't Sam …?

He had no answers to those questions, but the answers didn't matter anyway. The truth of it was all that mattered. He had a twelve-year-old son! A fine boy. Sam had done such a good job.

Sam.

Yeah … *Sam.*

The beautiful red-haired woman who had shouldered the whole burden of parenthood — walked the floor with a crying baby, sent a six-year-old off to his first day of school, encouraged him and disciplined him and prayed over him … *all by herself.*

Well, no more!

He would not let Sam carry the whole load alone anymore. He would …

Yeah, would what?

Rusty was unconscious, might never wake up.

And Malachi — the father to the rescue on a white horse … well, he might not live to see another sunrise.

Putting his hands on Sam's shoulders, he shook her, called out, "Sam, what's wrong?"

But instead of pulling Sam back into his reality, grabbing her seemed to draw Malachi toward hers. Toward *somebody's.*

Sparkling light. Snapping and popping and a "fried circuit" sensation welled up around Malachi and blotted out the rest of the world. He had time to wonder if perhaps sparklers now outlined his body as they outlined Sam's, and then Fearsome Hollow blinked out of existence. Malachi tried to struggle against the sensation, but it was as inexorable as a wave washing out to sea.

He blinked and opened his eyes ... somewhere else. Some*one* else.

Gabriel Dunn is chopping wood when he hears the voices. He stops, ax held high, then slowly lowers it to the ground and listens. He can tell by the tone that something is wrong, but it could be something no more threatening than a skunk wandering into town, which is what had set all the girls squealing three days go.

But he supposed it could be ...

Indians.

Maybe ...

Gabe's gut yanks into knot. Not because he is afraid, though he is afraid. But because he can feel his resentment leak back into him and he has worked so hard to get rid of it. Has prayed and asked for forgiveness. Has pleaded with God to take the rebellious spirit out of him. His father, an elder in the Society of Friends, had warned him, said a spirit like that was telling God, "I'm in charge, butt out. I will do it MY way."

That was a grievous sin, the sin of Adam.

"When you question the beliefs of the elders, you're questioning God," his father had said. "You're telling God that you know better how to run the universe than he does."

Gabe had been properly rebuked, knew his father was right.

And yet, he can't silence the voice in his heart that tells him to fight back. That he has a right, an obligation to take up arms to protect the weak from harm.

The voice could not be silenced, awakened by the news the travelers from Boonesborough had brought in the early spring. They'd described in graphic detail — that the women and children were not allowed to hear — how the Cherokee had attacked their settlement.

Gabe couldn't get the images out of his mind, of savages whooping and hollering, riding through the village, killing the livestock, animals and people alike. He'd believed the men who had driven the savages away were courageous, but when he said so his father had scoffed.

They weren't brave, his father had told him sternly. They were sinful.

It was a sin to take the life of another. The Bible couldn't have been more clear about that. Thou Shalt Not Kill. A simple command that meant exactly what it said.

"But Pa, what if they're trying to kill ....?"

His father hadn't even allowed him to finish, had slapped him hard across the mouth and called his words blasphemy.

Gabe had repented, of course. Had confessed his sin of rebelliousness and worked hard to win again God's favor.

But still ... sometimes when he lies in bed at night, imagining the scene the battle the men had described, he feels an involuntary swell of admiration in his chest. The men had risked their own lives to save their families, had protected the women and children who were defenseless.

"Gabe! Where are you, boy?"

His father is calling to him from the trail that leads from the village into the woods where he sent Gabe with his ax as soon as it was light outside.

"Here, Pa." Gabe drops the ax and goes running through the trees to the trail, where his father is racing toward him, leading a group of children. The children are quiet, not squealing in fear. They've been told to be quiet and they are obedient.

Gabe's father's eyes are huge.

"It's Indians, boy," he says, his voice tightly controlled. "Jeremiah saw them from the ridge. Cherokee, he thinks, not Choctaw. A raiding party headed this way."

Gabe has never felt fear before like he feels now.

"Take these to the cave. Hide them there."

"What are you—?"

"We're going to speak to them. Extend to them the hand of friendship and God's love."

"But what if they don't—?"

His father shoots him a look that silences him instantly.

"Take the little ones and go."

He reaches out and grips Gabe's arm.

"You're the oldest. You're in charge of the safety of all the children. Hide them and look after them. See that they come to no harm."

His father turns and runs back down the trail toward the village and Gabe looks into the terrified eyes of the village children.

The Campbells — Silas, who's nine, is holding Leah in his arms. She's a chubby little girl of eighteen months and an armful for her skinny oldest brother. David Campbell, seven, has hold of Silas's shirt tail, just holding it.

There are the Biddle twins that Gabe can never tell apart, the three Whitts — Ruth Ann's red hair flaming between her blond brother and sister, and the Southwicks. Even at two, Esther Southwick is smaller than Leah Campbell, and her brother Ezra, eleven, is carrying her piggyback, while their other two brothers hold hands behind them. The two Lancaster girls, Sarah and Naomi, and Lydia Mullins, holding her baby brother Matthew on her hip, bouncing him up and down, to keep him from crying.

Behind them all is Daniel, Gabe's little brother. Gabe knows the nine-year-old moved to the back to be sure nobody was left behind. Danny's like that. He's genuinely … good, in ways Gabe could never hope to be.

They all look to Gabe. He is the oldest, though only fourteen, and he will lead them. They all know what they are to do. They've been shown the cave where they are to take shelter if there is danger, but it is up to Gabe to be certain they get there safely and to stand watch over them until the danger has passed.

He can hear more shouting from the village, women, some of them screaming, and he turns toward the mountain.

"This way! Come on!" He gestures and takes off running through the trees, guiding the group of children running through the trees behind him.

Chapter Twenty-One

CHARLIE STARED at Sam as she stood frozen in terror, her hands clamped over her mouth. Light sparked all around her, pinpricks with sharp edges that felt like they were slicing into Charlie's corneas.

Malachi called Sam's name but she didn't respond. He grabbed her shoulders and shook her. "Sam, what's wrong?"

He instantly let go of her, almost like he'd been shocked, and Charlie thought he was getting ready to slap her cheek to snap her out of it.

He didn't, though, just stood with his hands limp at his sides and the same sparkler light that had appeared around Sam appeared around Malachi.

Charlie reached out to him, grabbed his arm — her mind trailing along a heartbeat behind the knee-jerk movement, warning her, "*Don't touch him!*"

Too late.

. . .

IT'S DARK. *Sarah Elizabeth Lancaster has never been as scared as she is right now, not even when she saw the rattlesnake on the trail and thought it was going to bite Ben, and she'd turned and run all the way home screaming.*

Not when she heard the bear growling in the trees and her father had grabbed her by the arm and flung her behind him, standing tall in front of the creature, his arms extended, shouting, with nothing more to fight with than the branch he'd picked up off the ground.

Pa had backed away slowly, shoving Sarah behind him. And later he'd yelled at her for putting herself in danger like that. Any fool knew you never ever got between a mother bear and its cubs. But Sarah hadn't seen the cubs until it was too late, and she'd had to get Naomi out of there.

Naomi never looked where she was going, humming to herself as she picked blackberries, never gave a thought to danger. Sarah was only ten and Naomi was eleven, but in every way that mattered Sarah *was the big sister.*

Naomi clung to her now, trembling and sniffling, and Sarah knows she has to be brave. But ...

Indians.

The very word makes her want to throw up. Huddling together in the darkness of the cave with the other children, she struggles not to cry. Naomi is crying, softly, they all have to be quiet and Sarah shushes her, but she won't stop.

"Shut your mouth," Ezra Southwick whispers at Naomi fiercely, getting right in her face. Sarah wants to smack him, but the boy is right. They have to be quiet.

Even with the crying and sniffling that's all around them, they can hear what's going on outside. A sudden whoop seems so close, like the monster is right there in the cave with them, that they all gasp, choke off screams.

The be-quiet *part — they all have to obey because if anybody breaks down, they all will break down and even though she is sure the Indians couldn't possibly hear the sounds of Naomi's muffled sobbing, they would hear it if* all *the children let go. So they huddle together, all of them quiet, trembling in the dark.*

The cave is not totally black. There are cracks in the stone walls, and the rock that covers the entrance doesn't seal it. Light shines in all around, and as her eyes grow accustomed to the darkness, she can make out the shadowed faces of the others.

David and Silas Campbell are by the door. David has his ear to the crack, listening. Sarah doesn't want to hear any better, what she and the others can hear without effort is so horrifying she might wet herself. Somebody already has. She can smell it, hopes it isn't Naomi.

They all can hear, but they can't respond. Can't give in to the terror in their chests that makes it hard to draw breath.

Wild cries! Screeching, monstrous whoops and yells. They sound so evil and vicious, full of hatred. Wild animals, snarling just out there beyond the cave.

And the screaming. She can hear women's voices, tries not to identify them, can't let herself know that one of them could be her mother. All the children know the screaming women are … what? What's happening to them? Are the Indians … hurting them? Killing them?

Her father and the other men — what's happening to them?

All the what's-happening questions whirling around in her mind are just Sarah's way of trying not to know, because she does know. Of course she does.

The wild savages out there beyond the cave walls are murdering their parents. Shooting them with arrows or hacking them apart with tomahawks.

She's crying.

She doesn't know when she started, but as she realizes she's crying she realizes the other children are, too. All of them. She can feel the sobbing shaking their bodies, but the sounds are muffled, every child crying in terrified silence. She wants to scream! Shriek! Run away, far, far away where … Naomi snuggles closer, muffled sobs wracking her body, and Sarah pats her back as they both continue to cry.

MALACHI WAS NOT aware of himself, except as an observer. Some part of him knew he was standing with Sam and Charlie beside the Carthage Oak in Gideon, but his attention was focused on what he could see out the eyes of a little boy named Gabriel Dunn.

GABE MUST TRUST in the elders.

Trust.

The.

Elders.

He huffs out each thought with a breath as he races toward the cave on the hillside, terrified children running as fast as they can behind him.

It's not a big cave, maybe twenty-five feet by thirty, but the ceiling is five feet from the floor so all but the oldest of the children can stand up in it. The cave is up on the side of the mountain, can't be seen from below, the perfect place to hide and Gabe leads his tribe of children toward it, hearing more and more horrifying sounds below as he races up the incline through the woods.

The Indians are crying out in horrible voices, savage cries that so terrify Gabe he feels like an iron band is clamped around his chest and he fears he won't be able to keep breathing. They sound so vicious. How will his father and the elders ever convince them——?

Trust the elders!

They are being obedient to the commands of God, not lifting their hands to smite down another, and God will protect them. God will look after them. He will not let those come to harm who have obeyed his commands.

Gabe believes that. He must believe that.

Except the screaming behind. The screaming …

The stone to cover the opening of the cave leans against the rock next to the entrance. *Jedediah Biddle is a stone mason and he fashioned the rock with his chisel so that it rolls easily into place to cover the cave opening. Once in place, all that must be done is toss brush on top of the rock and the entrance vanishes.*

Gabe staggers the last few feet through the trees and into the brush, where a path leads through the bushes to the small bare space in front of the cave.

He turns and calls out to the first child he sees on the path.

"You first. Get in!" Elijah Southwick, who is seven years old, staggers to a stop and bursts into tears.

"Stop that!" Gabe expects his voice to sound firm and commanding, but it is shaking as vigorously as is the whole rest of his body.

"It's dark in there."

"No it's not. There are cracks that let in light."

Gabe has been in the cave several times. The whole back wall is wet, where a spring oozes down the rock face and puddles in a rivulet that flows along the base of the cave wall. Gratefully it drips back out another crack a few feet away — otherwise the whole floor of the cave would be wet.

"Go on!"

Elijah's older brother, Ezra, puts Esther down on the ground, takes Elijah by the shoulder and shoves him toward the entrance, turns and grabs the arm of their five-year-old brother, Ezekiel, and pushes them all ahead of him into the opening, before ducking his head to follow.

Jonah Whitt, who is nine, pushes his little sisters Hannah and Ruth Ann ahead of him. Silas Campbell, also nine, is still carrying his eighteen-month-old sister, Leah, staggering under the weight. His younger brother, David, is still clinging to the tail of his shirt. The Lancaster girls, then the Biddles, then Lydia Mullins, eight, carrying her six-month-old brother Matt.

Gabe looks back over his shoulder to see Danny running down the trail toward him. The freckle-faced little boy huffs out, "Nobody got left, I made sure," before Gabe shoves him into the cave with the others.

The sounds from the village down the mountain somehow seem louder now, even though they are farther away. Indian war cries. Screaming.

It's a massacre.

No! He won't let himself think that, won't.

Danny said they were all here, but Gabe stands in front of the cave and calls out quietly anyway, "Who's missing? Anybody?"

"Where's Hope?" Grace Biddle cries. "Where—?" Then Hope grabs her hand.

Gabe turns toward the rock and carefully rolls it into place to hide the entrance. He pulls off limbs from the nearby brush and stacks them against the rock, brushes their footprints out of the dirt in front of the cave. Its hidden perfectly. There is no indication that there's a cave here.

Then he stands, panting. He can hear the children inside crying and he shouts at them through the crack between the stone and cave wall.

"Hush. Do you want them to hear you?"

Matt Mullins is wailing.

"Lydia, make Matt be quiet."

"I can't. He's scared!"

"Shut him up!" Gabe commands. He doesn't know what the little girl does, but the baby's cries cut off and now there is no noise coming from the cave.

Gabe looks back down the hillside. He must hide, too, climb up into a tree, or hide inside the limbs of an oleander bush. Or between the big stones where there was a rockslide in the spring.

But he doesn't do any of those things. Instead, he turns and heads back down the mountainside toward the river, the waterfall and the village. He has no clear plan in his mind, only obeys a primal instinct that compels him forward.

The closer he gets, the more horrifying the sounds become.

He climbs on a rock outcrop that sticks out of the ground behind a large sycamore tree on a rise near the edge of town. He clambers from the rock into the limbs of the tree, then moves slowly down the trunk until he can see out through the bottom limbs.

The horror rips apart his soul.

Cherokee are everywhere, going in and out of the houses, carrying possessions. Tools and clothing, food. One is gnawing big hunks of bread out of a loaf he has carried out of the Lancasters' house. Another is drinking greedily from the cask that contains wine Mary Whitt made from blackberries he and the other children had picked last summer.

Another Indian is … Gabe doesn't know for sure who the woman is. The Indian has hacked into her skull with a tomahawk and her face is gone. She has brown hair, so it could be Frances Biddle, Grace and Hope's mother. Or maybe Ruth Southwick. The Indian grabs a hank of her hair and pulls it out from her head, then uses the tomahawk to cut through the skin to remove the hair and the scalp.

Gabe sways, his grip on the tree limb loosens and the world grays out for a moment.

He cannot see his mother or father. But he can see a pile of bloody bodies and knows that must be the contingent of elders that went out to greet the Indians, to extend to them the hand of friendship and the love of God.

Suddenly, there is movement below him. He sees a woman crawling slowly toward the tree line. There is an ugly wound in her back and her whole dress is saturated in blood.

His heart freezes and gratefully he cannot make a sound, because if he could, he would have cried out, "Mama!"

She continues to crawl, leaving a snail trail of blood on the ground, slowly inching toward the trees.

Then one of the Indians spots her, drops the basket he is digging through and crosses the space between them. The Cherokee looks like the travelers had described — tall and skinny. His face is narrow and his nose looks as big and sharp as his tomahawk. There are streaks of black and red on his cheeks and his long black hair is tied in a braid down his back with a strip of rawhide. A single feather dangles from a leather band with beads on it around his forehead.

The savage takes a knife from a scabbard on his belt, pulls Mama's head up by the hair, and slices the blade across her throat.

Blood and gore gushes out over the front of her dress and she goes limp.

And Gabe is consumed with a rage he didn't know it was possible to feel. Rage at the monsters who are massacring his whole village. But rage, too, at the men who let it happen. *His father! His pious father who stood by and did nothing to protect his mother, just let the monsters murder her without raising a hand.*

Gabe leaps down out of the branches of the tree. He lands on the savage's back, slamming him to the ground and knocking the knife from his grip. Gabe reaches out, picks the blade up off the ground and plunges it into the monster's back all the way to the hilt. The man screams and Gabe pulls the knife out and stabs again and again and again, as the man makes horrible gurgling sounds in his throat.

Consumed by a wave of horrible red fury, he is only barely aware of the two Indians running toward him, tomahawks raised.

Then he is running through the trees, though he can't feel his feet striking the forest floor. He is small and quick and he knows these woods. He will—

A blow slams into his back, as if he'd been struck between the shoulder blades with a piece of the firewood he was cutting when ...

There is no pain, just the thudding pressure, the force of the blow that knocks him forward into the bushes. He tries to reach out his hands to cushion his fall, but finds that his arms no longer obey his commands to move.

And then the world goes black.

Chapter Twenty-Two

CLAUDE LETCHER GESTURED at the man below them and whispered to Shep, "He's digging a grave alright, just like you said."

"Wasn't me said, it was Abby."

She'd been right. Of course, Abby wasn't never wrong, didn't never get things confused. Never had. Shep was the absentminded one. He'd leave his car keys in the pocket of his other pants and have to go back into the house and get them. Or he'd lose them altogether and him and Abby'd spend half an hour looking for 'em. Abby never minded, though, didn't make fun or nothing, didn't get upset. She'd just grin and shake her head, kinda the way you done when you found an old shoe the puppy'd tore up. One time she reached over and pulled the collar of his shirt away from his neck, and when he'd looked a question at her she'd said she was just checking to make sure his head was attached tight or he'd lose it, too.

Shep felt the warmth of the memory and must have smiled because Claude asked, "What's so funny?"

Wasn't no sense in explaining it, Claude wouldn't get

the point. There was something serious wrong with that man. Shep'd always knowed it, everybody had, but he'd spent the last few days with Abby's brother and seen it up close and personal and he was here to testify that Claude Letcher was crazier'n an outhouse rat.

He ate ants. Serious. Shep seen it with his own eyes. He'd step on a trail of the red ones out in the woods, then lean over, pick one off the bottom of his boot and pop it in his mouth like it was a McDonald's French fry. He didn't never sleep, least Shep hadn't never seen him do it. Maybe he was one of them people who could sleep with they eyes open, cause Shep had never seen him close them except to blink. And that was another thing. He didn't blink often as normal people. He'd look at ya, his eyes open too wide, and just keep looking, not blinking for so long Shep wondered why his eyeballs didn't dry out.

Claude Letcher was not a man you ever felt safe turning your back on, and the crazy light he got in his eyes when him and Shep talked about killing them people made it clear to Shep that Claude was looking forward to maybe ripping them apart with his bare hands.

"I asked you, What's. So. Funny," Claude snarled and Shep realized the man was suddenly so furious he was grinding his teeth. "You hadn't ought to be laughing at me. Last man done that, I bit his nose clean off his face. Doctors never could sew the thing back on where it looked right."

We gonna have to put Claude down, Abby said inside Shep's head. Matter-of-fact like and in that flat not-Abby voice she used now. *Soon's we done here, we'll kill him.*

Claude was Abby's brother but 'parently kin didn't mean to her what it used to. Well, it was her call. Shep just done what he was told.

"Abby told me once I'd lose my own head if it wasn't

stuck on my neck. I thought it was a funny thing to say is all."

Claude nodded solemnly. "She told me when we was kids that I's dumber'n a sack of doorknobs." He paused. "I slapped her upside the head for sayin' it but it was funny."

Claude gestured to the man below them. The sound of his pick whunk-whunk-whunking into the ground carried to where the two of them were hidden in the undergrowth. "You sure we can't just shoot him now?"

"It ain't up to me. *Abby* says we got to wait."

Abby and Shep was like a glove and a hand. He was the glove, Abby was the hand. She was the one done all the moving, but he was right there with her, closer than his skin. And it was closer even than he'd felt to her before the world went mad. He'd always figured him and Abby had some-thing special, something most couples didn't have. And they had, but since the day he started picking her voice out of the whispered voices he could hear in his dilapidated shack, the two of them was closer than he'd ever felt to her before. He wondered what it was gonna be like once they killed these folks like Abby wanted. Once Abby and them others come back from wherever it was the Jabberwock'd put them. What would it be like to have Abby outside his body, standing there in front of him, talking to him, 'stead of in his head, thinking with him, thinking *for* him.

And he suddenly wasn't looking forward to that part. Once Shep realized that to have Abby back alive meant that he had to lose the Abby in his head, he wasn't at all sure that was what he really wanted.

"But we ain't gonna let him bury nothing in the hole he's digging, that right?"

Shep managed not to sigh in aggravation.

"I done said — *we* ain't the ones gonna stop 'em.

They's *others* gonna take care of that part. We just here to do what Abby says, to get rid of what they's planning to put in that hole. That's our most important job."

"But we get to kill these folks soon's the deed's done — right?"

The light shone bright in Claude's eyes.

"Just so's they end up dead, she don't care about the way of it."

Claude smiled. His rotted teeth put Shep in mind of the stumps of a forest after a fire.

MALACHI COULDN'T SEE. It was dark. Then it was light … just light, nothing to see, though he tried to open his eyes. No, not his eyes. Gabe's eyes.

THE WORLD SPINS CRAZILY when Gabe opens his eyes, so he closes them again immediately. The world fades away. When next he opens his eyes, it is evening. The shadows stalk among the trees and Gabe comes around in stages of pain.

He is lying on his face in the bush he was running toward. He can barely breathe. The agony in his back is so staggering that it grays out the world with every breath.

It takes the boy a while to put it together in his head.

The Indian killed his mother.

He took the knife and killed the Indian.

And then the others came after him and …

It is quiet now. The only sound is hard for him to place for a little while, then he understands that it is the sound of fire, the crackling of flames. He smells the smoke then, knows that the Indians must have set fire to the village.

He lifts his head and the motion stabs agony into his back so he lies his face back down into the stickery bush.

He must … what?

He must help. His father …

Is dead. Was one of the bodies he caught site of when he first looked down from the tree. The elders who …

He lets the thought go, or it merely flits away on its own out of his mind and is gone.

His mother …

Is dead, too. He watched her die.

Gabe should be dead, too. An arrow … a tomahawk … something was buried in his back. Why didn't he die?

Then he thinks about the children. Are they still safe? Surely they are. There is no way the Indians could have found them.

They are safe in the cave behind the big rock.

They are trapped in the cave behind the big rock.

It takes a long time for his slowed thoughts to process the understanding, the realization that the children cannot get out of the cave.

It was his job to hide them there.

And to let them out!

He tries to lift his head and the effort sends the world spinning away and darkness takes him.

He hears birds. The sound floats down to him where he is in a dark hole and he opens his eyes. There is light. It is day. The agony in his back takes the breath from his lungs so he lies still.

As he does, it all comes back to him. And he realizes what he has to do. He has to get to the cave and free the children.

He tries to move and the agony forces a grunt through his lips. Parched lips. He has been lying there long enough that he needs water to drink.

There is water in the cave.

But no food.

Gabe doesn't even try to crawl because he knows he will not likely be able to rise up on all fours. He merely scoots on his belly, extending his hands in front of him, moving his body forward, pushing with his legs.

He passes in and out of darkness. Can no longer feel the pain in his back and that is good, very good.

He drags himself through a small stream, eagerly drinking up the water, slurping it into his parched mouth. Sticking his face down into the glorious coolness revives him and he goes on.

It grows dark. Maybe it is night. Maybe the dark is inside his own skull. He knows he cannot keep moving, that he should pray for strength to go on.

That thought gives him strength, but not from God. The strength rises with his own anger.

God didn't protect the villagers. God just let everyone be killed. Like his father let his mother be killed.

And Gabe feels such fury at the … betrayal. He trusted God, the elders and his father. They all sat back and watched monsters savage his whole world.

He is almost angrier at them than at the Indians. If Gabe could kill them, he would. The elders. His father. God!

He would plunge knives into their backs again and again, while they screamed and made gurgling sounds in their throats.

He would kill them all. They deserve death.

But the children don't. His little brother doesn't. And so he crawls on.

Then he is on the pathway through the brush in front of the cave. It is light. Maybe daylight. Or maybe the last bit of brilliance from his dying soul is lighting his path.

Danny!

Danny, can you hear me? Answer me!

Silas, Ezra … Lydia.

Gabe calls out to them, but the sound is only in his head. His mouth and throat refuse to form the words.

There is no sound from inside the cave. Are the children still there? Of course they are. They are staying quiet.

Being obedient to what he told them.

As the elders were obedient, did what God told them.

As his father was obedient, did what the elders told him.

As he was obedient, did what—

But he wasn't obedient. Gabe didn't stay and look after the children. If he had been obedient ...

Gabe makes a sound then, a shrieking roar of rage and denial and hatred. No, this was not his fault. It was his father's fault and the elders' fault and God's fault.

It was Not. Gabe's. Fault.

Noooooooo!

The overpowering wail of rage moves over his lips and falls into the dust as a whisper on a breath, without strength or sound.

All his energy is gone. Even his raging hatred cannot summon his body to obey his commands. He will die here, now. The children in the cave will die there ... soon.

The raging torment rips at his soul, burns with a brilliant flame that provides no light to see, no warmth for the chill in his bones.

He would cry if he had tears. He would scream if he had breath. He would vent his fury on the universe ... but he cannot. It remains there in his soul, boiling in impotence as the world fades away.

Chapter Twenty-Three

IT'D ALL BEEN BRAVADO. Female macho posturing. Jolene Rutherford did *not* want to go into that dark hole and as soon as she'd bravely said she'd do it she regretted the words.

She was all the time doing stuff like that to herself. It amounted to daring herself to do a thing she didn't want to do and didn't think she could do. A way to paint herself into a corner so she couldn't back down. What an idiot.

She took a lungful of summer air that smelled a unique kind of *fresh*, an aroma equal parts pine cones and cedar boughs and maybe wildflowers and damp leaves and sparkling creeks and … mountain perfume. She'd found it nowhere else on earth, a fact she'd only realized when she came back home … home. Yeah, Jolene Rutherford was home.

Grabbing one more breath, like a diver about to take a plunge, she stuck her head and shoulders through the opening into the dark interior.

It smelled old.

Old had a similar smell no matter where you encountered it. A dark attic. A dank cellar. An old storage building. She couldn't have identified the components of the "old" smell, but the air she breathed into her lungs reeked of it. More than that, though. Infinitely more than that. It wasn't just old. It was dead. The air she pulled into her lungs had been trapped in that enclosed space for more than a hundred years, and she remembered reading somewhere that when archeologists opened up Egyptian tombs, they set out open jars to capture the air for study.

Maybe that air smelled like this, but she didn't think so. Those tombs were the opulent resting places of pharaohs and kings. This was the sealed crypt for a dozen, maybe two dozen people whose spirits had not rested easy since their deaths.

She felt that. Along with the cold — why was it so cold in here? And not just cold but … The hundred-year-old air was not the reason she felt it hard to breathe. It was the pressure. The oppression, the …

Her hand landed on a bone. It felt like a small tree branch and she couldn't help jerking back from contact with it. She should have brought the flashlight in with her instead of leaving it with Cotton to shine into the chamber around her. Yeah, she needed both hands, but …

She turned, pulled back out of the hole and snatched the flashlight out of Cotton's hands.

"Are you alright?"

"Absolutely not," she gasped. She shined the light in front of her now, ducked her head down and crawled the rest of the way into the chamber. The pile of bones was shoved up against the back of the hole with an open space in front of them big enough for her to move around. Though the bodies buried in the cave burial chamber had surely been laid out neatly, probably in rows next to the bones of those who'd gone before, these were not whole skeletons. This was a tangled heap of bleached-white bones — femurs and tibias and jaws and hips and skulls.

She reached out a gloved hand and picked up a bone and shoved it down in the green plastic leaf bag Cotton had bought. Then she forced herself to stop thinking about what she was doing, to just reach out and load these things, and they were merely *things,* after all, into the sack. She hurried then, didn't like the rattling sound the bones made when they clacked against each other in the sack.

Skulls. Leg bones, arm bones, spines and hips and fingers.

As she filled the bag with bones, she ventured farther and farther into the enclosure.

She handed the first bag out to Cotton. He took it and gave her a second empty bag. She filled it. And another. And another. On her hands and knees in the hollow place in the tree, she crawled around grabbing bones as fast as she could and jamming them into sacks for Cotton.

Then the words Rose Topple had said to Cotton rang in her ears.

"Mama knew she couldn't miss a single one, and the finger bone of a two-year-old ain't very big at all."

She slowed down, clamped her jaws together and struggled to calm her racing heart. She had to be just as careful as Lily Topple had been. She had to get them all, couldn't miss a single one. If a ten-year-old child had seined them out of the carpet of leaves/twigs/rocks and dirt on a forest floor, there was no excuse for her missing any of them laid out in front of her, glowing that eerie white in the flashlight beam.

She didn't fill the final bag Cotton gave her because there were only a few bones left. Once she'd slipped them into the bag, she slowly ran the flashlight beam around the darkened chamber, making sure there was not a single …

At first she thought it was a rock, one of those Lily had used to seal up the opening of the tree. Her flashlight beam passed slowly over it and then she jerked the beam back. Reaching out with hands that at some point had started to tremble violently, she picked up the little white rock, that was no rock at all but a small skull. A *baby's* skull. Couldn't have been more than six months old. She turned it over in her hand, marveling at how small it was. Then she forced herself to put it into the sack and keep looking. Starting at the back wall, she raked her fingers across the flashlight-lit floor in even, overlapping rows. Just like Lily Topple had done. She performed the operation twice before she was convinced she had covered every square inch of the interior of the hole in the tree. There were no bones left. This time, she didn't back out of the hole, but crawled out — forward into the sunlight.

"This is the last of them," she said, panting. Cotton took the bag and turned away.

Getting to her feet, she dusted the dirt off her knees and removed her gloves.

The hum of static was louder than when she'd gone into the cave. So was the whispering, louder and ... more urgent. And the sparkling cascade of twinkling light in front of the tree was so brilliant she couldn't look at it.

She squinted as her eyes adjusted after the darkened interior of the hole in the tree. Then she saw that Cotton had been removing the bones from the sacks and placing them in neat piles on the ground. Skulls, long bones, short bones, all arranged in kind.

"Seventeen," he said, his voice foggy. "Seventeen skulls."

"So the cave on the mountainside was the burial chamber for seventeen people."

"Maybe ..."

There was something he wasn't saying. She took a couple of steps and stood beside him.

"Do you see——?" he began.

And she did then. She hadn't noticed it in her haste to gather up the bones but there was no avoiding the reality of it now.

"So small … they're all … *children*."

Seventeen of them. Seventeen little kids.

"Why would they only bury their children in the cave? Why a separate place for them? Where'd they bury the grownups?"

And as soon as she asked the question, the answer fluttered on black bat wings in the back of her mind, a moth getting closer and closer to the candle flame.

The Jabberwock had told Lily Topple not to put them "back there." Jolene, Stuart and Cotton had talked about that, and hadn't come up with a reasonable explanation for why the Jabberwock wouldn't want the bones to be buried in their original grave.

The reality knocked Jolene's legs out from under her and she sank down onto her knees beside the bones.

The Jabberwock didn't want the bones put back in the cave because it wasn't a grave site.

The children hadn't been *buried* in that cave … they had *died* there.

Chapter Twenty-Four

THE SPARKLING, glittering brilliance was everywhere, but it didn't light the world. It was beyond Sam, all around her, encircling her — but *out there* where Sam Sheridan was. Not in here, though. In here, it was dark.

THE SOUND of the flies is a maddening hum. It is the only sound Grace Biddle hears now. It never stops. Never goes away. Flies drawn to the piles of feces in the corners of the cave. Not just corners anymore, though. It started out that way. Silas said the girls should go on one side of the cave and the boys on the other, though it is so dark here, so many of them ... but they know they should.

That was back when something mattered.

Grace reaches out her tongue to her dried lips, licks across them. The dribble of water down the back wall of the cave is all there is. You have to lick it off the rock. Her tongue is raw from licking and it's not enough, not for all of them.

Even though there are fewer now. Fewer every day.

She lets herself know for a few moments that the awful stench is not just where the children have used the toilet in the corners. They only did that for a couple of days, anyway, because after that they didn't eat so nobody had to go ... No, the stench is more than that.

Matthew Mullins was first. He was only eight months old. He got hungry, started to cry that first night but there was nothing Lydia could do for him except rock him, try to get him to suck on his thumb.

The baby had cried until he was so exhausted he fell asleep. The others slept too, in bits and snatches, that first night. Grace and Hope had and huddled together up against the cool of the rock in a little alcove near the back of the cave. In the beginning they did, the first couple of nights, before Grace lost track of time.

In the beginning, while they'd still believed someone would come.

But when Matthew died — he was the first — they put his little body there in the alcove. The cave ceiling was high enough to stand, for everybody except Ezra Southwick, who was the tallest. He had to bend his head over to keep from bumping it. The others could stand, but they had all knelt that day and said prayers for Matthew, who looked like a doll asleep, just lying there.

Sarah Lancaster had had to make Lydia let go of him, almost had to pry the baby out of her arms. She kept crying that she had promised her mother she'd look after him, take care of him.

Even in the dim light, Grace could see the baby's face clearly. It was pale. His eyes, sunken in his head, had been blue, such a bright blue. When they laid him in the alcove in the back of the cave and prayed for him, that first one, she had tried not to look at how sunken his eyes were. Because even with his shadowed eyes, he'd looked like he was just asleep. Beautiful.

And then he wasn't beautiful. Then he had ... his body had swelled up. His skin had ...

The stink was so bad, they all would have vomited, except they had had nothing to eat so they couldn't throw up. They didn't know then that the stink would get worse and worse, as one after another ...

Grace wasn't hungry anymore, though. At first, it was such a pain in her belly, she couldn't straighten up. Some of the children ate dirt, but it made them sick.

Esther was the next one after Matthew. She had just turned two years old — her three brothers sang happy birthday to her. Then Hannah Whitt, who was three.

Grace wondered why the little ones went first.

After that …

Grace can't think. Doesn't matter. Nothing matters.

It had already stopped mattering when Ezra went crazy. Even weak as he was, he attacked David, hit him, punched his face, would have killed him if he'd been able.

Fighting happened after that. Other bad things, too.

It didn't matter.

Grace turns her head with an effort and looks out across the bodies lying on the floor of the cave in the shafts of sunlight streaming in around the rock. She doesn't know for sure who is still alive — is only sure if they've been dead a long time because … the flies know.

They crawl across her face, try to crawl up her nose and at first she waved them away. Too many now. Everywhere.

She doesn't try anymore. It doesn't matter.

Her eye falls on the swollen body stretching the fabric of the dress made out of a blue flower sack. The one that matches her own. Mama liked to dress them alike, liked that when she did, nobody could tell which was which.

Grace closes her eyes. Wants it to be over soon.

Stuart had never in his life been happier to see anybody than he was to see Cotton Jackson and Jolene Rutherford. He had managed to keep his mind focused on digging, just digging, didn't let it stray out there into the growing certainty, confirmed by the skin-crawling sensation at the base of his skull, that he was being watched.

Watched.

So why just … *watched?*

The whoever-they-were out there in the woods the last time they'd come to Gideon hadn't just watched. They had opened fire, totally without warning, a barrage of gunfire intended to kill all three of them, would have, too, if the storm hadn't masked their escape. They owed their lives to the sudden rain that obscured them from the view of the killers in the woods.

Killers in the woods. Stuart almost burped out a bleat of laughter. Listen to yourself, man, he chided himself. *Killers in the woods.* Burying bones that some little kid picked up in the woods a hundred years ago and stuffed into the hole in a tree.

But the absurdity didn't track anymore. To expect "normal reality" really was absurd now. Stuart had … walked through the Looking Glass on Saturday when the road blew up in front of his car. And every minute of the time since then had been filled with one impossibility stacked up on another. He wouldn't allow himself to think that what they were doing was nonsensical, wouldn't work, because to believe that was to accept that he would never see his wife and daughter again and he flat out would not accept that, would never accept that, would keep looking and looking and …

The emotion of his thoughts, the anger and frustration and … yeah, fear … propelled Stuart McClintock past the point of exhaustion. Oh, he was in good shape. The go-to-the-gym-every-morning-before-work kind of good shape of a former athlete, who had *not* juiced to bulk up and was therefore not experiencing the awful side effects some of his teammates were struggling with.

No, he was just a big, strong man, who was angry and scared.

Stuart didn't even realize how exhausted he was, and hadn't attended to how much he had accomplished until he heard the sound of the car on the road and looked up through the sweat stinging his eyes to see his rented red Lexus turn off the highway and up into the cemetery where he was working.

He dropped the shovel and walked to where Cotton parked. The old man and Jolene got out of the car and the two of them looked around, then seemed to relax.

"There was all kinda weird stuff in town — lights and static," Jolene said, "but I guess all the weird stuff stayed there."

"And the bones …?" Stuart asked.

"They were just where Rose Topple told me they'd be," Cotton said.

Until that moment, Stuart hadn't really believed they'd find anything in that hollow tree.

"There are seventeen—" Jolene said.

"Seventeen?" Stuart was surprised. "I didn't expect there'd be that many people."

"Not 'people.' Seventeen *children*."

That didn't compute and he looked questioningly at her.

"Children. No grownups."

"Unless they were pygmies," Cotton said, "these are not adult skeletons."

"So these Quakers … what? Only buried their kids in the cave? Why—?"

"Jolene doesn't think that was a *burial* cave."

"I don't think the Quakers put their dead children in that cave. I think …"

She couldn't seem to get the words out, looked to Cotton to finish the sentence.

"They weren't *buried* there. They *died* there."

That totally did not compute.

"Are you saying … what are you saying?"

"It's the only thing that makes sense," Jolene said and it was clear she and Cotton had talked about it on the way back to the cemetery. "Remember how Rose Topple said she saw … scratches on the walls of the cave?"

Stuart felt the bottom drop out of his stomach.

"Solves the mystery of why the Jabberwock didn't want Lily to put the bones back where the miners found them," Cotton said.

"Remember it said, 'No, not there!' It didn't want to be buried in the spot where they … died."

"You don't think these bones were the accumulated dead of the settlement … or the children of the settlement? You think they … *died* in there?" Stuart couldn't get his mind around the concept. "Died of what?"

"Rose said the settlement of Quakers, jitter dancers, had been wiped out by Indians," Cotton said. "So we're thinking maybe—"

"Say you're a Quaker," Jolene said. "You don't believe in violence. You won't fight. In an Indian raid, what would you do—?"

"You'd hide your children to protect them," Cotton said.

"And if the whole village was wiped out—"

"Nobody'd hide their kids somewhere they couldn't get out of!"

"I'm not saying I've got it all figured out." Cotton let out a breath before he continued. "I'm sure whoever hid them didn't intend for it to go down the way it did. But for some reason … I think the Quakers believed somebody would survive to free the children, but something happened and … I don't know. I just believe that live children were sealed up in that cave."

"And died there." Jolene's voice was haunted.

They all stood silent. Stuart was shaken to the core by

horror. Seventeen little kids had … died. Thirst. Starvation. They had been sealed up together and *died.*

"Which certainly makes a case for why their spirits were so *disturbed*!" Jolene said. "These kids were the Haints of Fearsome Hollow. Spirits of the children who died unspeakably horrible deaths here. It fits." She turned to Cotton. "You've heard the stories — people heard little kids crying in the woods. These children haunted this hollow for a hundred years after they died."

"And then, when the miners scattered their bones …" Stuart's thought processes stopped there. "How?"

"The 'why' makes sense, but the how …" Jolene shook her head. "You got me, pal, I couldn't tell ya. Not 'how did the spirits stay here for a century?' That's not uncommon in the ghostly circles I travel in. But how did they somehow get the power to … to *take* everything? Take it where? What happened to the people who vanished, what *physically* happened to them? They were gone, along with everything inside the houses, when Lily came back the next morning — vanished *overnight.*"

"And a hundred years later, overnight *the whole county* …" Cotton let it go.

"Maybe it has something to do with time," Jolene said. "I don't know how, but clearly the Jabberwock has the power to … somehow control time. It aged those houses."

Stuart thought about the old house where he and Jolene had taken her equipment, the one that had been just like all the others — until it wasn't. The one belonging to the man who had blown a hole in the road. He opened his mouth to point out that the most recent of the Jabberwock's victims must still be physically present *somewhere,* because they had come …

That's what he'd started to say. But he couldn't find his voice. He had glanced over Cotton's shoulder into the meadow where butterflies chased each other from one beautiful wildflower to another. He saw what was slowly crossing the meadow toward the cemetery, scattering the butterflies and the bees.

People. Or not. Maybe not *people*. At least, not anymore. The other two saw the look on his face and turned to see. Jolene opened her mouth in a scream, but she seemed unable to propel the sound out of her mouth.

Stuart didn't know who the people were, but he suspected Jolene and Cotton knew. He did recognize the one in front, though, striding in a strangely gangly gate through the tall grass and flowers.

He definitely recognized that man. He was wearing the same tee shirt and bib overalls he'd been wearing the day he blew a hole in the road.

Reece Tibbits.

Chapter Twenty-Five

Fish had been among the first people to arrive on Main Street. He'd milled around as more and more people came walking up from where they'd filled every parking space in front of every building on the street, and he was sure for several blocks beyond it in both directions.

He kept his eyes down, kept moving, was afraid if he stood still for very long he would start shaking and then somebody'd notice it and point it out and before long his instructions to "go unnoticed" would be totally blown.

Pete had told him to look around the group for "leaders," people others would instinctively follow. He was supposed to call out to them, as soon as the shooting started — shooting! Seriously, *shooting!* He shook his head, focused on finding people who would help him herd the crowd to safety.

The first person who might possibly fit that description came down the street slowly, seemed as intent on not being noticed as Fish. He looked familiar, but it took Fish a moment to place him.

Sebastian Nower. Not in a pressed suit, clean dress

shirt, creases in his pants you could cut a finger on, and every hair in place. His rumpled suit accentuated his slat-thin frame, sharp elbows and shoulders. His skin was sallow, and hollow cheeks indented his face above a flesh-less chin that resembled the knob of a femur. Though he could not hide the signature attribute of the Nower family, an Adam's apple more prominent than his nose, this man looked like a derelict.

No, the politically correct term to use now was home-less person.

And Sebastian might right now be just as homeless as Fish. Maybe more so, if there were degrees of homeless-ness. Of course, Fish had been at it for a while, knew the ropes, where you could find shelter and maybe a bite to eat. Might be Sebastian Nower was too proud to go begging to his neighbors, hadn't had a solid meal since Viola evicted him on Monday.

Fish had seen where the Tacketts had pulled up the National Historic Landmark marker out of the front yard of the Nower House and felt a wave of renewed sympathy for the man. When somebody could just knock on your door and order you out of your own home at gunpoint ...

Whatever it was that Sam, Charlie and Malachi were doing out there in Fearsome Hollow ... it'd better work.

"What are you doing here, Fish? You ain't even got a car."

Fish turned and saw Bolyard and Delbert Scully. Carrying rifles. Standing there in the middle of Main Street packing rifles like it was the most normal thing in the whole world.

Fish had gotten to know the Scully brothers way better than he would have liked when he'd spent a miserable afternoon with the duo in a holding cell in the Beaufort County Jail — before Fish was finally recognized and released. He was sure they were among the unknown number of henchmen Viola had recruited to pull off her mass murder scheme here today.

His mind served up for Fish a revelation he'd just as soon not have considered. Judd, Lester and Pete were going to … *shoot* these guys. They might actually have only minutes left to live.

He shivered involuntarily.

"S'matter, Fish? You look like a man who could use a drink!" Bolyard said with a hearty laugh. He pulled a flask from his pocket and held it out.

"Uh … I'm trying to quit." Fish realized how ridiculous that statement was, but gratefully neither Del nor his brother, Scully — who'd break your nose if you called him Bolyard — had a full complement of sandwiches in their picnic baskets and they thought he was making a joke. They both burst out laughing.

"Riiiight … trying to quit …"

Then Del nudged Scully and indicated with his chin that Neb had come out on the top step of the school. Without a word, the two of them made their way through the crowd to the edge, turned and stood. Just stood there, feet wide apart. If you couldn't tell from their body language alone their intent, you were dumber than they were.

Fish turned the other direction and began searching faces again. Only a couple of people, but in a stampede it only took a cow or two to turn the whole herd, or so Fish had read somewhere.

Oscar Manning who owned Food Town. Wilbur Berg … who lived next door to Martha Whittiker. They said he'd found her body. And Skeeter Burkett, who had fished Hayley Norman's body out of the Rolling Fork.

They'd help. Or if they didn't, Fish would somehow

manage to do it all by himself. He was going to get this right! Wasn't going to be the person who got other people killed. This time Holmes Fischer would *save* lives, not take them.

~

THELMA JACKSON STOOD in the crowd of people gathered on the street in front of the West Liberty Middle School waiting for Viola Tackett to show up and get the signup process going.

Thelma almost didn't come. She didn't trust Viola Tackett any farther than she could throw the Washington Monument, but just like everybody else in the county, it wouldn't be long before Thelma's car ran dry. That'd be a problem since Thelma didn't own a horse and she was not up to walking these days. She felt like she had aged ten years since J-Day, felt the life being sucked out of her minute by minute by the imprisoning wall of the Jabber-wock and all the horror it was perpetrating.

Truth of it was, Thelma Jackson was *worn out.*

She wasn't sleeping well. Hardly sleeping at all, as a matter of fact, paced the floor in her house on Chimney Rock Pike, wandering around in the dark like she was looking for something, though she couldn't have told you what it was.

Even though the nights were cool, she had every window in the house open because it felt so stuffy inside — close, like a sealed-up attic, like there wasn't enough air in the house to breathe even though she was the only person breathing it.

And there was Cotton, of course, or what she called her "Cotton sightings." She hadn't shared that little bit of magic with Sam, Malachi Tackett and Charlene Ryan …

McClintock … when she had talked to them about the history of Gideon and Carthage, the Bible in Shakertown, and her interview with Rose Topple in the nursing home in Beaufort County. Oh, they had extended to her — what did they call it? The umbrella of mercy, meaning they would not laugh at her for whatever ridiculous thing she shared with them, and that should have made it possible to tell the whole thing. Maybe she would have it they hadn't been interrupted when Skeeter Burkett had brought in the body he'd found in the river — Rev. Norman's daughter, Hayley. And after that …

They never did get together again to talk about the rest of it, but she had left all her information there, all she had at the house. Most of the old records were in their storage unit in Lexington. And who did she think she was kidding? Thelma wasn't going to tell anybody about what she had experienced in her house almost every minute of every day since J-Day.

It was like Cotton was … there, just out of reach. And when she turned around quickly she would swear that she had caught a glimpse of him. Or not. Maybe she was imagining the whole thing. But she didn't think so.

Some nights, she would lie awake in bed and concentrate, try to … make contact in some way. It was crazy, but still. And it was like he was right there in the room with her, like she could sense his presence, feel his nearness. And so she wandered the house at night, seeking a Cotton sighting, trying to find what was obviously not there in the first place.

And then, late Monday afternoon, she felt a cloud of dread settle over her as real and palpable as a wet blanket. It settled around her and her heart began to hammer. She was afraid, but there was nothing to be afraid of. Still, her fear grew and grew until she was near tears, looking fearfully around.

She felt Cotton's nearness ... not like before, but like he was ... tuned up louder, maybe, the volume bigger and she could hear what had only been whispers before.

There was a sound like popcorn. Like popcorn in the microwave in the kitchen and you're standing in the living room. Not loud enough that you're even sure you heard it at all. Pop. Pop-pop-pop. Pop.

She found she was clenching her hands into fists so tightly her fingernails were gouging holes in her palms.

And then it was over. Abruptly over, and she found herself panting like she'd run a marathon, the way you gasp in air after something really terrifying has happened.

Ever since Monday, Thelma had felt like whatever separated her from Cotton was growing thinner and thinner. This morning, she'd even gotten a whiff of his aftershave. Which was crazy!

"Ya'll listen up, now. Mama wants to talk to you." That was the voice of Neb Tackett. He was standing on the top step of the porch in front of the school, beside his mother, who had a stern look on her face, glaring out at the crowd. "Come on, now, scoot in close so's everybody can hear." The crowd obediently shoved closer together, densely packed in the street before the porch steps.

Thelma glanced to the side and did not like what she saw. There was Jethro Bodean and the bearded Monroe brothers, Felix and Bubba. They were standing a few feet beyond the crowd of people ... and Bubba was holding a rifle! So was Jethro. No, this was not a good place to be.

Thelma turned in place and started to make her way through the crowd when Viola's words stopped her.

"You there, Thelma, c'mon back here. Where you think you's going?"

Thelma felt ice cold dread in the pit of her stomach. But she had nowhere to run. She turned back toward the front of the school building where Viola stood next to one of the huge white columns, but she didn't dignify the old woman's rude question with an answer.

"Matter of fact, come on up here and stand next to me." She gestured but Thelma didn't move, but she saw that Neb had already started in her direction. This was bad, very bad. "C'mon. You can be the first to sign up."

Sign up on what? Viola's hands were empty. Neb took three steps down off the porch to the sidewalk and took hold of Thelma's arm and yanked her forward.

She might actually have tried to break his hold and run away, but there was nowhere to go. The crowd was pressing in from all sides. But she did pull her arm free from Neb's clutches without appearing to snatch it away, and walked with as much dignity as she could muster across the sidewalk and up the stone steps to the top where Viola Tackett and her other son Zach stood waiting for her.

Viola looked at her with a smile that never reached her cold shark eyes, then turned her attention back to the crowd.

"Ya'll know Thelma Jackson, doncha? Thelma here is going to demonstrate how things is gonna go here today." Then Viola allowed the smile to slide down off her face. She reached into her bag and drew out a pistol, a big one, a revolver, and pointed it at Thelma's chest. "She's going to be the first." Then she cocked the weapon with a clacking sound that sent chills down Thelma's backbone.

~

JUDD HADN'T YET STUCK his rifle barrel through the space between the stones on the facade. It wasn't time yet. But he was ready to. On his knees, holding his rifle, peering around the side of the stone at the crowd below he spotted Fish wandering around like a lost puppy and hoped he'd pull his weight when the time come. Hard to put your trust in a man hadn't drawn a sober breath in more than a decade, but Pete knew him better than Judd did, and if Pete was okay with it, it was fine by Judd. Of course, it wasn't like Pete'd had a whole lot of choice about who he asked to help. What little time he'd had, he spent lining up Judd and Lester.

And maybe somebody else.

Might be Pete had asked ... well, any number of people to help out but *they'd turned him down.*

Judd didn't think that was the case. He liked to think that any man who'd been asked to step forward and defend a bunch of folks who couldn't defend themselves would have said yes. He wanted to believe that, so he did.

While he watched, Neb Tackett came out the front door of the school and walked to the edge of the porch and looked out over the crowd. Judd prepared to set his rifle barrel on the edge of the stone and hunkered down over it, ready to ease it out into the crack when the time came.

"Ya'll listen up, now. Mama wants to talk to you." That was the voice of Neb Tackett. "Come on, now, scoot in close so's everybody can hear." The crowd obediently shoved closer together, densely packed in the street in front of the school steps. Judd laid his cheek against the stock of his rifle, put his eye to the scope, and the crowd leapt into magnification, became the stitching on the back of a hat, some guy's bald spot, a woman with white roots showing in her black hair. Judd couldn't yet move the crosshairs onto a target, not until he pushed more of the barrel out between the stones. But it'd be a simple thing to do. This was going down just like Pete had said it would.

Then he heard a sound, a scraping sound and a crunch like feet on gravel.

He snapped his head toward the back of the roof. Obie Tackett was standing in front of the ladder leading from the roof to the ground. He held a 30.06 deer rifle trained on Judd's chest.

"I don't know what you think you're doing up here, but it's gonna be the last thought you ever think." He steadied his shoulder for the rifle's kick when he pulled the trigger, and Judd Perkins closed his eyes.

Chapter Twenty-Six

"Do you know what just happened?" Charlie's voice was breathless, her hands trembling, as she tried to shake free from the skeins of the reality that seconds ago was as real as the broken fingernails she had taken up chewing after she broke off all her fake nails the day she sat outside a kiln ...

Charlie was leaning against the back door of Sam's car, parked next to the massive tree. On the other side of the tree was a hole that had been filled centuries ago with rocks.

Malachi was leaned against the driver's side door with Sam in front of him.

All around them were sparks twinkling in the air against a background hum like static.

"I know what happened to me ..." Sam began. "What *seemed* to happen to me, but it felt so real—"

"It *was* real," Malachi said. "I don't understand how or why or ..."

They were breathing hard, as if they had run to this spot from a great distance. Panting. The reality of right here and right now felt solid enough. But then, so had the reality of … where Charlie had just been.

"Did you guys … were you in—?"

"*Inside* somebody else?" Sam asked. "Yes."

Malachi nodded but didn't speak.

"So what was it? Why …?"

Charlie's words trailed off and as they did they again became aware of the creepiness settling into all the buildings in the ghost town, and of the tension in the air. As if a thunderstorm lay just out of sight on the other side of the mountain, was lurking there where you couldn't see it, but any moment it would unleash growling thunder, arrows of lightning, and a roar of torrential rain. Pent-up energy was all around them, straining at the air, the might of it.

"Look at your watch," Malachi said, looking at his. When she looked down, the time was wrong. It said eleven o'clock.

"It can't be eleven o'clock," Sam said, looking up from her own watch. "We hadn't even left to come here at eleven o'clock."

"Mine's just broken." Malachi held out his arm for them to see his watch, moved it slightly as they looked so they'd realize all three hands — second, minute and hour — hung loose, swaying whatever way he leaned his hand. He took a breath and changed the subject. "What did you see just now?"

Charlie didn't know if he was asking her or Sam.

"I was … a little girl, a twin, six years old, her name was Grace Biddle and she was mad at her sister …" Sam got that far, then ran out of steam, and when she continued, her voice was airless. "The other children were playing hide and seek when the Indians came."

"Gabriel Dunn was the oldest, he was in charge of taking care of the others, of hiding them away—"

"In the cave, where they could still hear the Indians attacking," Charlie said. "Sarah and Naomi could hear the war cries."

Malachi stood up straight from where he had leaned back against the car.

"Gabe rolled the rock in front of the entrance to hide them," Malachi said. "He was supposed to ... he was *not* supposed to ..." He took a breath. "He went back to the village and got shot, or maybe a tomahawk ... he tried to get back, crawled to the cave, but ..."

The horror of it rolled over Malachi in a wave it was possible to see from the outside.

"They *died* in there." Sam had no voice or air to say it, but she did. "All of them. When Carthage was massacred, all the children ..."

"Those children were the voices we heard in the mist," Charlie said to Malachi.

"The children who watched us play hide and seek," Sam said.

At that moment, from some great distance and yet right next to them at the same time came the cries they'd heard and heard about, the mournful cries of lost children.

"The Haints of Fearsome Hollow," Malachi said, awe hushing his voice.

"Why did we ... why were we ... caught up in their minds?" Charlie asked. Neither Malachi nor Sam spoke, probably had no more idea than she did. Finally, Malachi was willing to hazard a guess.

"Because it happened here? I suppose ... And the reality of it ... the energy is still here, the power ..."

"Plates spinning," Sam said, and both she and Malachi looked quizzically at her. "E.J. said it when the stars got wonky, that the Jabberwock's got too much going on at once, trying to spin too many plates at the same time. I don't think our watches are broken. I think *time is* broken." She glanced at her watch and looked so surprised that Charlie looked again at hers. It was now half an hour earlier than when she'd looked only a minute or two before.

"Or the Jabberwock's control of time is slipping," Charlie said. "The others ..." She made herself say it, "Stuart and the others looking for us, they were supposed to be here at noon. And it's noon. Well, it *was* noon. That's a lot of things going on at once—"

It suddenly looked like a dimmer switch had been turned down on the day, and she felt her arms pebble with gooseflesh. It was so abrupt they all looked up, looked around, like a cloud had passed in front of the sun, but of course the sky was blue. The darkness was happening all around them, and had nothing to do with sunlight. The gloom around them was a palpable thing. The throbbing power behind it so strong they could feel it in their teeth.

Then the world began to ... dissolve. It couldn't have, but it did. The edges blurred and stretched and elongated. Not smoothly, but in a jerky-jerky fashion that for some reason reminded Charlie of the way a chicken walked. Reality hitched and sputtered. Sparks popped.

"An electrical transformer," Malachi said, his words hard to hear through the static. "A transformer when it blows ... sparks ..."

Great power flashed around them, unharnessed and out of control and it felt wrong, like somehow this wasn't the way it was supposed to be.

What took shape then in front of Charlie, Sam, and Malachi was a bubbling, boiling, cauldron of evil that stretched out into the trees around them and up into the sky above. Looking at it was like looking into the surface of the sun, dancing red and yellow light, boiling and bubbling

— except it somehow managed not to look bright but dark, not to give off *light* in any traditional sense. Instead, it generated an impossible *black light*, the boiling inky blackness they saw that had transported them to the Middle of Nowhere on J-Day.

How big had Charlie expected it to be? What form had she expected it to take? Her pitiful imaginings were the conjurings of a slug before it looks up at the elephant about to step on it. How could she not have envisioned it to be huge, monstrously big — a power strong enough to lay out an invisible barrier hundreds of miles long? An entity that could control time and the weather, change the stars in the sky. What would that kind of unrestrained power look like?

She was seized by an elemental terror that sprang from the core of her being, an instinctual fear of a thing so *other* that nothing in previous experience was a reference point. It wasn't *like* ... anything, except fire, though for all its boiling similarity, what emanated from it was not heat but cold. Charlie realized her breath was frosting, as it had done at Abner's house a week-long lifetime ... epoch ago.

And they'd thought they could somehow ... *defeat* a thing like this by playing games with it!

She noticed then that within the bubbling mass were points of light, other suns within the larger sun, that were the greatest part of it but not the whole, whirlpools of black light, spinning in tornadic fury. Those grew more and more distinct from each other, reverse photography of pouring cream into steaming black coffee and watching it spread out in tendrils and merge. Here, the boiling whole began to gather itself into individual whirlpools. They formed all across the surface of it. And then one of them oozed down to the ground in front of them, frothing and bubbling there. An indistinct form that quickly took on features, like a picture forming up in the developer's tray in a photographic studio. Another did the same. Then another, until there was a line of them distinct from, individualized against, the boiling black background.

Sam stepped to Malachi, who put his arm protectively around her. Charlie wanted to rush to them, huddle together with them in terror. But she had that sense you get … *don't make any sudden moves.*

So she crept slowly until she had joined Malachi and Sam, backed up against Sam's car, facing …

The creature was shrouded in mist, but it was clear to see. It was what Aloushous Hardy had seen in the trees, the thing the trapper saw rushing at him.

A deformed head, too large mouth, full of sharp, jagged teeth. Arms with long fingers ending in claws that looked like sabers. Eyes of flame. Different sizes, different shapes, all of them indescribable horrors. Anger, rage, malice pulsed off them like heat off a pot-bellied stove.

The Jabberwock.

Correction, the JabberwockS — plural — began to appear in a semi-circle in front of them.

JOLENE RUTHERFORD HAD SPENT the greater part of her adult life making it appear there was magic in the world. She'd tricked people into believing in spirits that weren't there, in occurrences she had faked. Oh, she believed in ghosts, or spirits, or phantoms, or wraiths, or apparitions — or just plain old spooks. But it was *intellectual* belief. Meaning now and then reality really did lend credence to the stories, demanded some level of acceptance, like a teaspoon full. Obviously, there was *something* to the tales people told. After all, Moses Weiss had found the ring a ghost had stuffed into frozen hamburger meat in a freezer, so there had to be some form of communication from one ... world, sphere, level of consciousness, *whatever* to the other.

But intellectual belief took up almost no space at all in her mind. Reality was the homeowner and belief in spooks just came by now and then and stayed overnight in the guest room.

Then she had watched the ceiling in her father's house bleed. *Bleed.* Okay, sure, it was a hologram, but a pretty sophisticated one, one that could not possibly have been generated by any equipment that currently operated in the real world.

And the faces. The identical faces that had appeared out of nowhere and told them to go away.

That and the real readings on equipment she'd used during her whole career to cook the books, confirmed that there was indeed "something" to all the ghost sightings.

But it hadn't been ghosts ... *spooks* ... that had gotten her firm and forever attention. The creatures that had attacked her and Stuart in Reece Tibbits's house were not gossamer, translucent floating Casper-the-Ghosts, dressed in nineteenth century high fashion and taken to slamming doors and moving candlesticks in historic old homes.

That woman's fingers had been real. Not filmy spirits. *Real.*

Real and cold ... and Jolene suspected, very, very dead.

That had been reality still in the husk.

What was crossing the meadow toward them was just as real. Leading the charge was the man ... the *thing* that Stuart had knocked down in Reece Tibbits's house. And only a few steps behind him was the woman who had tried to strangle Jolene.

"What in the ...?" Cotton Jackson was what passed for

"pale as a ghost" for a black man. His face was the color of ashes.

They exchanged looks.

"What are … what do we do?" Cotton's voice was a raspy whisper.

It was clear that they could escape from the things. They weren't charging across the meadow like a herd of stampeding buffalo. They were just … *coming.* The three of them could leap into the car and get the hell outta Dodge.

Instinct propelled her forward to do just that, crying out as she moved toward the Lexus, "We have to get out of here!"

"And leave the bones?" Cotton asked.

"Of course, leave them."

"We have to bury them," Stuart said. "It's the only way to appease the Jabberwock."

"We don't know that! It's a guess, that's all." She gestured toward the approaching creatures. "Why would it send those … those things if we were 'doing right by it'?"

"Maybe these creatures are … on their own," Cotton offered, "have their own agenda."

"The Jabberwock left that little girl alone after she gathered up the scattered bones." Stuart's voice was fierce and low. "You got a better idea to make the thing happy?"

The creatures had advanced halfway across the meadow by now, moving slowly, like lava sliding inexorably down the side of a volcano. Jolene looked at the ones she hadn't seen at the Reece house.

There was an old woman. Jolene gasped when she recognized her. She had aged … Grace Tibbits! Reece's mother. And there were two other women on either side of her Jolene didn't know.

A pregnant girl Jolene knew had to be Becky Sue Potter.

A man with a harelip.

Others she did know. The faces from her father's living room — Tungates, she couldn't remember their names. Fifteen, twenty, maybe more, closing on where the three of them stood rooted to the ground firm as fence posts.

Suddenly, Stuart stepped back to where he'd been digging and grabbed the pick. He hefted it like a weapon, spread his feet wide apart.

Cotton Jackson didn't move.

The closer the creatures got, the more detail it was possible to make out about them, and Jolene absolutely did not want to get a better look at them. They were so horrifying — it was almost overkill, like they'd come staggering off a movie set.

A stench wafted off them that made bile rise in the back of Jolene's throat.

Bloated, blackened faces. Flesh … *hanging off them*. And there were bugs, too. Jolene couldn't see them but she knew they were there. Like the ones that'd fallen off Reece's Tibbits's tongue.

She didn't intend to whisper, but that was all the sound she could make. "I don't think you can … how can you kill something, someone who's already dead?"

Then Cotton took a couple of steps back and picked up the shovel, holding it like a baseball bat.

That was the extent of their weapons. Two men with digging tools. A couple dozen *dead* things. Not good odds. Jolene turned and ran around to the other side of the car, leapt behind the wheel. Stuart turned toward her when he heard the car door slam, didn't question her decision to bail.

Terror was hijacking the body that had until just now belonged to Jolene Rutherford. Propelling her forward in a headlong, mindless rush. She was totally powerless to control it. But she could *direct* it, channel it to take her where she needed to go.

Jolene started the car, but didn't turn back toward the highway. She pointed the nose of the red Lexus toward the field of flowers and slammed her foot down on the gas pedal.

Chapter Twenty-Seven

MALACHI COULD FEEL Sam quaking at his side, pressed against him for …

Comfort, maybe. Certainly not for protection.

Any one of the creatures that now stood there in the gloom, rumbles of rage exuding from hoary throats, could rip the three of them apart without breaking a sweat. Perhaps it should have occurred to Malachi, the Marine, to come to the party armed. Wouldn't have mattered, though. There was no weapon known to man that would protect them from what stood there, the group of them, fanned out in a semi-circle.

Sounds came from the group, but it was impossible to tell which individual was making them. The voices were childlike and yet as old as crones. Innocent and yet full of evil portent and intent. Sincere and mocking. All and none. Both at the same time.

Play with us.

We want to laugh.

Can you play games with us?

We want to have fun.

Malachi had nothing to say to them. What were he and Sam and Charlie supposed to do, ask the monsters to count to one hundred while they ran off into the woods and crouched down behind a mulberry bush?

He understood then that the Jabberwock was … the *creatures* within it were, indeed, *children*. And children want what they can't have. These children wanted life and the childhood that was stolen from them. They wanted the horror of their deaths erased. They wanted … the Jabberwock just *wanted,* a communal desire that was unfathomable in its intensity.

When three little kids came running up into the woods, playing hide-and-seek all those years ago, the Jabberwock was drawn to them, came so close it could almost touch. He and Sam and Charlie had heard the children within it whispering to each other in the mist. The Jabberwock had basked in Sam's giggles, Charlie's bubbling laughter and Malachi's carefree vitality, warmed itself on their *life* like sitting in front of a crackling fire.

The witch had warned them, "You hadn't ought to have come, making it *want.*" She'd told them, "Don't you come back here, all three of you …"

But they *had* come back! The three of them returned on the night of graduation. And the Jabberwock had drawn near again. Sam had seen the mist swirling around the car, had heard the voices. The Jabberwock had wanted what the little kids playing hide-and-seek in the woods all those years ago had had, but graduation night, in an instinctive understanding, it wanted even *more.* It wanted the comfort, caring, touch, and tenderness it had seen between him and Sam. The essence of *life.*

The Jabberwock should have taken them that night. Malachi had no idea why it didn't, but after that, the chance was gone. It waited. Years passed. The aching *want* the three of them had kindled within the Jabberwock began to sour, turned blacker and blacker. Somewhere within the creature made of children was one with a heart of unspeakable rage. It was in charge of the Jabberwock now, calling the shots. That rage wanted only one thing — to kill ... *to stab the knife in again and again and again.*

There was nothing he, Sam nor Charlie could do that would satisfy the hunger of the Jabberwock now ... except die.

The creatures began to advance on them. He held Sam close. Her hair smelled like strawberries.

"... thirteen, fourteen, fifteen ..." She was counting unconsciously.

"Close your eyes," he whispered.

"... sixteen, seventeen."

She finished and burrowed her face into his chest.

Seventeen.

Malachi moved before he willed his muscles to carry him. He spun around, yanked open the car door and leaned into the vehicle.

A rumbling, growling sound erupted from the monsters. There was a sensation of taking in a breath before the charge. Malachi had seconds. Only seconds.

MALACHI HAD BEEN HOLDING Sam tight to his chest, cradling her there, and Charlie was huddled up against her on the other side.

He told her to close her eyes and Sam—

Malachi suddenly let go of his grip, turned and yanked open the door of the car.

What in the ...?

The movement provoked a communal reaction among

the creatures, an as-one growl that rumbled in more than a dozen ragged throats. A pride of hungry lions, they tensed to leap forward.

How unutterably foolish they had been to think they could beat this creature. Sam didn't want to die! Rusty needed her.

Please, no ...

Malachi was back now. He didn't put his arm around her but took her hand in his.

"Grab hands!" he commanded.

Sam snatched Charlie's hand and squeezed.

The nearest creature was only a dozen feet away now, looking at Sam, focused on her. She could smell it, a hoary scent of decaying flesh and rotting clothing.

Run! all Sam's instincts screamed.

But they were backed up against the car, surrounded. There was nowhere to run. The creature slowly drew back its arm to strike, to slash off her face as it had slashed off the face of the hitchhiker. It tensed and she cringed away, squeezing her eyes tight shut.

Rusty, she whispered, without making a sound.

"We're going to play a game," Malachi called out in a loud, powerful voice, milliseconds before the creature struck.

He lifted his free hand and Sam saw that he had a piece of paper in it.

"Red Rover, Red Rover, let ..." he read from the sheet, "... Jonah Aaron Whitt come over."

~

THE FRONT BUMPER of the red Lexus with Jolene Rutherford at the wheel slammed into Reece Tibbits like a bowling ball plowing into the front pin. The impact threw the body up into the air and it landed with a shuddering, sickening thud on the hood and crashed headfirst through the windshield.

Jolene screamed and kept driving, blind now, the half of Reece's body not inside the car blocking all but a small part of the bottom of the windshield that she had to hunker over the steering wheel to see through.

Wet sounds, thunking — as the car plowed through the group of … things behind Reece. Maybe the first was Grace Tibbits, or maybe his wife. The body didn't fly up into the air. From what Jolene could see, it was knocked backward and disappeared below the level of the hood, and she felt the front of the car lurch as the wheels thumped over it.

She mowed down others behind it, the car bumped and lurched like she was driving over potholes. Through her small space of unobstructed view through the windshield right in front of her, she saw a face for an instant before the headlight and grill connected with the body and knocked it off its feet.

It was the girl she believed must have been Becky Sue Potter. The pregnant girl. In something like slow motion, she saw the impact, watched the car strike the front of her body, the bulging belly. The girl's face remained blank, utterly expressionless, eyes un-focused, a mannequin on legs, then disappeared beneath the left front tire.

Then there was a grinding, hammering *thump,* the world exploded around her, and Jolene flew forward. She hadn't paused to put on a seatbelt when she leapt into the car, but Stuart must have turned the driver's side airbag back on because it deployed with a whooshing sound … no, actually that was the sound of the air rushing *out* of it as it collapsed in front of her.

The world spun and her mind blipped out a random

thought: teenagers did that. She'd read it somewhere. Kids stole cars and ran them into walls for the thrill of being saved by the airbag.

What followed was an odd silence that wasn't silence. It was muffled sound, and Jolene could hear it, could smell the strange aroma of the airbag deployment. Looking out the cleared windshield now, she could see what had stopped the car. She'd run headlong into one of the stumps obscured by the tall grass, though she wouldn't have noticed it if it'd been painted florescent yellow and flashing with strobe lights.

The impact had dislodged Reece Tibbits's body, must have sent it flying across the hood because she could see it in the tall grass and flowers off to the left. It was sitting upright, had been caught by a sapling, like he had decided to sit down and lean back against the little tree.

It would have looked like he was just resting there for a bit, maybe, except the body leaned against the tree had no head.

No. Head.

Time slowed then.

It took Jolene an enormous amount of time, a century, a geologic epoch to turn her gaze to the right. Reece Tibbits's head had been ripped off and now rested on the passenger side seat of Stuart McClintock's rented red Lexus.

No blood. There was no blood. Somehow that insane factoid registered in Jolene's consciousness.

Then the eyes on the severed head opened and looked sightlessly at her.

Jolene screamed, wailed soundlessly. Fumbling for the door handle, she finally grasped it and pulled and then fell out of the car into the grass. She scrambled to her feet and ran faster than it was humanly possible to run, crossing the distance back to the cemetery where Cotton and Stuart stood armed with digging tools to fight off monsters. Stuart held out his arms to her and she crashed into him, almost knocking him off his feet. He let her slide off his body to the ground before he took a grip once again on the pick. She twisted around to look back the way she'd come.

They were still coming. All of them. Even the one with no head.

Chapter Twenty-Eight

MALACHI GRIPPED Sam's hand tight and took a step away from her, extended their arms so their clasped hands hung down between them. A shudder went through the creatures in front of them, like the quaking of tall grass when some behemoth creature stomps through a field.

The thought that had propelled Malachi to the car had been like a meteor streaking across the black velvet of a night sky. He'd glanced at the paper in the car on the way to Fearsome Hollow, and the words came back to him as he stood there, Sam's whispered "seventeen" echoing in his mind.

The words noted in a diary more than two hundred years ago. "Mary Whitt was a white woman who'd been held captive by Indians for twenty-five years. She was a Quaker and they built a town called Carthage beside the waterfall on Troublesome Creek. Then the Indians come, kilt the men, carried off the women, and burned everything to the ground."

The words hadn't caused an itch in his mind when he first heard them, but they did now.

Kilt the men. Carried off the women.

What had happened to the children?

They'd been left behind. For which Mary Whitt begged their forgiveness when she listed their names in the Carthage Bible in Shakertown in 1825.

"Please, please forgive us."

Seventeen *children.*

Seventeen spirits standing before them, whose only claim to the humanity they all so desperately wanted, was on the piece of paper Malachi held in his hand. Their names.

An unnatural stillness replaced the throbbing tension of only moments before. It was a quivering in the air that was almost palpable.

Malachi repeated softly, "Red Rover, Red Rover, let Jonah Aaron Whitt come over." He gestured with his chin to his hand clasped to Sam's, held out. Waiting.

Nothing. No motion of any kind. Utter stillness. But the tension in the air grew, the sense of some great struggle happening on some plane you could perceive but couldn't see.

Then a creature on the far left began to move forward. You couldn't say the creatures walked. They had limbs and a gait that was a movement like walking but which didn't actually propel their bodies forward. This being moved across the space between them in something like a glide.

As it moved toward them, it shrank. Not withered, just got smaller, more condensed. Malachi realized then that the creatures were both spirit and substance existing at the same time in the same place. An utter impossibility. For all their deadly claws and teeth, they were ephemeral beings as well, with features as insubstantial as the mirage that glittered on the county line.

By the time the creature reached Malachi, it had

become a little boy. A horror of a little boy, but a child nonetheless. It … *he* had brown hair, a tangle of it that hung down past his shoulders. His face was a ruin. He smelled … of death. He merely stood in front of Malachi, colorless eyes that appeared blind peered up into Malachi's face.

Malachi let go of Sam's hand and extended his hand to the child. The creature, the boy, moved sightless eyes toward it, slowly reached up and took it, then turned to face the crowd. The shock of cold flesh on Malachi's was a jolt to his system, to his whole being, but he managed not to cringe away. Neither did Sam, when she reached out and took the boy's other hand.

The *four* of them stood now — Malachi, Sam, Charlie and Jonah Whitt, facing the sixteen other creatures. Malachi held up the paper to find another name, but before he had a chance to speak, a sound came from beside him and he looked down to see that the boy's face was turned up to his. He heard a small voice, a whisper, though he didn't see the child speak. And perhaps the voice was only in his mind. The voice was without inflection, robotic. But within the lack of inflection lay a depth of feeling it was impossible to miss. A longing, yearning ache in two simple syllables.

"Han nah."

Malachi found it, listed right below the boy's name.

"Red Rover, Red Rover," Malachi called in a loud firm voice, "let Hannah Elizabeth Whitt come over."

There was no shock this time. The mass of creatures was as still now as if they'd been carved from stone. But the sense of struggle was even more intense. Malachi noticed then that the light around them was … different. When he'd first seen it, the impossible black light with sparkles in it had covered the whole of them in a thick, malevolent blanket. Now, that darkness was *behind* them, a single impossibly black light that pulsed like a heartbeat in the gloom.

With only the briefest hesitation, another creature, one that had not been very large to begin with, began to shrink as it advanced. It became a little girl with hair in her face, her ratty skirt dragging on the ground. She went directly to the little boy and reached out her hand. This time, it was Sam who let go of the little boy's hand so he could take the small hand of his little sister.

Now the five of them faced the others.

Malachi searched the list for the same last name.

"Red Rover, Red Rover, let Ruth Ann Whitt come over."

She was maybe five years old. Her hair might once have been red.

The darkness throbbed. Malachi could feel the pressure in his ears. The pressure built, like going down in water, deeper and deeper. Great power was pulsing, struggling against the small creatures as they pulled away.

After the Whitts, the Campbells — a girl and two boys came to stand between Sam and Charlie.

The Lancasters, two girls.

When Malachi called out, Frances Grace Biddle, Sam gasped. Before the child reached her, she let go the hand of the child next to her and reached out both her hands to the approaching little girl. She took Sam's hands and Sam stood there for a moment, holding on, looking into the child's face, maybe into her eyes. Maybe she had eyes still.

Instead of joining the line, the little girl turned back to the pulsing mass and stood. Waiting.

"Her sister," Sam called to Malachi in what might have been a loud voice, but the sound was almost inaudible in his ears. "Her twin — Hope."

"Hope Abigail Biddle," Malachi called, and another creature joined the first one standing in front of Sam. They grasped hands with each other before they joined the line.

Then the game continued.

The Southwicks, three boys and a little girl, the smallest of all the children. Just a toddler.

With every one, there was a struggle of tremendous proportions. The pulling away was like a moon in the orbit of a planet, fighting to fly out into the darkness of the rest of the universe.

As the number of the creatures diminished, the brightness of the black light pulsing behind them faded. But in some way Malachi couldn't have articulated, he was certain that the dimmer light was growing more and more malevolent, more intense as its glow decreased.

Finally, there were two creatures left, but three names on the list. Malachi shot a questioning look at Sam, but she didn't see. So he called out to Lydia Faith Mullins ... *and* Matthew Isaac Mullins to "come over."

A creature moved forward and it became obvious that it was not one being at all but two. One of them was a baby the other cradled in her arms.

One last child now stood. Alone.

Malachi opened his mouth to call out the name and the pressure in his ears threatened to burst his eardrums.

"Red Rover, Red Rover, let Daniel Paul Dunn come over."

The darkness quivered, quaked like jello struck with a fork. A word formed in Malachi's mind, and from the surprised looks on Charlie and Sam's faces, it must have formed in theirs, too.

An anguished cry, *Danny!*

Then the final form separated from the mass and crossed the distance between them, that somehow managed to feel like a thousand miles, across a chasm of infinite depth. Malachi took the boy's hand, knew his face was freckled, *remembered* that it was, but he could find no trace of them.

Malachi had called out to all the children who'd died horrible deaths together in that cave more than two hundred years ago. They stood with him, Charlie and Sam now, facing a presence that they had left behind, a form in the almost complete darkness. It was an angry, bitter force, powered by rage, a boiling, bubbling caldron of hate. And even Malachi could feel its pull. A magnetic force, grasping, straining with all its will to drag back to itself what had separated from it.

And furious that it couldn't.

Chapter Twenty-Nine

STUART STARED in wonder as Jolene roared past him and Cotton and aimed his car like a battering ram at the advancing creatures. She hit Reece Tibbits square, a perfect shot, knocked his body up into the air before it crashed down on the hood of the car. She didn't stop there, just plowed ahead, striking one … two, three, more of the other creatures, running over them or knocking them out of the way before there was the awful sound of metal striking something solid. The back of the car rose up into the air as the front crumpled around … a tree stump. She'd hit one of the tree stumps.

As Stuart stood gawking, the driver's side door opened and Jolene fell out of it onto the ground. Getting to her feet, she staggered, fell, and lunged up again and then ran back toward where he and Cotton stood. He opened his arms and she crashed into them, knocking him backwards, and he let her slide off him to the ground.

They were still coming.

The bones!

"Jolene," he said without turning from the advancing

creatures. "Get the sacks, dump the bones into the grave." Adding urgently, "*Now!* Do it now!"

He almost followed with, "We'll hold them off" until he saw the headless body of Reece Tibbits lurching in their direction. The holding-them-off part probably wasn't possible. No, absolutely wasn't possible. They could *delay*, though. He was sure … he *hoped* they could delay the creatures. Keep them … busy long enough for Jolene to get the bones into the hole he had dug for them in the earth.

He turned back toward the advancing creatures, while Jolene staggered to the leaf bags, grabbed the first one and began to empty the contents into the hole in the ground at her feet. The creature out in front now was an older woman. She had white hair, but that was all he could tell about her — she'd been one of the bodies Jolene had run over, and there wasn't enough left of the features on her face for her own mother to recognize who she was.

Close behind her was the pregnant woman Stuart knew must be Becky Sue Potter.

She named it Marilee. Marilee because she liked it and Winona because that was her aunt's name. The baby didn't breathe. Never got a chance to breathe. It didn't stop breathing like the others did. Just stopped, not choked, just … stopped.

In a suddenly-old house down the road from Cotton Jackson's, Moses Weiss had spoken to the spirit of this woman, who was mourning the loss of a baby that never had a chance to draw breath.

Somewhere in his heart, Stuart managed to be grateful that this … *creature* was dead, had been long dead before the baby who'd never breathed had been … before Jolene crashed into her with his car.

He raised the pick over his head as the old woman approached. Tried not to conjure up what would happen when he hit her with it. It wouldn't stop her. She'd keep coming. They all would, overpower him and Cotton by sheer numbers.

As soon as she was within striking range, Stuart slammed the pick down into the top of her head. It split open like a cantaloupe and the death smell of the rot inside turned his stomach and he reflexively heaved, would have vomited but the woman with the pick in her head was on him then, clawing at his face with yellowed fingernails, scrambling to get her fingers around his throat.

He had body-slammed Reece Tibbits that day in his house, knocked him off his feet … but hadn't actually *touched* him … hadn't felt the cold Jolene had described feeling in the fingers that encircled her throat. He felt it now. Cold fingers with unimaginable strength closed on his neck, an iron band that instantly began to squeeze.

Suddenly, Jolene made some kind of sound, a cry, garbled, without form. He cut his eyes toward her as he staggered backward, pulling with all his strength to loosen the grip on his neck. Jolene had just dumped one of the bags of bones into the hole and had picked up a second, about to turn it up and pour out the contents, but had stopped, and now sat on her knees staring at the hillside that Cotton had said lay between the cemetery and the town of Gideon.

THEN SOME KIND of shudder went through the children — they were now "children" — who were holding hands with Malachi, Sam and Charlie. The attention of every one of them snapped in the same direction as perfectly as if a drill instructor had commanded an honor guard, "Eyes right!"

There was nothing there. To the right were no houses, only a steep hillside.

Then they began to move together. As they had functioned as one before, their will and intent forged again the total bond. Dropping the hands of Sam and Malachi and Charlie, they moved toward the hillside, a school of fish in perfect unison. And they changed, fluidly transformed from the shapes of children who'd "come over" to Red Rover. Though still small, each of the forms had claws and fangs and jagged teeth — and eyes that flamed.

They "flowed" up the hillside without seeming to climb it, but not seeming to float over it either. Up and up they went until they reached the top.

Then they vanished over the crest of the hill and were gone. As soon as they were no longer visible, the pressure on Malachi's ears eased, like some struggle was over.

The black presence hadn't gone with them, though, had remained, growing dimmer and dimmer as the children got farther away, growing uglier and angrier with every second that passed, still there, pulsing, boiling, frothing.

So full of hatred you could almost smell it.

Then the black formless mass coalesced into a single, towering form. The creature the trapper Jed Pollock had described. "A beastie twenty feet tall, teeth sharp as knives, eyes like the devil, come running at me out of the mist in the trees."

Malachi stood almost in the middle of the street, where the line of children had extended, and he began to back up slowly until he reached where Charlie and Sam stood together cowering in horror. The creature matched his movements. As Malachi backed up, it moved forward, closing the distance between them.

It hunkered down then, low to the ground as it approached, crouching as a lion crouches when it stalks its prey, coiled strength held barely in check, preparing any half second to launch itself at them.

"Get to the car," Malachi said to Sam and Charlie in a harsh whisper. "Get in the car and run."

Sam merely looked at him, took his hand then and squeezed it.

"No," she said, and stood resolutely beside him.

SHEP and Claude stared in shocked disbelief at the people who was walking across that meadow toward where that fella was digging a grave in the cemetery. Shep couldn't figure out where they'd come from. He hadn't seen nobody in the woods on that side of the meadow — though, just like him and Claude, if they hadn't wanted to be seen, you couldn't have seen them. But they wasn't hiding now, they just come walking out of the trees into the grassy meadow. Weird walking. Like walking was a hard thing for them, which didn't make no sense, but wasn't none of them people any good at it. They didn't stumble or nothing, just … kinda lurched along, like that man who had something, some kind of palsy, that his mama'd slapped him upside the head for staring at that time in the grocery store.

Except these was people Shep knew and they didn't have no palsy. There was Reece Tibbits, his wife and girls, and his mama Grace. There was the Tungates, too, Abner Riley and Ronnie's wife, Becky Sue, who was pregnant. He didn't know Ronnie's mother, hadn't seen her but one time, but he figured she was the woman walking, *lurching* along next to Becky Sue.

Then it occurred to Shep that every one of them people was among the ones who'd vanished. And more'n that, most of 'em, maybe all of them, was folks who lived in them houses that'd got old all of a sudden, like his and Abby's done. But here they was, right out here in the daylight, walking across a field, not disappeared no more.

Claude made some kind of sound, like a cough or a grunt or something and Shep turned to see him staring in that wide-eyed, unblinking stare of his at the people crossing the meadow.

"Them what you was talking about?" he asked, his voice all tight and strained. "Them as Abby said was gonna help out?"

In truth, Shep didn't know whether they was or not, but then Abby answered with his voice, "Yeah," so she musta been expecting 'em.

Then he seen Jolene Rutherford leap into that red car and drive off into that field, and wasn't but a second or two fore she hit Reece Tibbits, just run him over! Shep could hear that ugly whump sound it made when the car crashed into him. Reece flew up in the air and landed on the hood of the car and she just kept going, hitting others, *aiming* at 'em, until there was an awful *bam* sound when she hit one of them tree stumps. She stumbled out of the car and took out running to where the men was standing in the cemetery, holding up a pick and shovel as weapons.

Claude made another sound then, a strangled sound, and when Shep turned to look at him, his mouth had dropped open, unhinged like as if his jaw was broke, and he was shaking his head back and forth real slow, a look on his face of …

Shep turned back to the meadow to see what Claude was staring at, and he almost cried out his own self.

Reece.

As Shep watched in horrified wonder, Reece Tibbits climbed down off the hood of that car, and went right on walking, same as the others.

And he didn't have no head.

Claude liked to choked then. He jumped to his feet and began to back away, mouthing words he wasn't saying, then he turned and high-tailed it off into the woods, crashing through the undergrowth, bulling his way through.

Shep looked down and seen that Claude had dropped his rifle in the dirt before he took out. Shep's heart was hammering so loud he couldn't hear nothing but the pounding sound, felt like his face was all blowed up like a balloon and blood would come squirting out when it burst. He felt like running away, too, woulda if he coulda got control of his legs so he could stand up.

Then movement caught Shep's eye and he turned to the right to see … what?

What was that coming down the hillside from Gideon? It was — looked like a bunch of kids. They wasn't walking funny like them folks in the field. They wasn't walking at all, really, just moving real fast down the hill toward the cemetery and the meadow on the other side of it.

Shep stared. The closer they got, the more horrible they were. But he couldn't stop gawking. Couldn't breathe or think, hadn't never in his life seen nothing so … awful. Turns out Claude had run off before the real scary stuff even showed up.

Chapter Thirty

Lester Peetree had almost forgotten how quiet the Ruger was with a suppressor to silence the gunshot. He heard only the familiar coughing sound, then watched Obie Tackett fly backward off the roof of the drug store where Judd Perkins crouched behind the facade overlooking Main Street.

He immediately swung the rifle barrel back toward the school and the porch where Neb was calling out to the crowd. He searched with the magnification of the scope the space *behind* Neb, between him and the school doors. Viola Tackett would move into that space any second now, and the instant he had his crosshairs fixed on her head, he would put her down.

Hers would be a kill shot. He'd opted for a body shot on Obie Tackett, likely not fatal but he'd only had seconds to sight in when he spotted Obie out the corner of his eye, stepping up off the ladder onto the roof of the building behind Judd. Obie'd been knocked off the ladder backwards. His body'd fallen straight down two stories to the concrete behind the store. If the bullet hadn't killed him, the fall had.

There was a blur of movement behind Neb, and Lester could hear Viola's voice addressing the crowd. He couldn't *see* her, though. She had moved to the side of the porch instead of the front, talking to someone she saw in the crowd. The white pillar blocked Lester's shot. He kept the crosshairs trained on the edge of the pillar. The instant Viola poked out from behind it, he'd fire.

VIOLA STOOD next to the white stone pillar, scanning the crowd while Neb got everybody to squeeze in nice and tight. As she watched, one after another of her "boys" was winnowing casually toward the outside edges of the crowd.

She was looking for … who should she pick to make the first sacrifice for her cause? Hmmmm.

Ah, *there.* Thelma Jackson had just turned and started to move out of her spot down front in the center of the crowd toward the back.

"You there, Thelma, c'mon back here. Where you think you's going?"

Thelma turned back, but with an attitude. Like maybe she didn't like taking Viola's orders. Well, we'll see about that.

"Come on, you can be the first to sign up." Neb had grabbed hold of her arm and was making sure she done as she was told. He pulled her on up the steps to stand in front of Viola beside the pillar. She was a big woman, probably even taller than Sam Sheridan. A thought flashed through Viola's mind and was gone as quickly as a comet across the night sky.

I bet Rusty's gonna be tall when he's a man growed —
with both his mama *and his daddy* tall like they was.

She smiled then, brief but genuine.

Viola looked out past Thelma at the crowd. They had
grown restless when Neb dragged Thelma up onto the top
step, like maybe they didn't think she'd been treated with
proper respect. Viola asked 'em if they knew Thelma,
which they all did, of course. That was one reason why
Viola'd picked her to be first. Wasn't likely anybody in the
county didn't know her, or at least who she was, her being
a teacher for all them years. She was well liked. Perfect
choice for the first person to shoot.

Though it wouldn't really count as killing a somebody.
Wasn't like she was white, a real person. Still, she'd do just
fine.

Viola told the crowd she was gonna use Thelma as a
demonstration of the way things was gonna go today, then
she pulled her .357 magnum pistol out of her purse and
aimed it at Thelma, and the crowd gasped — grumbling
and rumbling moving through the people like watching
sheet lightning firing off inside a cloud.

"She's gonna be the first." She cocked the pistol. She
talked to the crowd, but never took her eyes off Thelma's
face, was enjoying the deer in-the-headlights look she saw
there. "Somebody killed my Essie, drove by the Tackett
House yesterday and shot her down like a dog."

That brought gasps and muffled voices from the crowd,
too. Oh, everybody knew Essie'd got shot. Viola couldn't
have kept a thing like that quiet if she'd wanted to. But it
was likely most people didn't know the specifics of what'd
happened.

Least the people who wasn't there didn't know. She
addressed her next words to the folks who *was* there.

"You're out there right now, listening to my words — the one who kilt my little girl." She turned her gaze from Thelma to the crowd now, but stayed where she was with the gun leveled at Thelma's chest. "And you others is out there, too, the others as was in the car when the shot was fired. I'm talking to you now, and I ain't gonna mince words. If you step forward and tell me who done it, I will let you live. You got my word on that — won't touch a hair on yore head. But if don't nobody step forward ..." She turned her focus back to Thelma. "Ima shoot Thelma Jackson."

A rumble of denial and protest belched out of the crowd, loud and raucous. She hoped wasn't nobody in the crowd packing, though it was likely that somebody out there had a gun. Folks here carried their firearms with them wherever they went. That was why Viola was standing kinda outta sight, behind Thelma, up next to the pillar — in case somebody decided to take a shot at her.

"And then I'm gonna get somebody else up here ... and I'm gonna shoot them, too." She let her rage growl out through her voice. "And Ima keep killing people one after another until *somebody* tells me who killed my Essie. You folks got to the count of three."

Thelma Jackson just stood there, didn't say nothing at all and that surprised Viola. She expected the woman'd drop down to her knees, maybe, beg Viola not to kill her, cry and holler and plead for her life. But she didn't do none of those things, just looked at Viola, and the look in them eyes! Viola almost stepped back from the fierceness of it.

"One!" Viola called out.

You coulda heard a mouse in house shoes tiptoeing across a cotton ball it was so quiet.

"Two!" She didn't call out this time, just said the word normal. Wasn't nobody didn't hear her. She knew they thought she was bluffing, didn't really think she'd do it.

Well, they was about to get the surprise of they lives.

She lifted the pistol up and aimed the barrel at Thelma's face, took a half step toward her so it was only inches away from her forehead and called out,

"Thre—"

She never got out the rest of the word.

LESTER DIDN'T HAVE A SHOT!

Viola was almost completely concealed behind the white pillar on the porch and Thelma Jackson was in front of her.

Lester listened to her speech about how she was going to keep shooting people until somebody fingered the person who'd killed her daughter. His eye never left the sight on his rifle. He had set the crosshairs of it, fixed on the edge of the pillar Viola stood behind. The instant she showed herself, he would squeeze the trigger.

She began to count.

"One!"

The barrel of the pistol edged out beyond the pillar where Viola was pointing it at Thelma Jackson's head. That was all, though. Should he take a shot, try to hit the gun barrel, knock the pistol out of her hand?

Could he make a shot like that at this distance?

He'd threaded bullets through inch-wide gaps in the vegetation of a jungle a hundred yards away. But he was twenty years old at the time and he hadn't fired his sniper rifle since.

"Two!"

Thelma had a second, maybe two to live. Lester sighted on the pistol barrel and began to squeeze the trigger.

"Thr—" Viola moved. Lester shifted his aim and fired.

Chapter Thirty-One

Pete no longer felt the pain of the gravel digging into his bony knees. As soon as he heard the sound of Viola Tackett's voice, he placed the barrel of his M1 in the slot between the stones and lowered his face to sight in on a man in a black tee shirt, one of the armed men standing out from the crowd. That's when Pete saw that Lester didn't have a shot.

Maybe Pete was wrong. Maybe from Lester's angle …

It was impossible to tell for sure, but from where Pete crouched on his knees in the gravel on the roof, it appeared that one of the big white pillars on the porch of the school was between Viola and Lester. She stood beside it, not out on the front of the porch with Neb. And Thelma Jackson was smack in front of her.

Pete *did* have a shot. From his position, he would have to thread a needle around Thelma, but he could see more of Viola than Lester could.

Maybe Judd had a shot, too. Pete couldn't tell. But he knew Judd would never take the initiative to deviate from the plan even if he did. In truth, Pete wasn't even sure Judd was going to be able to hold up his end of the deal, but wasn't no way to find out a thing like that in advance. He'd often been surprised by which soldiers froze and which ones brazenly ran into enemy fire. They often weren't the ones he would have picked for bravery.

Viola began to count.

Should Pete take the shot?

He was no sniper! He'd shot expert on the firing range half a century ago, and he was good enough to bag a deer every season. At this almost point-blank range he could easily take out the targets he'd been assigned this day, no doubt about it. Shooting M1 like he was, body shots would be kill shots.

But this wasn't a body shot. If Thelma moved, even an inch …

"Two!" Viola cried.

If Pete fired, he might miss and kill Thelma Jackson.

If he didn't fire, Viola Tackett would put a bullet through Thelma's forehead.

Pete began to squeeze the trigger.

"Th—"

Viola suddenly lurched backward, blood spewing out of her shoulder, the pistol flying out of her hand.

Nobody in the crowd had any idea what'd just happened, but Ned Tackett was standing on the front of the porch, facing the crowd and their rooftop positions. When Pete called out, "Drop your weapons, all of you! Hands—" Neb lifted a pistol and fired and a chunk of the facade a couple of feet from Pete exploded into dust.

Pete snapped his sight back on the man in the black tee shirt, who was turning now, raising his rifle. Pete dropped the man in his tracks before he could get off a shot, the boom of his rifle setting the tinnitus in his ears singing.

And then the rhythm took over. He'd forgotten about

the rhythm.

Fire!

Fire!

Fire!

Change the magazine.

Wrack the bolt.

Fire!

Fire!

Fire!

The crowd exploded, people screaming and hollering and running ever which way and Pete had to pick his shots careful.

Return fire clattered into the building, sent chunks of stone exploding off the facade, stinging his face. Pete Rutherford didn't hit nothing he didn't aim at that day, and what he did hit crumpled to the asphalt.

JUDD'S HANDS were shaking so violently he could barely hold onto his rifle. Obie Tackett had been standing right there, a gun pointed at Judd — and then he lurched backward, never even let go of the rifle, just flew off the back of the building and was gone.

Like he hadn't never been there to begin with. No gunshot; he was just gone.

For a moment, Judd wondered if he'd imagined the whole thing. It'd happened so fast. He'd heard the feet-on-gravel sound. He'd turned. Obie'd said something about … asked what he was doing … and then there was a spray of red and Obie disappeared.

Judd's head snapped to the post office building down the street, but he could see nothing. Of course he couldn't. He hadn't heard nothing, neither. Lester had shot Obie

Tackett and not a soul in the world knew it'd happened except Judd Perkins.

Lester Peetree had saved Judd Perkins's life.

That's when Judd's hands started to shake and he was afraid he was going to throw up. Or wet his pants. He did need to go something fierce.

Then he heard Viola's voice from below, and that was the signal. Soon's he heard her start talking, he was supposed to sight in on a target.

He lifted the rifle and put the barrel in the slot. The barrel jumped around like a man with a bee in his drawers and Judd couldn't seem to grab hold of himself.

They was counting on him. He had a job to do.

And he thought of E.J.

"I HAVE A PLAN — not a very good one, but it's the only shot we have. You start the tractor, engage the power take-off and unhook the clasp on the barn doors. I'll open the doors, get Buster's attention and then dive under the PTO." Judd has trouble following E.J.'s train of thought. His confusion must show on his face because E.J. says, "He'll come after me, his fur'll get caught in the spinning PTO and ..."

And it'll wrap that dog around the shaft, crush him to death instantly. But the PTO ain't but maybe two feet off the ground.

E.J. must see that on his face, too, because he says, "A skinny guy like me, I'll fit."

"What makes you think you can outrun—?"

"I don't, actually. That last part is just ... you know, a Hail Mary. I figure he'll take me down as soon as I turn around and start running ... well, hobbling."

"But E.J., if Buster gets you, he'll kill—"

"He's already killed me, Judd. It'll take a while, but I'm as good as dead. He's rabid and I'm not vaccinated. Without that vaccine, the

*best doctors in the best hospital in the world would just have to stand
by my bed and watch me foam at the mouth."*

Judd just looks at him, flabbergasted.

"Rabies is an ugly way to die, Judd."

"So's getting your throat ripped out by a dog," Judd whispers.

*"True that. I'd rather die in my sleep at some time after my one-
hundredth birthday. As soon as Buster took a hunk out of my leg, that
stopped being an option. Of the available options, I pick number two.
It's the only chance we have to save Julie and Michelle."*

Judd actually backs up a step, shaking his head.

"I don't know about this, E.J. ..."

*"Yes, you do, Judd. You do. You don't like it and neither do I. But
you know, if you've got a better plan, let's hear it. If you don't, we go
with this one."*

AND THEN E.J. Stephenson walked right out into the jaws
of a mad dog.

Judd felt the jittery sensation melt out of his body like
frost when the morning sun hits it. His grip steadied. He
pushed the rifle barrel out through the opening and put his
eye to his sight. It was a Diamondback HP 3-12x42 scope.
He'd once dropped a deer with it at seven hundred yards.

With huge magnification like that, it was hard to
maneuver at such close range, but he was expecting that
and compensated.

He placed the crosshairs of the scope on the back of a
John Deere cap. He saw oil stains and dirt on it. The
bottom was frayed, like it'd been chewed on. Maybe a
puppy'd got it. He moved the crosshairs down, could have
counted the hairs on the back of the man's neck. Down
from there he found a single red square in the man's black-
and-red checked shirt and fixed on it.

Viola was counting, shouting out numbers.

One.

Two.

She didn't get the whole of the next number out and Pete's voice rang out from atop the Hair Affair Beauty Shop and Nail Salon. He only got a couple of words out before the first gunshot rang out and a heartbeat after that, Judd heard the crack of Pete's M1 rifle.

The checked-shirt man was moving, lifting his rifle as he turned. Red and black squares blurred and Judd pulled the trigger, saw blood spurt out a hole the size of a baseball.

Moving the sight instantly to his next target, a skinny man wearing a dirty tee shirt and jeans who had a pistol and was firing wildly at the rooftops. Judd planted a shot square in the center of the smiley-face logo on the front of the shirt.

Ping! A bullet ricocheted off the facade an inch from Judd's face. Another hit the top of the facade next to him and knocked out a hunk of plaster. Now, Judd was aiming at moving targets, men dodging around, diving for cover. He knew how to lead a shot, aim where a bolting deer was *gonna be*, not where it *had been* and he dropped the man who'd fired the shots at him. Then he swung the rifle to the right, tore out a bearded man's throat and fired at another bearded man who'd taken cover behind a parked car. He missed, blew a hole in the trunk of the car. Movement caught his eye and he watched a man dive on his belly behind a mailbox. Another was running across the street right toward Judd. He followed the man with his sight, rising as the guy got closer and closer, and pulled the trigger right before the man disappeared from view.

Judd was no soldier, but his friends who had served in the military always said you never heard the shot that hit you. Turned out they were right.

Chapter Thirty-Two

STUART MCCLINTOCK COULD BARELY SEE, his eyes beginning to bug out of his head from the pressure around his neck. What he could see was a horde of … what? Small … beings … *children* were gliding down the hillside toward them. Jolene had squeaked out a little cry, would have backed away but she was on her knees beside the grave. She did all she had strength to do, simply fell over on her side and curled up in a fetal position, making some fear sound that was a little like sobbing.

Surely the old lady choking Stuart couldn't see. But she somehow knew the children were coming. At first, she froze like she'd been unplugged. Then seemed to have renewed strength for the attack because her attention snapped back to him and the pressure on his neck grayed out the world on the edges. Sparkles and spots. No sound. Light fading.

A force slammed into Stuart from the side, into him and the woman choking him, staggering them both, and suddenly one of her squeezing hands let go of his neck. He would have reached up with his own hands to pry loose the other hand, but he was so nearly unconscious that his limbs refused to obey his commands.

Suddenly the other hand let go. Stuart lurched back, gasping in great lungfuls of air. And as light returned to the world he could see through watering eyes why the woman strangling him had let go. Her arms were no longer attached to her body. The child ... *thing* that had ripped them off knocked her off her feet backwards and Stuart sank to his knees, his head bowed as he felt a rush of cold pass by him. It broke around him and Cotton and Jolene like a wave breaking around a rock and flowed back together toward the creatures crossing the meadow toward them.

One of the women Jolene had run over was nearby and two of the children tore into her. Literally tore into her. Without making a sound, they attacked her with claws and fangs, ripping her apart. Maybe that was the most horrible part, that the whole thing happened in silence, not the snarling of animals who attack a prey, no screaming from a wounded animal, no sound of any kind except scuffling sounds as the creatures were torn apart and thrown to the ground, where the other children swarmed over them, ripping and ...

One of the larger children launched itself at Reece Tibbits, who made no effort to fend it off. Some part of Stuart's mind informed him that Reece likely couldn't see the attack coming, given that he had no head. Reece staggered back, but didn't go down. Another of the children joined the first, ripping and slashing at Reece's body. It grabbed hold of Reece's arm and slashed, pulling and clawing until the arm came off but the stump didn't bleed. The woman who'd been strangling Stuart hadn't bled, either.

The pregnant woman had made it to Cotton. He

slammed the shovel down on the top of her head, a crushing blow, but she merely staggered back a step from the momentum of the shovel hitting her, not from any injury. The whole top of her head and front of her face was smashed in, but she lurched forward again, arms extend, and Cotton wasn't quick enough to lift the shovel again for a second blow and she grabbed him around the throat. He dropped the shovel and grabbed her arms, trying to free himself, staggered back and tripped over the shovel, went down heavily on the ground with the woman on top of him.

Two of the children attacked the two grappling on the ground. One of them sliced claws across the woman's back, opening up groves deep enough to have reached vital organs. There was no blood. The second bit into one of her arms, slashing with dagger teeth. Then the first child ripped through one of the woman's arms, almost severing it, breaking her hold on Cotton's neck. The other child grabbed the woman's body and flung her backward onto the ground. And then they were all over her, clawing and biting and tearing and …

Stuart looked away. To Cotton, he croaked, "The bones!" Then he crawled to the spot beside the grave where Jolene lay, curled up in a ball, sobbing, crying, screaming, all and none of them.

"Jolene." He shook her shoulder. "Help us. We have to get the bones into the grave."

She uncurled enough to look at him and then turned her head toward the carnage, but he grabbed her chin and forced her face back to his.

"Don't look that way, look at me, focus on me now and help me."

He crawled toward the nearest leaf bag and Jolene got to her knees and picked up the one she'd dropped on the ground. Cotton helped Jolene lift it, and the three of them emptied the bones into the grave. They made an awful clacking sound when they hit the bottom, skulls and leg bones and arms and fingers and toes.

Words came back to him.

I was careful. Didn't miss a single one. And the finger of a little two-year-old kid, why that ain't very big at all.

Lily Topple had faithfully picked up every one of the bones the miners had scattered in the woods and Stuart was just as careful to empty into the hole every bone in the sack.

Cotton and Jolene did the same, tossing the empty leaf bags aside. The carnage was still going on around them. The sounds were not screaming, the sounds were the awful thwacking sounds of arms yanked off, sucking thuds as … he wouldn't let himself look and he dragged even his thoughts away.

"Dirt," he gasped, forcing the word out his swollen throat.

They crawled to the pile of dirt he had shoveled out of the hole and began shoving the dirt back in with their bare hands. The shovel was right there, but Stuart didn't have the will to get it where Cotton had dropped it. To do so, he would have had to attend to what was happening, the battle, the war going on around them and he knew to do that was to lose his very tenuous grip on sanity.

They shoved the dirt into the hole, got behind the pile and pushed with all their strength. The bones vanished beneath the dirt. They piled it higher and higher on top of them, until they had filled all the hole. Then they shoved dirt up on top of it, making a mound of sorts, patting it in place with their hands.

At some point while they were working, the battle had ended. Stuart dared to glance in the direction of the meadow and saw carnage that would haunt the dark halls of his nightmares for the rest of his life. Not a single, complete body, nothing but parts, arms, heads …

As the children were … completing their task, they came one by one to stand around where Stuart and Cotton and Jolene knelt beside the mound of dirt. The growing cold of their nearness chilled Stuart to the bone.

And then it was done. The three looked at each other. All the children were gathered in a circle around them, monsters he couldn't look at, even though their bodies had somehow … changed. The claws and dagger teeth were gone.

"They was the horriblest creatures ever was on the earth … They couldn't help what they was. It weren't their fault." Jolene whispered the words Rose Topple had said to Cotton.

Somehow, Stuart managed to stagger to his feet. He put out his hand and helped Cotton stand, and then Jolene.

"Put the rocks on top."

A few feet from the grave was a pile of rocks Stuart had dug out of the hole. He stepped to it, picked one up and fit it down tight on the loose dirt on the top of the grave. Jolene did the same, as did Cotton.

The encircling audience merely watched. He stole looks at them while he worked. Their eyes were sunken back in their horror faces and they didn't look at him. He was glad. He didn't want to make eye contact because he feared if he did he would somehow be able to feel the pain, horror, loneliness and anger these children had been feeling for two hundred years. He suspected to feel that was to die.

When they had fit all the stones on the top of the grave, Stuart said, "Hand me the marker."

The crude cross they had made was lying beside the empty leaf bags, and Jolene took a step toward it. There was a piece of something … he saw her shudder, then resolutely reach down and pick the marker up off the ground.

Stuart jabbed the pointed end of the marker into the dirt and shoved as hard as he could, then picked up a rock and hammered it in the rest of the way until it was stable.

The words on the marker. They hadn't known when they were printing them yesterday, how very appropriate they were.

"May these children of God rest here in eternal peace."

This, what they'd made here today, wouldn't last. In a few months, not even a year, the dirt would settle, the marker topple. But Stuart vowed at that moment that he would return, if he was ever able to come back, that he would make for these children a resting place that would last centuries. But right now, this was all they had. It would have to be enough.

He straightened up from hammering the cross into the ground and looked at Jolene, then Cotton. They hadn't planned beyond the grave and the marker, any more than to say they would "have some kind of service."

What would that be?

Jolene was standing directly behind the cross, with Stuart on one side and Cotton on the other. She reached out and took their hands.

"Close your eyes," she whispered. They closed their eyes.

Then she began to sing.

"Amazing grace, how sweet the sound, that saved a wretch like me …"

Stuart was shocked at the sound. She had an incredible voice, rich and strong, something lower than a soprano but not quite an alto. She reminded him of the women, and men, he'd seen stand on the fifty-yard line and sing the national anthem. Perfect pitch, voices loud enough to carry.

Cotton joined his voice to Jolene's and the two of them sang the next stanza together. "I once was lost, but now am found. Was blind but now I see."

Cotton's was a rich baritone, thick and strong. Stuart was imagining it, of course, but it seemed that the sound of the two of them was the most beautiful music he had ever heard, the voices of angels. Stuart knew the song, of course, all four verses. His grandmother had seen to it that Stuart's bum was on a pew in church every Sunday morning, Sunday evening and Wednesday for prayer meetings.

So he joined in. He didn't really want to because their voices were so hauntingly beautiful, he was reluctant to spoil it with his own ordinary, garden variety voice. But he wouldn't mess it up too bad — his throat was so swollen his voice was ragged, and he'd hardly be able to make any sound at all. He whisper/sang the words along with them, though, because this was something they all three had to do.

"Twas grace that taught my heart to fear, and grace my fear relieved. How precious did that grace appear, the hour I first believed."

It wasn't his imagination, the sounds did echo against the sides of the mountains, reverberated and repeated until it sounded like the Mormon Tabernacle Choir was standing around the grave of children dead two centuries, bearing them away — finally — into a peaceful eternity.

Stuart kept his eyes squeezed resolutely shut through the song, so he didn't see the children ... leave. But he did feel their presence diminish. The cold encircling them and the grave from the ring of children had felt like standing in a walk-in freezer.

He could actually feel the air warming, the temperature around them rising. As a warm summer breeze washed over him, he opened his eyes. The children were gone. Jolene's eyes filled with tears and they spilled down her cheeks. Stuart reached out to pat her arm and his breath caught in his swollen throat. His gaze had strayed from her face to the meadow beyond.

And he saw two things that froze his blood.

The first was that the bodies — *pieces* of bodies — were gone. How they could have just *disappeared*, vanished like that? He didn't know. But he couldn't imagine how they'd gotten there in the first place, either.

The second thing he saw was a man striding through the field where once there had been wildflowers. The man was Shep Clayton, who'd been sitting in a 100-year-old shack all alone the day Stuart had arrived in Nowhere County. Stuart had been struck by the look on the man's face that day, had thought at the time that here was a man who had looked into the abyss and the abyss had looked back. That man had a rifle raised to his shoulder, aimed at the three of them.

Chapter Thirty-Three

"GABE, IT'S NOT YOUR FAULT."

The monster stopped in its tracks, hesitated.

"You just wanted to fight back, to try to save your mother. The rest ... just happened."

The lights that had been glowing inside the bubbling blackness from which the creature had come, were growing dimmer. As they did, the creature shrank.

No less fearsome, horrible, dangerous. But it grew smaller, and somehow seemed to draw away from them, into some kind of hole in the universe, growing less and less, like a specter viewed through the wrong end of a telescope.

Malachi could feel the creature's anger, the boiling rage, which wasn't diminishing because of what he was saying. Something else was sucking the energy out of it — the *absence* of the children. They constituted the greater part of its power and *something* was happening to them on the other side of that hillside.

Its fiery eyes fixed on Malachi's and dozens of images filled Malachi's mind, as if blown into his head by an enormous storm. People, faces — dozens, hundreds, whirling around in a frenetic whirlwind. Feelings, too. Emotions. Like sparks off a blown transformer, emotions flashed off the creature. Hate, anger, sorrow, jealousy, resentment. Sparks of them connected to some circuit inside Malachi and he *felt* the emotions as if they were his own. He felt angry, then sorrowful, then jealous. The accumulated power of the emotional onslaught was staggering — and then he got it. The faces … the feelings were taken from *those people.*

The strength and power of the creature was what it had taken into itself from the people it had absorbed.

Nothing good, though. No laughter or joy. The creature sought only evil, sucking all the darkness from the people of Gideon a hundred years ago. But it didn't stop there. It had continued to absorb negative energy. The mist in Fearsome Hollow fed on the darkness around it. Was that why so many people in Nowhere County were depressed? Was that why they hated Nowhere County, wanted to leave, had no love or loyalty in their hearts for it?

Or was it the other way around? Had the people simply turned sour on their own, lost interest in the place when the businesses went belly-up, the schools closed and people moved away — and the Jabberwock had merely fed on those emotions, growing meaner and stronger.

Was the Jabberwock the cause or the effect?

Malachi didn't know. What he *did* know was that he'd be a fool to think that the creature before him, consumed by rage and hatred, could be talked out of it by sympathizing with the young man whose darkness had been the seed of it all, the boy who had died and left the children sealed in the cave.

He literally felt the motion in his arm when the hands on his watch began to whirl furiously.

Something was happening to time. It was passing too fast. Or too slow. Static, that awful sound they'd each heard when the Jabberwock kidnapped them out of their lives and their world two weeks ago suddenly roared around them now, rumbled and buzzed and—

Music.

Singing.

The static was instantly silenced.

Malachi looked around, and realized he wasn't imagining it. Sam and Charlie heard it, too.

"Amazing grace, how sweet the sound, that saved a wretch like me. I once was lost but now I'm found, was blind but now I see …"

A huge chorus was singing, hundreds of voices in perfect harmony, the sounds reverberating off the mountain tops.

Every word seemed to hit the creature like a drop of acid and it writhed from the impact.

But its tremendous power seemed to grow more intense as its form grew smaller. Even as it shrank, it was still a monster capable of ripping them apart. And it was preparing to do just that. It hunkered before them, the lion in a crouch, tensing to jump.

The music grew louder. Where could it possibly be coming from?

"Through many dangers, toils and snares we have already come. Twas grace that brought us safe thus far and grace will lead us home."

A roar, a bellow of pure hatred, erupted from the creature. It tilted its head back and … screamed. An animal cry that was somehow human, too.

Then it settled, turned its fiery gaze on the three of them and hunkered down again.

They had one, maybe two seconds to live.

Sam suddenly whispered urgently, "Join hands." Charlie and Malachi complied. It would be good to hold on in death, bound together.

The Alphabet Gang.

The Breakfast Club.

The three of them standing together on the brink of eternity, no weapons. Utterly defenseless.

Or were they?

Nothing stood between the mighty Jabberwock and the three of them — they had brought to Fearsome Hollow nothing to fight with. Except each other.

Something held the monster back. Could it be that their bond to each other was protecting them? The creature's rage grew brighter even as it shrank. And then the darkness bubbling in the air settled around the creature like a cloak. Mist shrouded it and it sank back into the darkness.

Hoary words formed in all their heads.

This isn't over. I'm not done—

"... once was lost, but now am found, was blind, but now I ..."

At the final word in the last chorus — "see" — the creature was gobbled up by its own boiling blackness and withdrew into the mist. The mist rose up off the ground and retreated into the trees.

And vanished.

SHEP WAS AS HORRIFIED as Claude, struck speechless, wanted to cut and run just like Claude had done.

It was Shep's dread, not Abby's. And once he let it loose, it grew bigger and turned into fear. Finally, for the first time since he'd seen his house all changed and life as he knew it gone forever, Shepherd Clayton was afraid. Terrified. So scared he couldn't breathe, even.

And he cried out, like a little kid calling for Mama in the midnight dark.

Abby!

Not with the voice that come out his mouth but inside his head.

But Abby didn't come.

He cried out again, terror and anguish welling up from his soul.

Abbbbbby!

Abby was gone, wasn't in Shep's head no more.

But there was *something* in his head still, it just wasn't Abby no more.

What was there inside Shep had lost all resemblance to the sweet girl Shep'd thought glowed like them fiber optic cables when she was sitting beside baby Cody's bassinet in the hospital. Wasn't no trace of the girl who'd put Earl up to telling Shep she had a crush on him when they was in junior high school, the teasing woman who had told him his head would fall off if he wasn't careful, the voice he had picked out of the whispers in their house when he come home and everything was gone.

That voice had been sweet Abby, the sound of her talking reminding him of little bells ringing. He had noticed when he stopped hearing that sound when she spoke in his head. It had been gone a right smart while, but the voice had still been Abby, just with a different sound, that's all. But still Abby.

Now, he didn't have nothing.

He didn't have Abby in his head, closer than his own skin, directing his every move, and he didn't have the real Abby with the striking blue eyes looking up at him. He just had … the *presence* in his mind.

And the presence was all rage and anger and hatred. Nothing kind and sweet and loving like his Abby'd been. The rage that filled Shep's whole being was as overwhelming as being washed away by a flash flood.

It was the Jabberwock, of course.

And a horrible thought occurred to him that maybe … maybe it had been the Jabberwock all along, maybe it hadn't never been Abby there, just this angry creature.

When Shep done what this thing was directing him to do, would he get Abby back, like all them other folks, would she come back with all of them?

Only maybe they weren't coming back at all.

Maybe that part had been a lie, just what the Jabberwock told him to get him to do what it wanted. Maybe Abby was … gone. For good. Maybe all them people was.

But, of course, it didn't matter what Shep Clayton thought. Wasn't nothing in life up to him now, and his soul shrank back in horror from the rage of the thing that wasn't even pretending to be Abby anymore. The thing was like something bursting up out of a shell, stretching out to its full size, a horror of anger and evil, hatred. It was all things black and foul, and it shoved Shep Clayton aside like batting a gnat out of its face.

Shep watched his hands grip his rifle, felt his lips draw back in a smile and his body rise to his feet. Wasn't no hiding in the woods no more.

He would walk across the meadow, stand right in front of them people so he wouldn't miss this time. Then rage would flow out from him, hatred and revenge and he would …

Blow. Their. Heads. Off.

Yes!

They saw him coming but didn't run, just stood there and looked at him. He laughed at that. Actually laughed out loud. Even a rabbit had the sense to run when it seen the fox coming. He approached closer and closer.

Shep was suddenly sorry. The Shep who hunkered down in himself while the black vileness marched forward. Abby hadn't never told him to kill them people. Abby wouldn't never have told him to do a thing like that. The voice in his head hadn't never been Abby at all.

The Jabberwock had tricked him. And Shep had wanted Abby so bad he had let it happen. Now it had come to this.

Shep looked out through eyes he no longer controlled and saw fear on the faces of them three people. And he was sorry.

STUART WATCHED in horror as Shepherd Clayton crossed the meadow to the cemetery, his gait firm and steady, holding a rifle the way a man held a gun when he'd grown up with one in his hand. It'd been Shep, of course, who'd shot at them in the rain on Monday. Why? There might have been a rational motive, but Stuart doubted it. The man striding toward him had driven away from rational a long time ago and likely couldn't even see it anymore in his rearview mirror.

Shep had been trying to kill them two days ago, but his plans had run afoul of the storm.

He wouldn't miss this time, though. No storm, a few puffy white clouds clinging to the mountaintops like hot air balloons.

Closer.

"You hadn't ought to have messed in what ain't none of your concern," the man said, but there was no emotion in the words, no sense of the kind of wrath that would send a man out with a rifle to shoot three people he barely knew. The voice sounded as toneless and lacking inflection as an automated attendant.

Beside Stuart, Jolene was shaking her head slowly in denial. He wasn't touching her, but still could feel her trembling. The woman was just about *done*, was clinging to … sanity, herself, her soul … with broken fingernails. This — a whack-job with a rifle — was simply a bridge too far.

She whispered, "Please … don't."

But the man couldn't have heard, and would have paid her no mind if he had. He ignored Cotton, too, focused on Stuart as if they were the only two people present.

Cotton retreated a single step, slightly behind Stuart, but stopped there and held his ground.

Think!

Do something!

What?

Stuart could grab the pick he'd tried to use on the … or the shovel.

The guy would drop him as soon as he leaned over to pick it up.

A random line from some forgotten movie: *Never bring a knife to a gunfight.* The same went for picks and shovels.

The emotion that had been absent from Shepherd Clayton's voice was very much present in his face. His eyes were boring into Stuart. The intensity of hatred twisted his features into such a rictus of rage that he was unrecognizable.

Stuart tensed his muscles, got ready. He would launch himself at the man as soon as he got within range. Wouldn't just stand here and be executed.

But he knew he'd be shot as he did so. What was it the movies also said? *He'd be dead before he hit the ground.*

Stuart McClintock was about to die.

Three or four more seconds.

He summoned Charlie's face, smiling, holding Merrie close.

One more step.

Charlie! was the last thing Stuart thought as he began to release his tensed muscles. But before he could spring, several things happened right on top of each other.

A woman's voice from somewhere nearby screamed, "No!"

Shep's eyes cocked in that direction for only an instant. And then the roar of a gunshot filled up the world.

Chapter Thirty-Four

FISH STARED in horror as Neb Tackett dragged Thelma Jackson out of the crowd and hauled her up onto the porch of the school to stand in front of Viola.

Neb! — who was the person Viola was looking for, but she didn't know it. Fish was convinced Neb had killed his sister, accidentally shot her, then made up the drive-by-shooter story to cover his tracks. And now Neb planned to stand by passively while his mother killed no telling how many innocent people, too cowardly to confess what he'd done.

That wasn't going to happen, though. Viola wasn't going to kill anybody this day. Pete, Judd and Lester would see to that. Not one of them was an all-star, a hero, but all of them were solid and dependable. You could count on them.

Fish trusted that they would be able to pull off their plan to stop the massacre. Each had a role to play, and Fish would carry out his duty with the same dedication and determination as the men who were now crouched and ready, rifles aimed at the would-be murderers below.

Viola said she was going to start with Thelma, and would then select one person after another until ...

It took a great force of will for Fish not to look down the street at the post office, or turn and look up at the rooftops across the street. He'd seen where Sebastian Nower had stopped in the crowd, looked right and left at Oscar Manning and Skeeter Burkett.

Viola started counting. Fish tensed. Then two things happened one on top of the other. Pete Rutherford's voice called out something, Fish didn't get anything but the word "surrender," and Neb Tackett took aim and fired a pistol at him.

The world all around Fish exploded in pandemonium. The rumble of gunfire echoed between the buildings and the stunned crowd took about half a second to panic, was a heartbeat away from running madly off in all directions.

"This way," he called out in the orator's voice he hadn't used in years. It boomed out above the noise. He grabbed a woman he didn't know and an old man who might have been Henry Goodbody and shoved them toward the sidewalk, as gunfire continued to rattle around them.

"Oscar, help me get everybody to the *bank,* out past the fountain," he yelled at Oscar Manning, who had started running toward the other side of the street, and literally turned on a dime and began running toward the sidewalk in front of the school, grabbing others and shoving them along ahead of him.

"The bank!" Oscar yelled. He got it, understood that was the only way out. "Get to the bank!"

"This way!" Sebastian Nower cried, and the combination of their three voices turned the herd. Almost as one, the panicked crowd stampeded across the street to the sidewalk in front of the school. They hit the sidewalk like a wave washing up on shore and Oscar called out something unintelligible and the wave flowed to the right toward the bank courtyard down the block.

Fish hung back, everything happening too fast around him.

Men had been shot, were lying in the street. A man … looked like one of Angus Scully's sons, had hunkered down behind a mailbox, though, and was firing up toward the rooftop of the drug store building.

Some other guy Fish didn't know was behind a parked car, blood gushing out of his leg as he fired off one shot after another at the roof of the beauty parlor.

Suddenly, Sebastian Nower appeared a few feet in front of Fish, yelling for people to "run to the fountain" and shoving them that way.

Then time and life slowed down, like some slow-motion scene in a movie where a drip of water falls gently out of the sky and lands in a pond, making an ever-widening hole in the water's surface.

Fish looked past Nower at the porch of the school … right down the barrel of Viola Tackett's pistol.

VIOLA TACKETT THOUGHT a mule had kicked her. The force of the blow flung her backward away from Thelma Jackson, knocked her off her feet and she slid across the concrete and banged her head painfully.

She hadn't even stopped sliding when the world erupted in *gunfire*.

What the—?

She noticed her own shoulder then and the pain hit at the sight of blood gushing out a hole in her flesh and down the front of her shirt.

She'd been shot in the shoulder.

Wasn't no life-threatening wound, though, and she dismissed it. She'd been hurt worse. Where was her gun? She searched the now empty porch — Neb and Thelma Jackson were gone — and saw the pistol lying near the edge of the porch to her left.

Rifle shots rumbled from the rooftops across the street — where she'd sent Obie a few minutes ago to investigate that sparkle.

Not now … she'd think about that part later. Now, she focused on the gun, dragged herself toward it, fast as she could, eager to shoot the lights outta whoever was firing at her.

Her right arm didn't work right with her shoulder shot, so she reached out her left hand and picked up the pistol. After rolling over, she pushed herself up to a sitting position against one of the pillars and pointed the gun with her trembling left hand at …

What …?

Couldn't see nothing on the roofs.

People was running ever which way.

It was a big pistol, heavy, and Viola was trying to hold it with her left hand, aim it at *something*. She had six shots and she was determined to *kill* somebody — *anybody* — with one of them.

She fired up at the rooftops. Again. And again. Bam! Bam! Bam! The gun roared, but wasn't no way to hit somebody behind cover up there, not with a pistol anyway.

She was getting weak. Her left hand holding the gun began to shake.

"Mama!" It was Zach. He was standing over her, looking bewildered and frightened.

"Help me up," she demanded. Standing upright, she'd be able to shoot and *hit* something.

Zach started to take her right arm, seen the blood and

grabbed her left arm instead, the one holding the gun. He pulled upward—

Then red mist exploded out of Zach's left temple.

There wasn't no gunshot. They was just suddenly a hole in his head and blood splattering in her face. He'd been pulling upward, and when he went limp, he collapsed on top of her, pinning her down with his lifeless body.

Viola blinked gore out of her eyes, couldn't move or breathe, turned her head … and seen Sebastian Nower, not fifteen feet away.

He was standing there hollering, telling people to "make for the bank, out past the fountain."

She couldn't do much aiming, lying on her back under Zach like she was, but she was able to lift the pistol and point it in his direction. She fired, and a chunk of asphalt at his feet splattered upward. He didn't notice and she lifted the pistol, got it pointed at his belly. As she pulled the trigger, there was a blur of motion and Sebastian disappeared.

She pulled the trigger again and the hammer landed on an empty chamber with a hollow clacking sound. Again and again. Clack, clack. Out of ammo, and the shape she was in, with Zach on top of her, wasn't no way she could get to the extra rounds in her pocket.

They was a gunfight going on in the middle of Main Street in Persimmon Ridge, Kentucky. Didn't take but one glance to see her side was losing.

~

IT WAS like a series of still photographs.

Click-click. Viola Tackett is sprawled on her back with one of her sons — Zach — on top of her.

Click-click. A close-up of her face. The look of violent

hatred and anger had so twisted her features she is hardly recognizable.

Click-click. Viola lifts her gun, an enormous pistol, and the barrel is pointed right at Sebastian.

It seemed to Fish that time slowed down, way slower than Jabberwock time, so slow the world was magnified into credible detail.

The sounds of screaming and gunfire were frozen into a single sound, high, loud, screeching and rumbling all at the same time.

He could smell his own fear sweat, somebody's after-shave lotion, and a whiff of … was it cordite, from the gunshots.

He thought he actually watched the cylinder on Viola's pistol move as she began to squeeze the trigger.

And he knew then what he had to do. Seemed to have all the time in the world to consider the decision and the ramifications of it.

Holmes Fischer had been the unwitting instrument of death three times. The lives of three people had been snuffed out by something he had done. It wasn't a particularly thorny philosophical consideration to determine that he owed a great debt to the universe.

And now the universe had shown up on his doorstep in the form of Viola Tackett's pistol and demanded payment in full.

It was long past Fish's time. And besides, he was so very, very tired of living.

So Fish leapt. He'd never been particularly agile or athletic and years of alcohol saturation had done nothing to improve his motor skills. Even so, he took note that there was a singular grace to his movements, a fluidity, and a speed he was totally incapable of mustering.

In real time, all his musings took place between one

heartbeat and the next as he was already leaping forward with his hands extended as far as he could reach. Slapping Sebastian Nower on the back, Fish knocked him sideways. The forward momentum of his lunge carried Fish into the space Sebastian had just occupied.

The bullet aimed at Sebastian hit Fish instead, entered his body on the left side, ripped a hole there the size of a baseball. It shattered a rib and sent shards of it along with the bullet tumbling like a buzz saw through his chest. It shredded his heart. Then it tore out his right lung as it veered toward his back and blasted an exit hole the size of a grapefruit.

Fish was dead before he hit the pavement.

THE CROWD HAD SCATTERED FAR WIDER than Pete'd hoped it would. Though Fish gathered a considerable number of people in a rush toward the sidewalk, panic still hit folks like a bomb, sending men, women, old people and little kids skittering off in every direction, all of them screaming their lungs out.

Pete had dropped two gunmen quick, Judd had got that many, too, looked like, maybe more, before the others leapt for cover and returned fire.

Parked cars, light posts, a mailbox, even a fire hydrant, now blocked most of his shots — but the men below just kept dropping. Both Pete and Judd were firing at the dude behind the mailbox, their bullets thunk, thunk, thunking off metal on the front, when the man suddenly flew sideways and lay still in a growing pool of blood.

Another of Viola's gunmen was shielded from the rooftop shooters behind a parked car when all at once his head snapped to the side like somebody'd smacked him and a spray of pink mist splattered all over the car's grill.

Lester.

The gunmen hunkering down behind whatever cover they could find that stood between them and the other side of the street were completely unaware that they were wide open to the sniper shooting down the street from the Post Office.

Lester dropped one after another. None of them knew what hit them.

Then a voice rang out from behind the big metal switch box for the traffic light on the corner.

"Stop! Hold your fire. I give, I give!"

The man belonging to the voice threw his gun out into the street. Gunfire from the men around him stopped, too.

"Don't shoot," somebody else yelled and another rifle skidded across the asphalt and came to rest against the dead body of a man in a black-and-red checked shirt.

"Hands in the air, all of you," Pete called out. "Get out in the middle of the street where I can see you."

More weapons hit the asphalt and two men stood, one with blood streaming out of a hole in his thigh, another with a bleeding arm. Other men followed their lead, hands raised high and staggered out into the open, looking up at the rooftop where Pete's voice was coming from.

One of them stumbled and almost went down on one knee next to a rifle somebody'd dropped, and a hole exploded in the asphalt in front of the rifle. There'd been no sound of a gunshot. The men looked around, frightened, aware for the first time that gunfire could come literally from anywhere.

Another man threw out his weapon then, and rose up from between two cars. He might have been intending to hide, see if he could pick off the guys on the roof, but thought better of it when it was clear they weren't the only, and maybe not even the worst, threat.

Only then did Pete rise slowly to his feet, his rifle trained on the small group of men looking up at him. The whole shootout hadn't lasted more'n a couple of minutes. It'd felt like a lifetime.

Pete turned and hollered at Judd, "Anybody moves, you blow—"

Judd wasn't hunkered down with his rifle stuck through the slot in the facade of the Hair Affair Beauty Parlor roof. He lay splayed out on his back. It was clear to Pete, even at this distance, that Judd was dead.

Chapter Thirty-Five

CHARLIE WATCHED, stunned, as the thing, the black monster crouching to lunge at them and rip them apart … shrank back into the mist and vanished.

Sam squeaked out a sound of some kind, a cry. Malachi made some kind of sound, too, maybe a grunt like when he got tackled.

Then there was silence.

No, not silence. Not the unnatural awful quiet of the presence sucking all the air and energy out of the world. The normal silence that wasn't really quiet at all. A bird called from the trees and another answered. The raucous cry of a chorus of cicadas buzzed in the distance.

A warm breeze kissed her cheek.

"What …?" Sam's voice was small and trembling.

"Did you hear … music?" Charlie asked.

"Singing!" Sam said, and Charlie turned in the direction the children had gone, up the hill and over the top to the other side. "It was coming from there. We need to …"

She didn't finish because she found herself moving that

way, an instinctive thing, with a sense of urgency she didn't quite understand.

Sam was behind her and they had both taken several steps before they realized Malachi hadn't come with them. Charlie looked over her shoulder and stopped in her tracks, and Sam almost stumbled over her.

Malachi was standing still, his hands at his sides, his head tilted up, looking at the sky.

She followed his gaze, but couldn't see what he could possibly be staring at. Empty sky—

Sam cried out beside her, something very like a sob, and Charlie turned to her. There was the most incredible look on her face, unreadable, emotions too tangled to identify. But there was nothing negative in the look. Not fear or the ever-present dread that had sunk its teeth into their souls two weeks ago and wouldn't let go.

The look was primarily … wonder.

Maybe … joy?

Charlie finally looked up, trying to figure out what the two of them …

There was nothing, just … and then she saw, really *saw*.

Her hand flew to her mouth and tears squirted out of her eyes and down her cheeks too fast for her to wipe them away.

A simple thing, really. Nothing to get all excited about. Just puffy white balls of fluff against the bright blue of the sky above the mountaintops.

Clouds.

Clouds!

She turned then and ran to the hillside, clambering up it, clawing her way faster and faster. She didn't understand her urgency, but gave in to the instinct. There was *something* on the other side …

Staggering across the small top of the hill, Charlie

looked down the other side. She saw a cleft between two steep mountains where a meadow lay just beyond a cemetery. A red Lexus with the lid of the trunk up was parked next to what looked like a fresh grave and there were three people beside it — two men and a woman.

Charlie took in that whole scene in the first second she stood on the hilltop. In the second second, she saw that the people were two black men and a white woman. In the third second, she saw that the bigger of the two men was Stuart.

It was. *It was Stuart.*

In the fourth second, she saw the man crossing the meadow toward them. He had rifle to his shoulder, pointed at them.

Sam was suddenly beside Charlie and a single word escaped Sam's throat.

"Shep?"

Shepherd Clayton.

There might be ten different men in Nowhere County named Shep. Might be a hundred, or a thousand. It didn't matter, *this one* was Shepherd Clayton. Charlie knew that in her bones. That was Abby's husband, striding across the meadow with a rifle pointed at Stuart.

Abby Clayton, the monstrous creature that had shambled out of the shadows in Merrie's bedroom and told Charlie she had locked Merrie in the airless kiln.

Abby, who had shot Malachi.

Abby, who had exploded, blown apart in the Middle of Nowhere.

She'd been so desperate to get to "baby Cody and Shep" that she'd have killed anybody who got in her way. Now, her Shep had a gun on Stuart, and Charlie had no doubt he was every bit as ruthless and crazy as Abby had been.

This could not be.

This *would* not be! Not *now.* Not after they'd all been through. Not after the world had finally been set aright. Charlie would not lose Stuart now!

She screamed.

With every fiber of her being, with her very soul, Charlie McClintock cried out in horror and anguish, a shriek that tore out of her throat in a wail that almost sounded like the cry of some dying animal.

"Noooooooooo!"

STUART'S EARS rang from the blast of sound.

The rumble ate up the world and he tensed for the pain.

Nothing.

As he watched in amazement, a small, red hole — no bigger than a nickel, really — appeared in the chest of the man pointing a rifle at them.

The rifle dropped to the ground at his feet, but the man stood for a moment longer, the raging fury that had twisted Shep Clayton's features into the mask of a monster melted away. He lifted his eyes, and for an instant, they met Stuart's.

There was a look in those eyes at that moment. It appeared in a flash and then it was gone, the eyes unfocused and the skinny man folded up and crumpled to the ground. Stuart would think about that look often, ponder it, consider it. The doubt might come then, later, that maybe he hadn't seen …

But there was no doubt in that first moment. That instant when Stuart and Shep connected, soul to soul, the look in Shepherd Clayton's eyes was *gratitude.*

Stuart turned slowly to Cotton, who still stood with a pistol in a two-hand grip, pointed at the spot where Shep Clayton no longer stood. Stuart reached out carefully to the gun, gripped it and pulled gently. Cotton let go of it, took a step back and gasped for air.

Stuart stooped and knelt beside the still body of Shep Clayton, whose eyes were open, but now they stared sightlessly upward.

"Where did you get …?" Jolene started to ask Cotton but ran out of air before she finished the question.

"Borrowed it from a friend when I went to Carlisle yesterday," Cotton said. He seemed to be having trouble drawing in enough air to speak, too. "Wasn't gonna come back out here again today defenseless."

The nickel-sized hole was on the left side of Shepherd Clayton's chest, right below his collar bone. At a range of less than fifteen feet, Cotton had fired the bullet directly into his heart. Stuart continued to kneel where he was because his knees suddenly felt like they might not want to hold him upright if he stood. He still had the pistol, couldn't think what to do with it so he just laid the weapon carefully on the ground beside Shep Clayton's rifle.

He got to his feet then without stumbling, but clearly he was not fully in possession of his faculties because he was imagining things. Looking around to see who had screamed, he saw … *Charlie* … running down the hill.

It was so crisp and clear that his heart almost leapt out of his chest in longing for it to be real.

Then he heard Charlie's voice, calling his name.

Cotton and Jolene had turned and were staring at the hillside where the children had floated down. They saw the people, too. A man and two women. But the woman racing ahead of the others was … looked like …

Charlie.

Couldn't be.

Absolutely Could. Not. Be.

He started running without consciously willing his feet to move. Had no sense of crossing the distance between where he stood beside the dead body of Shepherd Clayton and where Charlie … Charlie? *Charlie!*

Then she was in his arms. He could feel her, *feel her.*

She was calling his name, sobbing, clinging to him.

It was real.

Dear God in heaven, it was real.

PETE STOOD in the middle of Main Street beside Lester Peetree, removed in some way from the pandemonium so that he was aware of it happening, but wasn't connecting to it in any real sense. He recognized that packed-in-cotton sensation from battle where the whole world was kinda on mute. It would pass.

He felt more exhausted than he had ever felt in his life, felt like all the energy he had ever had, had been expended on that rooftop and now he was just negotiating reality on fumes.

Though he was moving fast as he could, it seemed to take him an hour to get from the roof of the beauty parlor to the roof of the drug store, where Judd lay. Most of the top part of the right side of his head was missing. In that detachment that enabled you to do impossible things, Pete made a mental note to make sure Doreen and the girls didn't see Judd this way. Then he'd climbed down the ladder off the building, liked to fell twice his legs was so weak, and found Lester Peetree waiting for him there, beside Obie Tackett, whose dead body was draped over a sawhorse standing beside the rear door of the building.

He'd landed on the sawhorse on his back, and kinda broke in two over it.

They was lots of dead bodies around, but it was gonna have to be up to other folks besides Pete Rutherford to make arrangements for them and tend to the wounded. He'd done his part. It was over. Lester helped out, of course, and he'd be the one packing the dead bodies away at Bascum's. Oscar Manning's girl Chastity, Skeeter Burkett, Thelma Jackson, Raylynn's Aunt Effie Bennett, and Eula Mae Reynolds were taking instructions from the O'Conner kid, name of Brian, to patch them up as had got shot. The boy had *said* he was in medical school until he'd broke his leg and had to come home to his parents' house outside Twig. Though E.J.'d borrowed his medical school books for reference, Sam had had her doubts about what the kid'd been telling his parents about his education. Still and all, best as Pete could see right now, the boy did appear to know his way around a bandage.

Oscar Manning had … manned up, so to speak, and took Viola's boys who could still walk "into custody," whatever that meant. What he planned to do with 'em, Pete didn't have no idea and didn't plan to ask. He could hear Viola grumbling and cussing so she'd made it through. Two of her boys didn't — Obie and Zach. Neb was fine. He'd took one shot at the rooftop, but soon's bullets started flying, he'd crawled under a parked car and hid.

Pete was sure he knew most of the dead men sprawled out in pools of blood, but he didn't look at their faces, didn't have no desire whatsoever to see who they was.

"You might ought to sit down," Lester said, putting his hand on Pete's arm.

Reality returned to the world then, no cotton wrapping, nothing muted. He could hear the war zone of pain cries from wounded men, horror cries from women that somebody should have kept out of the street, and the smell of blood and cordite. Across the street, Bri Haggarty stood on the sidewalk, gaping. Pete hadn't seen her in a month of Sundays and he sure hoped none of the dead was her kin. Then the shock on her face blossomed into a huge smile, so if any of them was her people, Bri musta been real glad they'd got shot. Mamie Scully sure wasn't. She'd knelt down beside one of her boys — he didn't know which one — and was wailing.

Pete opened his mouth to tell Lester he couldn't sit down because he was afraid he might not be able to get back up again but didn't get the chance to say anything — because that's when he heard it.

Everybody heard it at the same time, turned as one toward the end of the block where the unmistakable sound of squalling airbrakes filled the air. They all gawked as the big black bus turned the corner and drove slowly up the street toward them, then stopped in front of where Pete and Lester stood — to keep from running over them, and other people both dead and alive.

The bus was a big sucker, one of them things that had bulging-out tinted windows and side mirrors that hung down like the antenna of an ant. Black and shiny, with the words Cumberland Mountain Tours emblazoned on the side.

The implications of the sight were so staggering that it totally knocked the wind out of everyone on the street and they just stared in slack-jawed amazement. Hadn't nothing been able to get out of or into Nowhere County since J-Day almost three weeks ago. This bus obviously came from outside, so did that mean …? Had Charlie, Malachi and Sam …?

Pete's gaze yanked back to Bri Haggarty on the other side of the street, a look of joy on her face that'd melt frost off a windowpane. Now that he thought about it, there'd been nobody standing in front of the drug store and then Bri just ... appeared, so did that mean ... ?

There was a whoosh and a soft whumping sound and the door opened. In the sudden silence on the street, it was easy to hear the sudden hysteria on the bus as passengers got a good look around them. The driver come stumbling down the steps — starched blue uniform with the name Reginald Blackaby stenciled above the right pocket and the bus company logo above the left.

What kinda mama names her baby boy Reginald?

The driver didn't get all the way out of the bus, paused on the bottom step and looked out at the carnage in horror. Understandable. It wasn't like he'd been expecting to find a battlefield full of dead and dying people when he'd rounded the corner at the end of the block thirty seconds ago.

Mr. Blackaby looked at Pete and Lester, and Pete saw sudden fear in his eyes. Wasn't until then that Pete realized he still had his M1 rifle in his hands.

"What ...?"

That was it, the only word the man seemed able to form.

"Can we hep you with somethin'?" Pete prompted, and hadn't meant any humor by it, but when he saw the look on the man's face and considered the situation, he had to swallow as hard as he could to hold onto a bleat of inappropriate laughter.

Pete's words shocked a knee-jerk response from the bus driver.

"The map doesn't show ... it's not on ... I'm lost. Where are we?"

"You ain't nowhere," Lester said, matter-of-fact as pass the mashed potatoes. "But you ain't got to the center of it yet. The *Middle* of Nowhere's another couple miles down that way."

Pete turned away then, his shoulders shaking. He thought he was laughing, but then he felt the tears on his cheeks and realized he was crying.

Chapter Thirty-Six

THEY WOULDN'T all fit in Sam or Charlie's houses, had briefly considered holding the event in the auditorium of the West Liberty Middle School, but ditched that idea quick. Liam had died there. Too many bad memories of that place. Even though Pete Rutherford's map had been framed and hung permanently on the back wall of the room, it still …

Then Sebastian Nower had stepped forward. Sam didn't even know how the man knew they were looking for a big place to hold Thanksgiving, but he'd found out somehow and graciously invited all of them to consider using the Nower House.

He didn't have to ask twice.

In truth, Sam had never been inside the Nower House, had always wanted to see it, and discovered to her delight that it was as ornate and beautiful as she had always imagined it'd be. It stood like a beacon now on Main Street with its fresh coat of paint and the National Historic Landmark sign restored to the front yard. Apparently, Sebastian's brush with losing his house, however briefly, had made him realize how much it mattered to him. Almost losing a thing has a way of doing that to you.

Charlie'd wanted to pay to have the whole Thanksgiving gig catered, but Sam had said she wanted to do it. Charlie had pointed out, in her no-nonsense Charlie way, that this would not be a small gathering.

"I know you love to cook, can whip up a meal for all the blond men in the Norwegian army in fifteen minutes and not leave a single dirty dish in the sink," Charlie had said. "But we're talking fifteen … maybe twenty-five people." The final number depended on how many of Lester Peetree and Sebastian Nower's families managed to attend.

And it was a little intimidating, but Sam had forged ahead. Thanksgiving was her hands-down favorite holiday, much better than Christmas because there was none of the hassle. No wreaths/garlands/Christmas lights to haul out and put up. No tree to decorate, gifts to purchase and wrap. Just good food. Lots of good food. And Sam did love to cook.

She was enjoying this a little more than some other Thanksgivings of her life, when she'd dreaded the struggle to fit into her jeans carrying the extra pounds she would put on. This year, she was in *deficit*. She could eat all the turkey and pecan pie and candied sweet potatoes and mashed-potatoes-and-gravy she wanted. She'd lost fifteen pounds. She didn't imagine anybody in the county had gained weight in June, but fifteen pounds was a lot even for a woman her size.

"I'll be in charge of the kitchen and order the rest of you around like a drill instructor," she'd told Charlie.

Sam had put Malachi in charge of the turkey. He could buy the thing, figure out how to cook it, do the cooking and the carving. All things turkey were his problem.

Charlie had gotten light duty. Given that, for her, making toast was a culinary challenge, she'd considered cutting up celery and chestnuts for the dressing a stretch.

Jolene Rutherford, who'd taken what she'd called a "spook sabbatical" to take care of her father, Raylynn Bennett and Thelma Jackson had insisted on bringing "covered dishes."

Sam leaned over and peeked at the rolls that were browning nicely in the oven — one of three in the Nower House! Sam's stove had a single oven, limping along. She had to keep a thermometer resting on the rack because the temperature in it waffled up and down like the warble in an off-key soprano.

She straightened up as Merrie plowed through the kitchen, chasing a little dog with white feet that looked like it was wearing gym socks. That one was Poopy. Or maybe Santa Claus. No, Santa Claus had big claws.

Sam could not imagine how the child had talked Charlie into letting her have *three* puppies! But maybe it was Stuart who had caved, couldn't resist when the little girl batted those big blue eyes at him.

That man would have done anything to make up for the hurt he had caused his wife and daughter. It had been some colossal mistake, had had something to do with loaning his credit card to his best friend, so he could surprise someone with a trip to Hawaii ... or something like that. The explanation had made perfect sense when Charlie had told her about it, but Sam couldn't remember now. It didn't matter anymore.

"Twinkle Sparkle, you gots to get back in your kennel," Merrie cried as she barely avoided a head-on collision with E.J., who was still not steady on his feet, even with a cane.

"Comin' through," he cried, trying to clear a pathway for the giggling little girl.

Malachi came up behind Sam and held out a piece of turkey. "Taste test," he announced, and dangled it above her nose like a treat above a dog.

"What difference does it make how it tastes? It's not like you can do anything about it now."

"Ah, but Pizza Hut still delivers."

He smiled at her and she smiled back. That was all, just a moment and it was over. They were still finding their way, seeing how things worked out, taking nothing for granted. That was enough. More than enough.

~

CHARLIE SAW MALACHI dangle a piece of turkey over Sam's nose and snatch it away like he was training one of Merrie's puppies. *One* of Merrie's puppies. Charlie shook her head. Stuart had likely wondered how on earth she'd gotten talked into such a thing — and she hadn't gotten *talked into* anything. Stuart must have sensed that, because he'd never asked.

Charlie heard his voice from the other room and stood very still for just a moment, listening. E.J. and Pete had goaded him into telling stories about the Pittsburgh Steelers, not that it took a lot of goading, and she loved the energy she heard in his voice.

It had hurt so bad to think Stuart had ...

Charlie wouldn't go there. The Jabberwock had damaged her in so many ways but like everybody else, she'd been in survival mode at the time and just soldiered through. In the months since, however, she suffered something akin to Malachi's PTSD. She'd wake up with a jolt, tangled in the skeins of a dream about singing a lullaby outside the locked door of the kiln. She'd sometimes be overwhelmed with a wave of despair, the residue of that awful time, and there was no cure but to go and be near Stuart. She didn't tell him about it, of course, didn't admit why she'd suddenly found it absolutely necessary to look for a lost *whatever* right where he happened to be sitting. She thought he knew, though.

"Merrie, watch where you're going," she cried, when the little girl almost bowled E.J. over. Charlie was concerned that he was still so weak, but Sam had been reassuring — said that what he'd been through simply required a long recovery time. The series of rabies shots and his immediate allergic reaction to them had hammered him. In his weakened state, with the obscure staph infection in his leg wound, his blood pressure had tanked and he'd almost died. A full week in the ICU, and another three in the hospital later, he'd emerged rabies free ... but looked like a returning prisoner of war. Raylynn had promised she'd come up with yummy deserts to fatten him up.

Raylynn and E.J.

Nobody knew quite what to do with that, including the two of them. He was thirty-two years old. She was seventeen, a *teenager* — in years only, though. In maturity level, Raylynn Bennett was a strong young woman. She'd had the state police waiting at her house when her father came rolling up the driveway in "After."

"After" was what they'd all come to call those nightmare crazy days when the Jabberwock disappeared and they all suddenly had to deal with the magnitude of the horror it'd caused.

The bull had been kicked out of the china shop ... but oh, the dishes it had broken in its rampage there.

And what exactly had "it" been? That depended on who you asked.

A gaggle of scientists from every known persuasion had

descended on Nowhere County when the testimony of literally thousands of people established that yes, there *really had been* an uncrossable barrier on the county line, and yes, people really had been *transported* somehow to the Middle of Nowhere when they crossed it.

Yes, they'd lived for two weeks *somewhere* — a place where the time was too fast or too slow, the stars were wrong and the weather never changed.

And yes, it *really had* appeared — for more than two weeks — that the entire population of the county had vanished.

And yes, houses really had aged a hundred years overnight.

Their stories had been corroborated, if corroboration were needed, by the collapsing hulks of the ancient houses that littered the county like empty gum wrappers and by the three piles of cars out in the woods in Fearsome Hollow. A squirrel hunter had happened on them. Pete and Jolene had gone out to see them before the cars got hauled away, said it was quite a sight.

More than thirty, or so she'd heard, vehicles had been stacked one on top of the other in three gigantic piles. Pickup trucks, farm trucks, cars — the Chrysler Cirrus she'd rented at the airport, and Billy Dan Singleton's souped up, Nascar-wannabe Chevy. They appeared to be undamaged except, well, being piled up one on top of the other had pretty much totaled them all.

The legions of law enforcement who descended on the county in the wake of the High Noon Shootout on Main Street had been tripping over each other trying to figure out what had happened, who'd shot whom and why.

All the legal issues were a pile of spaghetti that would never get completely untangled. For one thing, the Breakfast Club and their friends hadn't admitted to everything that had happened. Why bother?

Why drag Toby Witherspoon through some kind of court proceeding about his father's shooting? The boy had been scooped up by the state Department of Child Protective Services until his grandmother from Louisville had come to claim him.

Why make Cotton Jackson deal with the legal fallout of killing Shepherd Clayton? Cotton had tossed into the Rolling Fork River the pistol he'd pulled out of his waistband that day, then told the friend in Carlisle from whom he'd borrowed it that he'd lost it, and bought the friend a brand new one. "Somebody" had called Shep's family, and they found his body in the Gideon Cemetery. He had, after all, been driven crazy by what'd happened. No telling who had shot him.

There'd been nobody to call about poor old Moses Weiss, though. He had no family they could find. She and Stuart had paid to have him committed to a first-rate nursing home in Lexington, had moved Rose Topple there, too. Every now and then, Cotton or somebody from the Breakfast Club paid them a visit.

Relatives filed missing person reports on all the "vanished" people — the Tibbitses, the Tungates, Abner Riley, the Potters and all the others. But Charlie knew nobody would ever find Reece or Grace, Harry and Roscoe, or ... They were just *gone*. Absorbed.

The bottom line in all the investigations was that everything would get swept under some rug somewhere, no matter how big a lump it made.

All the law enforcement agencies were playing CYA, each blaming the other for why they had never investigated all the reports of "vanished" people. When you were unwilling — and they all were! — to admit that something supernatural had been the cause of all that had happened, it was hopeless to try to unravel it.

Oh, they did jump on the cases that didn't involve smoke and mirrors. Viola Tackett had gone down hard. Murder — at least one provable count. Sebastian Nower had watched her shoot Holmes Fischer. Attempted murder — the line of people willing to testify that she'd tried to kill them stretched out for blocks. Grand larceny — she stole a house, for crying out loud. And a laundry list of other charges. Neither she nor Neb — who'd survived the shootout by jumping off the porch and hiding under a parked car — would ever see the light of day outside of prison.

Unless they did.

Stuart had warned her and the others not to expect that the criminal justice system was going to provide the justice they all were looking for. Couple the shenanigans of defense attorneys, the disparity of testimony against her, her age and health — the gunshot wound to her shoulder had shattered it, and she'd require multiple surgeries to repair it, would probably never have full use of her arm again. All those factors … Stuart had wanted to be sure Malachi understood that the fat lady might not yet have sung on his mother's life.

"The law is whatever the judge says it is," he had said, using a phrase Charlie'd heard him use dozens of times about other cases. "Juries are fickle. Just about anything is possible."

MALACHI WENT BACK into the laundry room next to the kitchen where he'd snatched the piece of try-it-and-see-what-you-think turkey off the majestic bird he'd set on top of the dryer for want of a better place to put the behemoth foul. He had wanted to get a Superman tee shirt to wear for Thanksgiving, only with the letter T instead of S. T for Turkey Man. He took his responsibilities in that regard to heart and had spent the better part of the week before Thanksgiving talking to every little old lady up some hollow who was renowned for her cooking skills. He had taken Rusty with him on a couple of those trips, and the boy had seemed perfectly healthy. Intelligent, inquisitive, witty. He was just about the finest twelve-year-old Malachi had ever met, but then his was not exactly an unbiased opinion. Sam hadn't yet said anything about Malachi to Rusty. There was no hurry. She was determined that everything about the situation among the three of them should evolve slowly and naturally and Malachi trusted her instincts. She'd certainly done a great job parenting so far!

But he could tell Sam was still concerned about Rusty's health. He had languished in some state between a coma and simple unconsciousness for a week at the University of Kentucky Medical Center in Lexington. Then he had just opened his eyes and looked around, like he'd taken an extra-long nap.

The doctors didn't know what to make of the readings they got on their EEGs, CAT scans and other tests. There was absolutely nothing on any test that would explain why Rusty was still unconscious, and when he awakened, the doctors didn't know why that'd happened either. They had merely sighed in relief and pronounced that he was fine.

Sam wasn't so sure. It wasn't like Rusty had fallen down and hit his head. He had gone through the Jabberwock *twice*. Only one other person on the planet had taken more than a single ride and Abby had arrived dead in the parking lot of the Middle of Nowhere on her third trip, with a swollen body that exploded.

Sam knew there didn't likely exist tests that would determine the damage or lack thereof of an encounter with a supernatural being that was made up of seventeen children who'd died two hundred years ago and an entity created from rage that had fed on the evil in people's hearts for more than two centuries.

The Breakfast Club, AKA the Alphabet Gang, had spent hours trying to figure out exactly what had happened in Nower County, Kentucky, between June 3 and June 20, 1995. They were certainly more likely to come up with an explanation that the army of "experts" who swarmed over the county like locusts — because all those dudes were looking for a rational explanation and everybody who'd lived through it knew there wasn't one.

Their own discussions of why quickly morphed into discussions of "what if?" It was a lot more fun to get together and listen to Stuart wax eloquent about his grand plan to make Nowhere County the best getaway resort in the East. He'd fallen in love with the place, saw enormous potential. He and Charlie certainly had the financial means to pull it off, and Stuart had been lobbying Malachi to go in together with him to make it happen.

Who knew? Maybe he and Stuart could actually put Nowhere County on the map — for real.

"I couldn't tell, I need more data," Sam said. He turned to find her standing in the doorway of the laundry room. "Dark meat this time." Malachi obediently cut off a slice and started to hold it out above her mouth but she snatched it out of his hand. "I don't do Stupid Pet Tricks." She popped it into her mouth and chewed it thoughtfully.

"Needs more … something."

"Salt? Pepper. Oregano. WD-40?"

"Something. Give me another piece."

He cut one off and handed it to her, and then she

pronounced that, "… actually, it may have too much … something."

"You're just messing with my head. Fool with me and you'll have to find some other patsy to be Turkey Man next Thanksgiving."

Next Thanksgiving.

They stood for a moment, basking in the warmth of that, then Sam went back into the kitchen.

That evening, he and Sam were together on the back porch of the Nower House, recovering from turkey-induced tryptophan comas. Charlie had insisted on hiring a cleanup crew and Sam hadn't been too proud to refuse and they could hear the rattle and bang of pots and pans in the kitchen.

A small creek ran along the edge of the backyard. It was dry in the heat of summer, but it had been an unusually warm and wet fall and the water could be heard babbling over creek pebbles even from the back porch.

"You'll be sorry," Sam was saying. "I have accumulated something like ten miles of Christmas lights and Rusty always insists we put every one *somewhere* on the house."

"I'm almost as good at putting up Christmas lights as I am at …"

He stopped, looked out past Sam's shoulder at the creek. At the mist on the creek. She followed his gaze, then looked questioningly back at him.

"It's just creek mist," she said.

"Don't you think the weather's a little too cold for creek mist?"

Obviously, she hadn't thought about that.

"I suppose I could look up the atmospheric conditions that create mist over a body of water, but—"

"It's nothing." He put a smile on his face and turned back to her. "If you're going to investigate something, see if you can find out how to *fry* a turkey. I hear that's the going thing."

He put his arm around her shoulders. She leaned into him and he groaned inwardly at how very good that felt.

One step at a time. Just one.

He looked out at the mist and remembered the voice from the mist in Gideon that day. He knew she was thinking about it, too, even though she was pretending she wasn't.

This isn't over. I'm not done …

It was a chilly night, but it wasn't *that* cold and he felt Sam shiver. He shivered, too.

The End

Bailey Donahue was supposed to stay dead…

After witnessing her husband's murder, Bailey is ripped from her life and decorated away in the Witness Protection Program. Too bad the sleepy town of Shadow Rock was the wrong place to hide

Get Black Water today!

A Note from the Author

Thank you for reading *Nowhere People.*

If you enjoyed this book, you please consider writing a review on your favorite bookselling site so other readers might enjoy it too. Just a couple of sentences would mean a lot to me.

Thank you!
Ninie Hammon

About the Author

Ninie Hammon (rhymes with shiny, not skinny) grew up in Muleshoe, Texas, got a BA in English and theatre from Texas Tech University and snagged a job as a newspaper reporter. She didn't know a thing about journalism, but her editor said if she could write he could teach her the rest of it and if she couldn't write the rest of it didn't matter. She hung in there for a 25-year career as a journalist. As soon as she figured out that making up the facts was a whole lot more fun than reporting them, she turned to fiction and never looked back.

Ninie now writes suspense--every flavor except pistachio: psychological suspense, inspirational suspense, suspense thrillers, paranormal suspense, suspense mysteries.

In every book she keeps this promise to her Loyal Reader: "I will tell you a story in a distinctive voice you'll always recognize, about people as ordinary as you are--people who have been slammed by something they didn't sign on for, and now they must fight for their lives. Then smack in the middle of their everyday worlds, those people encounter the unexplainable--and it's always the game-changer."

Also By Ninie Hammon

Nowhere, USA

The Jabberwock

Mad Dog

Trapped

The Hanging Judge

The Witch of Gideon

Blown Away

Nowhere People

The Taken Saga

The Taken

The Changed

The Hidden

The Saved

Through The Canvas Series

Black Water

Red Web

Gold Promise

Blue Tears

The Unexplainable Collection

Five Days in May

Black Sunshine

The Based on True Stories Collection

Home Grown

Sudan

When Butterflies Cry

The Knowing Series

The Knowing

The Deceiving

The Reckoning

The Fault

Stand-alone Psychological Thrillers

The Memory Closet

The Last Safe Place